DOMINICANA

ALSO BY ANGIE CRUZ

Let It Rain Coffee

Soledad

DOMINICANA

Angie Cruz

FLATIRON
BOOKS
NEW YORK

DOMINICANA. Copyright © 2019 by Angie Cruz. All rights reserved. Printed in the United States of America. For information, address Flatiron Books, 120 Broadway, New York, NY 10271.

www.flatironbooks.com

Designed by Donna Sinisgalli Noetzel

Library of Congress Cataloging-in-Publication Data

Names: Cruz, Angie, author.
Title: Dominicana: a novel / Angie Cruz.
Description: First Edition. | New York: Flatiron Books, 2019.
Identifiers: LCCN 2019012554| ISBN 9781250205933 (hardcover) |
    ISBN 9781250205926 (ebook)
Classification: LCC PS3603.R89 D66 2019 | DDC 813/.6—dc23
LC record available at https://lccn.loc.gov/2019012554

Our books may be purchased in bulk for promotional, educational, or business use. Please contact your local bookseller or the Macmillan Corporate and Premium Sales Department at 1-800-221-7945, extension 5442, or by email at MacmillanSpecialMarkets@macmillan.com.

First Edition: September 2019

10 9 8 7 6 5 4 3 2 1

For Dania, my mother
Para todas las Dominicanas
For all our unsung heroes

PART I

THE FIRST TIME JUAN RUIZ PROPOSES, I'M ELEVEN YEARS old, skinny and flat-chested. I'm half asleep, my frizzy hair has busted out from a rubber band, and my dress is on backwards. Every other weekend Juan and three of his brothers show up past midnight all the way from La Capital to serenade the good country girls in the area who're eligible for marriage. They're not the first men to stop by and try at me and my older sister, Teresa.

For years, people stare at me, almost against their will. I'm different than other girls. By no means pretty. A curious beauty, people say, as if my green eyes are shinier, more valuable, to be possessed. Because of this, Mamá fears if she doesn't plan my future, my fate will be worse than Teresa's, who already has her brown eye on El Guardia, who guards the municipal building in the center of town.

That night, the first out of many, three of the Ruiz brothers park their car on the dirt road and clang on Papá's colmado's bell as if they're herding cows. The roads are dark under the cloudy sky and the absence of the moon. The power outages can last fifteen hours at a time. There'd been some chicken stealing, and our store had been robbed twice in the past year. So we keep everything under lock and key, especially after Trujillo was shot dead. In his own car! After being El Jefe for thirty-one years! This amuses Papá. All his life he had to look at Trujillo's photograph, along with the slogan: God in Heaven, Trujillo on Earth. No one could help laughing at his mortality. Even God had had enough. But Trujillo didn't go in peace. La Capital is in chaos. A tremendous mess. No law or order to speak of. Full of crazies. Visitors from the big city tug their lower lids, warning us to remain vigilant. So we're vigilant.

Mamá, Teresa, and I huddle near the house while Papá walks toward the darkness with his rifle in shooting position.

My brothers, Yohnny and Lenny, and my cousins, Juanita and Betty, are asleep.

It's us, it's us, Juan yells out in the dark. Everyone knows who the Ruiz brothers are because they travel to and from New York, returning with pockets full of dollars.

Behind Juan the two other brothers wave their instruments in the air and laugh.

Come, step forward, Mamá yells, and soon they sit in our front yard, beers in hand, talking about New York, politics, money, and papers.

When Juan proposes, he's drunk. Slurs, Marry me. I'll take you to America. He trips over himself and pushes me against the wooden fence. Tell me yes, he insists with his lit breath and his thick sweat dripping over my face.

Papá doesn't care for politics, and he knows not to trust a man in a suit. He goes for his rifle, and Mamá stands between them, laughing it off in the way she does where she shows all her teeth and dips her chin to her neck, then flirtatiously looks away. She grips Juan's shoulder and guides him back to the plastic lawn chair to sit with his brothers, who have all had too much to drink.

When Juan sits, his chest folds toward his round stomach, and his jaw, the corner of his lips, his cheeks, his eyes all droop: a sad clown. Juan stares at my knees, which come together tight tight as if I hold a secret there for him to discover.

The three brothers can't be more different, same parents but different faces and heights. And wait until you meet César, Hector says. They all wear suits and clump together near Juan like a band on a stage. Their eyes glassy and pink. Their instruments their crutches.

This song's for you, Juan says to Teresa, who cowers under Papá's watchful eye. But all the time he's looking at me. Teresa's thirteen going on twenty, born kicking before the sun had risen. She swings her skirt side to side in anticipation. This is before El Guardia will ruin her chance to get out. Ramón, the oldest, strings the guitar, and Juan looks to his brothers as though to make sure the chickens are in the coop, and like a real showman he gets on his feet, turns around, and there we are.

Bésame, bésame mucho . . .

He sings the song low and thick and full, filling a void in my chest. A block of ice melting. His voice is amplified by the dark sky and the stillness of the night. I close my eyes to listen. What is it that I hear? His sorrow? His longing? His passion? All of it?

Como si fuera esta noche la última vez
Bésame, bésame mucho,
Que tengo miedo a perderte, perderte después . . .

When he's finished, Mamá and Teresa jump up to clap. A scattered applause. Another one! Another one! Teresa says, unaware that Juan is singing to me.

I know then that one day the earth will rip open underneath my feet and Juan will take me away. Tears rise. I don't know how or when, but a ravenous world waits outside for me.

Girls, to bed, Papá announces with the resonance of a cowbell. He places his rifle across his thighs, pissed like I've never seen him. Two of his sisters had been taken by military men, back when Trujillo lived.

We should hit the road, Ramón says, and stands up lean and tall like a flagpole, always polite, always apologetic for his younger brothers who can't control their liquor.

Before Juan leaves, he bends over to look right into my face. I stare straight back into his eyes as if I have the power to scare him. He makes a gesture of retreat and suddenly pounces toward me and barks, loud and insistent. Bark. Bark. Bark. I jump back and away from him, trip over the plastic bucket we keep by the door to fetch water. He laughs and laughs. His large body shakes when he laughs. Everyone laughs except me.

Mamá makes nice and tells them to come back soon, and don't be strangers, and that the best of girls are worth waiting for. Maybe we'll go eat at your restaurant in the city one day, she says, knowing well we never go to La Capital or eat at restaurants.

THE DAY TERESA STEALS AND SLIPS INTO MAMÁ'S FAVORITE dress to sneak out to see El Guardia, Mamá declares Teresa a lost cause and my marrying Juan becomes her top priority.

Did you see her leave?

No? I lie.

Mamá's white dress fits Teresa tight in all the right places, including her knees. She moves as if her heels have wheels attached to them, her body full and womanly. Una mujerota, Yohnny says. Her heart-shaped lips always part because she has big teeth that give the impression she wants to kiss you.

Just thinking about boys getting their way with Teresa and having folks say how she's fast and hot and loose makes Mamá clench her fists and pull out her hair. So much so, she has a bald spot at the nape of her neck dedicated to Teresa's escapades. But no amount of whipping or hollering keeps Teresa from sneaking away to be with that man.

The first time she snuck out, Mamá screamed so loud the clouds dumped so much rain our land flooded. All morning, me, Teresa, Lenny, Betty, Juanita, and Yohnny swept away water from the house, filling buckets upon buckets.

I had watched Teresa toss off the hair rollers one by one and finger her dark locks. It had taken Juanita one full hour to blow out Teresa's thick uncooperative hair. But it was worth it. She shook her hair out so it danced around her face—a beauty queen.

Mamá's going to kill you, I whispered, trying not to wake Juanita and Betty, who share a bed with us and whose limbs tangle up when they sleep. They purr like kittens. A sheet separates Lenny and Yohnny from us. It hangs from one side of the room to the other. So threadbare that when the lamp is on, before we all go to sleep, we are able to see each other's silhouettes against the faded blue-and-yellow-flowered print. Lucky for Teresa, when they sleep they might as well be dead.

Sleep now, you're dreaming, negra.

Teresa shuffled about like a mouse. The night was ripe with chirping, screeching, croaking, miserable frog mating sounds, right outside our window. Papá says it's because love hurts.

What if Mamá doesn't let you come back? What if something happens to you? I said, already worried about our parents hurting later. Because where we live, there's nothing but dark. Not a house for at least a mile. And the electricity always in some kind of mood. On and off. On and off.

Teresa's eyes shone. Come see, El Guardia's right on the road, waiting for me.

I tiptoed to the window. Bright moonlight illuminated the top of the palms.

I'll be back before everyone's up. Don't you worry about me, little sister.

But why can't you wait and be with him in a proper way? He can announce himself and ask for your hand. How do you know if he has serious intentions?

Teresa smiled. First of all, Mamá will never accept him. One day you'll understand. When you fall in love, you have to play it out even if everyone calls you crazy. That's why they call it falling. We have no control over it.

I don't ever want to fall in love, I said but then thought of Gabriel, who can't look me in the eye without blushing.

Love's not a choice for you to make, Teresa said, and blew out the sage burning in the hotpot to kill the funky boy smell Lenny and Yohnny make in the night.

Teresa glided out of our room. She looked back at me and winked, licked her lips as if life itself is the most delicious thing she ever tasted. I imagined my mother, young like Teresa, cut from the same cloth, how much they look alike. Pin-pún, la Mamá, is what everyone says when they first see Teresa. Pin-pún!

EVERYONE HAS AN ARRIVAL STORY. THIS IS JUAN'S. THE first time he goes to New York City he has only an address and twenty dollars in his pocket. The bus drops him off at 72nd and Broadway on an island filled with benches and passed-out junkies. His heart races when the cars honk and helicopters fly overhead. He has always liked adventures, but the way the city is already pushing him to move so quickly, he knows that to gain control of such a place will require time. He locates the building number and finds a busted front door. Climbs the five flights of stairs hauling his suitcase. The lightbulbs in the lobby, missing. The musty smell of the damp rugs reminds him of caves he visited as a child. Oh, how he loved the caves—the slippery rocks, the darkness, the pounding of the waterfall—the sweetest reward, after the trek through the muck.

He takes a deep breath. He can do this.

When he finally knocks on the door, a scruffy old man answers.

Ju, ju, Frank? Juan asks. Frank is the Italian man who rents rooms.

Yes, yes.

And with that he waves Juan into his first apartment: a small room with two mattresses. One stripped down, topped with a neatly folded pile of sheets and a towel. On the neighboring mattress, a man asleep, with a pillow covering his face, to block the streetlight coming through the bare window.

Ten dollars a week. Every Sunday. You understand?

Jes. Thenk you, Juan answers in English. He had learned Yes, sir. Thank you. Dollars and cents. No, sir. Numbers one through ten. OK. Time o'clock. Taxi, please. Trains.

Gotta girl back home? Frank asks.

Oh shit, you speak Spanish? Juan almost cries in relief.

Because we don't allow girls in here, Frank continues. Not for a week or a night.

Up until now, Juan hasn't really thought about me. But he does plan to marry me because, as Ramón says, a good country girl is what a man needs to keep him out of trouble.

Frank prepares coffee and serves them in two mismatched espresso cups.

Heard there's some good work at the hotels down on 34th Street, Juan says.

Frank juts out his chin. Is that all you got to wear?

Juan's thin wool coat doesn't even have a liner. From a closet in the hallway Frank pulls out a three-quarter-length coat, thick wool herringbone with a furry collar.

You don't want to die of pneumonia waiting on that line.

Juan notes the worn-down cuffs, the exposed layers of muslin. The lining ripped to shreds.

We try and keep the lights off to keep the electric bill down. Everyone minds their business here.

A boom goes off outside. Juan jumps.

Be careful at night. The junkies will kill you for a buck. A desperate man is a dangerous one.

Juan gives ten dollars to Frank for the week's rent. Sips the coffee and realizes he hasn't eaten dinner. The portions on the plane were small. It's already dark, and he doesn't want to spend his money on food in case he can't find work right away.

Maybe I should sleep.

Bathroom at the end of the hall. Good luck tomorrow.

Juan tucks his baggage upright next to his mattress. The medium-size towel on the bed is thin and frayed at the edges but smells clean. He lies down fully dressed. His shoes by the bed. The other man snores. Juan's stomach growls. He looks at the clock and thinks about the chocolate cake they served him on the plane. Or was it a cookie? It was crunchy outside and moist inside, like nothing he had had before.

YEARS GO BY AND JUAN KEEPS COMING AROUND WITH HIS brothers for free beer at all hours of the night, flooding me with promises. Come with me now? Let's get the justice of the peace, Juan says to me more than once. Never did I see a green-eyed bird like you, and his bloodshot glassy eyes would stare into mine, making the fuzz on the back of my neck rise.

From birth, Mamá says, my eyes were a winning lottery ticket, inherited from my grandfather from El Cibao. She talks proudly about Papá's family, even though they'd cut us all off after Mamá married Papá thinking he would take her far away from Los Guayacanes. Ever hopeful, Mamá had ignored warnings that those people don't mix with blacks. And here we are, still in Los Guayacanes.

Maybe with Juan we can all get the hell out, she says.

Teresa had already stepped in it by getting knocked up by El Guardia. Their eyes only had to lock once, she told me, for her to feel the burning low in her stomach and between her legs, his desire like a fist pushing up into her crotch. This is how Teresa talks.

One day you'll discover it, she says to me in secret and winks, knowing that Gabriel's no longer a boy just running after freight trains. He's awake, Ana, and if you allow it, he'll bite.

Her teeth gleam whenever she talks boys with me.

Mamá too. It doesn't matter if Juan's intentions are serious or not. Mamá has lived long enough to learn a man doesn't know what he thinks until a woman makes him think it. So right when I get my period at twelve and eight months, she undoes my pigtails and pulls my hair back tight so no kinks escape, so my eyes pull at the ends. When he visits, she makes me wear my Sunday dress I had outgrown a while before. It pushes the little fat I have up and around my chest for all to see. Juan's often too drunk to know the difference between a dress and a potato sack, but she colors my lips pink. When I talk the lipstick bleeds onto my teeth. Unlike Teresa, I don't smile easily. Mamá makes me sit with the brothers, my dress rising high up, the backs of my thighs sticking to the plastic chairs.

Pregnant Teresa is made to stay in the house with Juanita, who is sixteen, and Betty, who is fifteen, so Juan has no distractions. Yohnny, who's a year older than me, and Lenny, who still doesn't know how to blow his own nose, sit a ways away and make faces, imitating the Ruiz brothers, who are in their fancy suits and stumble and slur all their words. The men talk in a loop: about papers, the value of the dollar, the baseball games they gamble on. One year they complain about President Balaguer's inability to keep his promises, the next they celebrate the coup and how Bosch won the election. We finally have a democracy! they cheer. And then it's back to money, papers, money, papers, money, papers. They talk as if we aren't even there until Mamá changes the subject.

I don't care who's president, but if things don't get better soon, we won't be able to keep all of our land. Especially the land by the sea, Mamá says, emphasizing all our land, the sea.

Ramón suddenly sits upright. Ah . . . maybe one day you can show us around? he asks Mamá but looks at Papá.

Oh, Papá's discomfort with these city men, fat and thick, dressed in dark wool suits even when they're sweating, bragging about their trips to New York, the properties they plan to buy, their restaurant dreams. Full of stories, full of hope. Ay Papá, in his worn pants and thinned shirt, listening to Mamá go on and on about the fertile land and the view.

I've never met a man who works harder than my husband, she says, and looks pleadingly towards Papá, who replaced the rifle on his lap with the scowl on his face.

Is that true, are we selling the land? I ask Papá.

Papá isn't a liar, so he says nothing. I may not have a chair to sit on, he often says, but I have my word. He may not care for the way Mamá flirts and how prematurely she mixes me up in things, but he does respect the Ruiz brothers. When they borrow money, they pay it back with interest and on time. When they lend money, they write it on paper, so no one gets screwed. Everybody knows that the Ruiz brothers' word is gold in the bank.

More beer for anyone? Mamá chimes in.

The next day, when we're alone, Papá says out of nowhere, Ana, I want you to be happy.

I'm happy.

You know what I mean. He looks at me as if waiting for a smile, or a squeal or a clap of joy. Everyone's always telling me to smile, even when there's nothing to smile about. Smile, Ana! You're a pretty, young girl! You haven't seen the worst of life yet! So sometimes I smile so that people will leave me alone. But this time no smile comes.

Papá has already drunk two beers, and with the hot sun it might as well be four. His eyes dip at the edges, and his free hand rubs on his knee, which is sore from working long days watching over our animals and land.

Are you happy? I ask him. His tanned leathery face is like looking at the sea at night.

JUAN DISAPPEARS FOR MONTHS AT A TIME TO STAND ON
line to get work at the New Yorker Hotel.

The wind slaps his face. His thin blood gels, his bones ache, and just when he thinks he'll die from the cold air filling his lungs, he begins to count the number of days he'll stay in New York: one hundred eighty. It's enough workdays to pay for his trip and save some money to take back with him. He counted twenty-eight years because it was his age. Nine, his birthday. Four, the number of Ruiz brothers, two of whom are on their way to New York to work alongside him, and one who had tried to bear the winters but returned back home. Juan counts the men on the line. One, two, ten, fifteen. He's the sixteenth on line. His stomach growls from not having dinner. The piece of bread he stole from Frank's fridge only opened his appetite. The men all stare at the side door of the hotel. He wants to return to his room and huddle near the heater.

The guy in front of him says, Tuck in your pants. Keeps the heat in.

But Juan doesn't want to look like a punk.

Finally the door opens and a woman runs out wearing a furry black hat. A real movie star. Bright red lipstick on pale skin. She walks up and down the line as she looks at her list. She picks her men and waves the rest away.

That's all for today.

Juan grabs her arm to get her attention.

Get off of me.

I'm sorry, but I need work.

Try us tomorrow. Everyone needs work.

As handsome as me?

This is the Ruiz charm. They all have a light in their eyes, not eagerness but an indisputable certainty.

Wait here. I'll see what I can do.

She disappears into the building. Juan sits by the door to wait. A man walks over and offers him a cigarette.

She ain't coming back for you. Don't be a pendejo.

All the other men have left. He had been told this was a sure thing.

Juan buys a coffee from the back of a van. He grabs the cup with both hands to warm them up and sips it slow. His heart speeds up each time someone opens the side door. It's the garbage. It's someone leaving work. It's a person flicking a cigarette butt outside. What's the time, he asks some kid. He decides he'll wait for only an hour. He counts the seconds. The minutes. He counts too fast. He slows down. Loses count because his fingers are numb. The door opens. The woman runs out. She doesn't see him.

Excuse me, he yells after her.

Are you crazy? It's below zero today. You should go home.

I need work.

I told you, I have nothing.

You told me to wait.

She looks around, searching for a way to flee Juan's desperate eyes.

I'll work for free today. You'll see how good I am. And then tomorrow you'll choose me for sure.

The woman sighs. Go inside and ask for José. He'll give you stuff to do. I can't pay you for today, but you can eat lunch with the others.

Thank you. Juan's face lights up, and he grabs her hand to kiss it. You're an angel, he says, and runs in through the side door, escaping the cold.

WHEN JUAN DOESN'T VISIT FOR A LONG WHILE, MAMÁ makes me write him letters. Tell him how hot it's been. Unbearable. How you long to see the snow. How handsome he looks in a suit and that your favorite color is green to remind him about your eyes. They're unusual. Maybe it'll inspire him to bring you a gift. Tell him how well you're doing in school. How you love numbers so much, you dream of them while you sleep.

In this way Juan and I are the same. I too count the steps to school, how many times the teacher repeats herself. Even the impossible things I count, like the stars in the sky, the limoncillos on our tree.

Tell him how much you enjoy to cook. Be specific. Don't just say food, say pescado con coco, so he knows you're the kind of woman who's not afraid to debone a fish or grate coconut.

What kind of woman is afraid to grate coconut? I ask, but Mamá keeps talking.

Invite him to visit during the day so you can cook him a proper meal at a proper time. Say how much you would enjoy feeding him. That you miss him and would like to see him again.

But that's not true, I say.

Oh, who cares what's true. Look, what is the truth? Letters are a lasso, words on a page that we fling out, hoping, hoping.

What about what I want?

What do you want, Ana?

I don't know.

If Teresa was a duck she would've saved herself from El Guardia, Mamá says. Now she's stuck with bad seed. Her life is basically ruined. Ruined! Ducks can reject unwanted sperm, only allowing in the sperm they want. They choose the best duck to make their babies, not just any grubby, ill-looking duck. And they sleep with one eye open unless they have some other duck on guard. Learn from the ducks, Mamá says.

RAMÓN SAYS HE DELIVERS ALL MY LETTERS, BUT JUAN doesn't write back. He's preoccupied with work, and all that is New York.

Listen to this one, Juan says to the guy standing on line in front of him.

Anything to get my mind off the cold.

Two friends see each other and one says, Don't know what to do with my grandfather. He bites his nails all the time. Then the other says, I had the same problem with my old man, but I fixed it.

How? You tied his hands?

No, I hid his teeth.

A cluster of men burst out laughing. So hard they don't notice that the lady dressed in black with her furry hat is pointing at them.

Maybe you're all having too much fun to work, she says.

It's the first time Juan sees her smile. Even if she treats him like every other guy on that line, Juan tells Ramón she has a thing for him.

A Puerto Rican chick who works management likes an off-the-boat spic like you? Keep dreaming, my brother.

You'll see, says Juan, determined to prove it. He's bought a red scarf for fifty cents on the street that really makes him stand out among all the other men who wear grays and browns.

When she sees him she does a double take.

Hey you, how's your English? she asks Juan.

Bedy good.

We need a doorman today. Someone called in sick.

He notices her wedding band.

Seguro que yo speako English, he says, chasing after her.

If you mess up, you'll never work here again.

Sí, señora.

Don't call me that. You make me sound like an old woman.

I'm sorry, señora. I mean señorita.

Ask for José. He'll give you a uniform and tell you what to do.

Gracias, señora. You're very beautiful, señora.

You're totally crazy, she says, and laughs with him.

And your name? Juan finally asks.

Caridad. Caridad de la Luz.

From that day on Caridad picks Juan from the line, for various positions. He trains to set tables in a formal way: forks for each of the courses, placed to the left, and knives to the right, bread and butter plates above the forks. He learns the difference between white and red wineglasses. How to fold napkins to look like birds. One day he hopes his restaurant in Dominican Republic will be as fine.

He enjoys bussing tables over the monotony of washing dishes in the kitchen, but working the door even more, because the tips are good and he's working alone. Even if by the end of the day his jaw hurts from smiling and his feet ache from standing, Juan would rather be busy, because when he stops he gets lonely and sad and misses Santo Domingo and all the girls back home who never turn him down. The women in New York are complicated. Women like Caridad are complicated. Many are married, waiting for their husbands who are on active duty, ready to fight some war. These women want to be taken out, to talk and talk.

Ramón reminds Juan that he's in New York to work, not to get into women trouble. He tells Juan he needs a quiet girl like me, from a good family.

So with a nudge from Ramón, Juan mails me a money order for five dollars, for my needs, he says, and a necklace with a green stone, because of my eyes.

His note is very to the point: Ana, please wait for me.

PAPÁ SAYS EVEN ONE DROP OF WATER COULD FILL A bucket if you wait around long enough. Between Mamá's letters, the free beers, and yearly visits, Juan Ruiz finally asks properly for my hand in marriage. I am fifteen. Juan is thirty-two.

He shows up, during the daytime, with Ramón. Sober, or as sober as I have ever seen him, not flailing his arms or grabbing at me, at Mamá, the chair, a tree, to hold himself up. For the first time ever, I see him. Really see him. He even takes off his suit jacket. In only a tailored vest and without the shoulder pads, his shoulders become small, less threatening.

Ana? Juan says in such a serious way everyone stares with bated breath. I wear my Sunday dress, a faded yellow one I can't breathe well in. Frizz crowns my head. My tongue dry, my throat aching. I knew this moment would come from the first serenade. Juan towers over me. I focus on the thin gray lines on his vest, the way they intersect at the lapels. The sweat running down his cheeks over the incoming stubble. I try not to look at him. But they all stare. Teresa stands close by with her son on her hip. My mother's teeth are exposed, her lipstick caked on her bottom lip. Yohnny and Lenny lie on a bench like overheated dogs, so thirsty, their tongues hanging out of their mouths. I look for Papá, who stands quietly, defeated.

Where is your rifle? Where is your scowl? I want to scream.

What is it? I ask. Has my lipstick already stained my teeth?

And suddenly, Juan pulls out a handkerchief from his pocket and wipes all the lipstick off.

What are you doing?

I push him away.

You don't need that stuff. You don't need anything, he says. You're the most beautiful thing I've ever seen.

He's undone just by looking at me. I open my eyes wider. Hold my chest higher, and a smile escapes the side of my lips.

Everyone wants something from a man like Juan—a visa, dollars, a good word, a ride in his car, a free meal in his restaurant. Even if my mother wants all those things, I keep my grace.

Will you be my wife? he asks.

Ramón stands behind Juan, as if without him there, Juan will split, run away, take it all back. And I understand then that maybe Juan doesn't want to marry me after all. They are here for my parents' land.

I could've said no. Teresa's mouth, tight lipped and pursed in disappointment. You have rights, she said days before. You're the boss of you.

I look to Papá for an answer. Go ahead, answer him, Papá urges.

Mamá grabs Papá's arm in solidarity, an unusual gesture, understood by Ramón because he smiles and shakes my father's hand as if I have already said yes, although nobody cares what I want.

Yohnny and Lenny run about singing:

I like to be in America . . . everything free in America, olé.

In minutes the adults distance themselves to make the arrangements. Yohnny and Lenny grab my hands and spin me around like they did in the *West Side Story* musical we had seen at the theater in the center. Juanita and Betty run out and join in the celebration.

Wow, prima, you're so lucky, Betty says. Don't forget to send me something.

Me too! Juanita's voice, laced with a mix of envy and hope. After you see all those bright lights, I bet you never coming back here.

Get the refrescos, Mamá yells over to Yohnny. We have to celebrate.

Teresa stomps back into the house and watches everything transpire from the window. She holds her baby in her arms, tighter, closer to her chest as if to keep me from reading her thoughts. *Who would cover for her when she snuck away? Who would do all her chores?*

Then it really hits me: I'm leaving. Dread and fear and excitement ripple through my body. Once I leave no one will ever treat me the same. My life will be a load of gossip material for Juanita and Betty, who lost their parents in a flood and have lived with us ever since I can remember. I'll be the woman with dollars, and fine clothes, and beautiful skin from all the good lotions Juan will buy me in America. I will be given lists upon lists, with orders to be filled.

EVERY BRIDE DESERVES A NEW DRESS. SO MAMÁ TAKES ME to Carmela's in San Pedro de Macorís for a fitting.

But I have school, I say.

You don't need to go there anymore.

But I can't not go. I haven't said good-bye to everyone.

From the moment I say everyone she intuits I mean Gabriel, and she won't let him ruin everything now.

Mamá wraps a scarf over her head and pulls the keys for the motoconcho off the hook. And without any hesitation she swings her leg over and sits on the scooter and yells, C'mon, get on!

She takes up most of the seat, but I manage to slip on behind her. The sun blares above us. She hands me an umbrella and waits for me to open it. After some fits and starts, the motoconcho peels onto the road, leaving a cloud of dust behind us. For a long while, we're alone on the narrow road, miles of cane fields on each side. I hug my mother, press my head against her sweaty back and taste the ocean on her skin. You would think we're close.

Then suddenly the clamoring of tin pots, the tooting of the ships, the stink of sedentary water inside the numerous potholes hits us. Cars and scooters compete for every inch of the city streets. The Malecón bursts at the seams, people shopping, hanging, talking, drinking. Selling lottery tickets and coconuts. Men whistling and hissing at Mamá, whose skirt hikes up, exposing her thick brown thighs, even thicker next to all my bones.

Cochino! she yells back at the gaping mouths.

Not a good one in that bunch, she says, and demands I hold on tight as she pushes through the traffic, around the park in the city center, the only refuge, shaded from the blazing sun by palmettos and almond trees.

Mamá pulls up to Carmela's house, the only one on the block made with concrete. Once painted red, now a faded pink, with dwarf palm trees cluttering the front yard.

Carmela! Mamá yells through the iron gates.

We peek into the house. Through the window, I make out a headless dress form and back away. Mamá glares back at my watery eyes and chin pressed against my neck.

Cheer up, she says when Carmela comes out to greet us. Her hair tightly wrapped around her head in a tubi. A smile that takes up half her face. This is the beginning of great things for you. For all of us!

Carmela leads us to her bedroom. There are a few reams of fabric on a shelf. A black metal sewing machine sits on a small table by a window. A bald bulb hangs from the ceiling. A loud standing fan turns to and fro near her work chair. A rope extended from one side of the room to the other displays pinned fabric pieces and magazine photos of dresses ordered by past customers.

Bad news, Carmela says, there's not an inch of white fabric in town. The communion ceremonies are in two weeks, and every girl between six and eight is dressing up like a bride.

Mamá fans herself with a McCall pattern she found on Carmela's table.

I smile to myself. Maybe this is a sign that the marriage will be postponed—or better yet canceled.

What other colors do you have? Mamá asks.

What? flies out of my mouth, startling them.

Other colors, Carmela? my mother repeats.

For a bride? Carmela sucks her tooth in disapproval but pulls out three possibilities. A shiny gold lamé—a definite no—black linen, and a roll of red cotton.

Mamá fingers the red fabric on the sewing table.

It's more pink, a flaming pink, Carmela says. She turns around and pulls out a large piece of white lace from her storage cabinet. She stands behind me, placing the lace on my chest so that Mamá gets the effect.

There are no mirrors in the room for me to look at myself. I'm supposed to be in school. Gabriel, my only friend, will wonder where I am. I can't go off to America without saying good-bye.

Mamá scrutinizes the flaming pink and white lace.

It's so bright. Don't you have anything else?

I have black, but she's not going to a funeral. Carmela pauses here and I sense she's been saying otherwise behind our backs.

I like the black, I say.

Mamá shoos my hand away. Carmela, make her something pretty in the pink. And put on as much white lace as you can. I don't want anyone thinking my daughter's indecent.

We walk out into the midday sun. Mamá opens the umbrella. She locks her arm into mine. Pulls me over to sit on the cement-block ledge of Carmela's house. The waft of fried fish and plátano makes me hungry. Ants march over a fallen apricot. Songs from radios, playing inside of living rooms and kitchens, compete for my attention. Across from us some men have set up cardboard over stacked crates to play a domino game. Women line the wash in their front yard. Two boys play catch.

Mamá reveals a cigarette she has hidden in her bra.

You smoke?

Only on special occasions.

She stops a passerby and asks for a light, then waves him away. After taking a drag, she passes the cigarette to me. I make a face of disgust.

Lesson number one to survive this life, she says through the acrid smoke, learn to pretend. You don't need to smoke if you don't want to, but you can use it to act like one of those movie stars.

I'm not that way.

She leans her head back, takes a drag and exhales. The sun behind her draws her silhouette. We have the same lips and eye shape, large and wide. The same coarse hair at our napes.

When she comes back for air, she winks and smiles at me.

They're gonna eat you alive in New York if you don't change that pendeja face. You need to toughen up, Ana. You think I like being the way I am? But your father has no backbone. Never fought for anything in his life. Not even me.

But you always say he came after you.

Ha. You better open your eyes before someone else opens them for you. You hear me?

That day, Mamá was a wolf pushing away her pup.

You go to America and pretend you don't care about what he and his brothers are talking about, but you listen carefully and take notes. He comes from a family of hard workers, good men, entrepreneurs. We can learn from them. The Ruiz brothers started poor like us. But they work together. Not like my family or your father's family, a bunch of uneducated and greedy idiots only out for self. And now the Ruiz brothers are going to be our family too. Ramón wants to build on our property, and with this marriage we're now bound. This is important for us—your father especially because soon all our fruit trees will be barren. The cherries are already rotten, the mangoes mealy.

But every fruit tree has had a bad year, I remind her. Some years they don't bear fruit at all.

And you'd count on that? These people own a restaurant in the capital right by the sea. I bet it's a fancy one, with cloth napkins on the tables, chandeliers in the main room, bathrooms with bidets and tiled floors. And in New York, Juan is working with his brother to start not one business but many. They are detailed people. Organized people. People with intelligence. You want to study, don't you?

Yes, I want to study, maybe have my own business. I fight to hold back the tears.

Mamá takes the last drag from her cigarette and puts it out on the ledge. She picks up my chin so tenderly, she takes me by surprise.

I promise nothing bad will happen to you. You go to New York and you clean his house and cook him the kind of food that will make him return home every night. Never let him walk out of the house with a wrinkled shirt. Remind him to shave and cut his hair. Clip his nails so women know he's well taken care of. Demand he send us money. Demand he take care of you. Make sure you sneak some money for yourself on the side. Women have necessities. And whatever you do, stay strong. Don't allow your-self to be tempted or derailed by anyone. The city is filled with predators, and you're just a girl. My innocent little girl. I'll come to America as soon as you send for me. We'll all go to New York to be with you, and together we'll build something. I swear to God who's my witness.

Do I really have a choice? What kind of future waits for me or my brothers if I stay?

Think of your Tía Clara—her daughter married a man who works in New York, and every month he sends the family money. He never fails. They have a cement floor and a new bathroom.

I don't want to cry. But I cry.

Oh mi'jita, please. Stop it. Now everybody's looking at us. You're being ridiculous. Look at those kids. You see those kids?

Mamá points at some barefooted boys carrying baskets of bags filled with peanuts and peeled oranges. Do you know what your brother Yohnny is doing every day while you and Lenny spend your mornings at school?

I turn away. Mamá grabs my chin and makes me look through my tears.

And as soon as Lenny can write his name and add his numbers he will be out there, too.

Yes I know. I know. Every day, I press Yohnny's shirts, only so he can get them dirty again while carrying baskets twice his weight, then sitting by the road to wait for someone to buy Papá's fresh meats and fruits. Knowing he's not allowed to come home until he sells everything.

Please try and be happy. It kills your father to see your sad face all the time.

I REFUSE TO LEAVE LOS GUAYACANES WITHOUT SAYING good-bye to Gabriel, who is the only one who actually cares about anything I have to say. The next morning, before Mamá wakes up, I prepare to go to school. Heat the coals for the morning hot chocolate, slice the bread. I let out the chickens, check their water and food. I envy their freedom. How they walk about without a care in the world. I sweep away the layer of dust that drifts into our living room while we sleep. Look over the two photographs we have: one of Papá and Mamá when they married, and a portrait of all the family by a tourist who took it and mailed it to us three years before. Our only photograph with all of us together.

The sun's still low, the animals tucked under the trees and bushes. I slip into my Sunday dress and shuffle out.

I walk quickly, until my mother can no longer yell out my name to call me back. I carry my notebook and a sharpened pencil. I cut across the field of overgrown weeds and wild tobacco and skip over rocky patches of grass. I delight in the scrape of bushes and brittle branches on my arms, as if they themselves are saying, Good-bye, Ana, remember us. I recite my numbers and spell words in my head. D-e-s-e-o: Desire. A-l-t-u-r-a: Height. P-r-o-g-r-e-s-o: Progress. It's all for the best. It's all for the best.

By the time I arrive to the one-room schoolhouse I can't breathe. I sit on the side of the road to reorient myself. Am I dying? An emptiness, deep in my gut. It hurts. I hunch over my legs to calm myself down. *Breathe, Ana, Breathe*. This cannot be my last day of school. How in the world does anyone say good-bye to everyone they love, to everything they know?

Soon after, Gabriel emerges from the sun, an out-of-breath angel pedaling up the hill. Sweat beads crown his temples.

You okay? he asks. His thick eyebrows come together.

Hoping he will understand, I say, I can't be here. He stares at me and then my body bolts. I run away from the school in denial of the inevitable. I find an opening in the fields.

Let me go! I yell back to Gabriel. I'm marrying Juan, punto and final.

I run by men working in the fields, lifting their machetes, bending at the knees, chopping the cane close to the ground. Chop. Chop. Chop.

Wait up! Gabriel is standing on his bike, pedaling faster. There are snakes.

Where? I stop and yell, and jump.

Everywhere, he says, laughing as he reaches me. Better to leave before they find you.

That's not funny.

Out of breath, I walk back to the main road. He trails beside me on his bike.

Let me give you a ride home.

No, just go away.

He takes my arm gently and pulls me so I look at him. It's a beautiful day. Not a cloud in the sky. The green foliage iridescent. If it were any other day I would shy away from him, but Gabriel's persistence lifts my feet off the ground.

Wanna go swimming?

The beach is only a mile away, and yet I haven't touched the sea in months. What a strange thing for him to ask. But not stranger than Juan Ruiz asking for my hand in marriage.

He says, I take care of this house with a pool, for some gringos. They let me use it when they aren't there.

Is that true?

Yeah, man. They're real relaxed.

Okay, I say, and hop on the bike. He pedals fast, cuts across fields, dirt roads. He tells me to hold on, and I grab his waist; our bodies bop and bump over pebbles and branches. He pedals up a hill I've never known of and behind a wall of fragrant flowers I've never seen. He parks his bike in front of a colonial-style house that stands overlooking the valley. There are iron gates everywhere with huge padlocks, and Gabriel has all the keys.

Been working with them for two years. You can't tell anyone because once people know this house is empty, forget about it. They're real nice gringos.

You sleep here too?

When they aren't here, yes. I'm the watchy man.

Diablo, you're good at keeping secrets.

He pumps his arms to show me his small muscles and says, Wanna check out my room?

I've never been alone with a boy that isn't my brother. My mother's voice rings in my ear: Don't stick your foot in it. You can ruin everything.

I follow him on a tiled path around the house, and he unlocks a gate into the service room. It's furnished with a twin bed, a table, a ceiling fan, a window overlooking the pool, a chair, bright red sheets, matching curtains. A small television, a shower stall and sink. The walls painted in a bright yellow and the concrete floors a dark red.

The service room is a far cry from the one I had to stay in when I worked for a family in San Pedro for two weeks. My room was in the back of the house. The bathroom had no door. The floors hadn't been finished. They had asked me not to use the toilet in the main house. They assigned me my own dishes and glasses, explaining to the children how countrywomen carry illnesses because we live with our animals.

Gabriel even has a television. I haven't known anyone with a television.

Maybe I could live in this room with Gabriel and cook and clean for the gringos . . .

The fabric on the bed is so soft, gringo sheets. What other secrets did Gabriel have?

Let me show you the pool.

Gabriel stands at arm's distance, shy and gentlemanly, unlike brutish Juan, who pokes and pinches as if I'm some animal. I follow Gabriel, who caresses the pool water to check the temperature.

Still early, so it's a little cold, he says. Then he takes off all his clothes except for his underwear briefs, and jumps in head-first.

You coming? He waves to me. I have swum in my underwear plenty of times with Lenny and Yohnny but not with a *boy* boy.

I won't look, promise, he says, and turns around and waits.

I take off my dress.

Don't look! I yell because I don't own a bra. I jump in. The cold water slaps my skin. I yelp. Gabriel laughs. Backstrokes across the pool. He flips to swim on his belly. I watch him nervously. I only know how to float.

I'll teach you, he says.

But then you can see me.

My arms and hands cover my breasts. They're two small lumps, but I still cover them.

Not for nothing, says Gabriel, but I got more stuff to show than you do.

He flexes his pecs.

You bastard, I say, and splash water at him, and stretch out my arms wide, and lean back to float. He places his hands under me. Above me, the sun presses its warmth on my skin. Water fills my ears. For a moment I pretend I'm alone, just me and the sun.

Now paddle your feet, Ana. As fast as you can.

I paddle, splashing water into both our eyes.

He climbs out of the pool first and puts a towel on the floor for me to sit on. As if to keep from looking at my body, he points to the view of the valley. The clouds drift far away, teasing us with their presence, the land thirsty. It hasn't rained in weeks. He sits close enough to skim his fingers on my leg. The hairs on the back of my neck awaken. How much time has passed? We sit there in silence; his arm brushes against mine, my heart races.

So what if I stick my foot in it? What if I turn my head to meet his lips?

I wait for him to lean over, but he doesn't. He props his weight on one arm, then the other. He acts as if we had all the time in the world. But I don't have time, so I kiss him, right on the mouth, covering my breasts with my hands. Our full lips closed tight like our eyes, they press against each other like soft pillows. My insides spin around as if I'm still in the water. A thread pulls up between my legs, through my heart and up my throat. Don't pull away. Don't look at me. Not yet. Not yet. What have I done? Is this what Teresa and Mamá have warned me about? The trouble ahead, that once you start you can't go back. When we part, we both giggle. I clamp my legs together, open my eyes wide, pull in my body tight tight tight all around, covering every point of entry. He looks away embarrassed.

I should go, I say. If I don't get home soon my mother will kill me.

Let me take you home.

He mops the edges of the pool as if to erase our time there together. I clumsily put on my dress, afraid to stay another minute, afraid of myself.

After he drops me off a few feet from my house, he says, I'll see you tomorrow? His smile takes over half of his face.

Okay, sure. I pretend my life isn't about to be turned upside down.

Mamá isn't home when I arrive. What a relief. I rush over to my room to look in the mirror to see if Gabriel's kiss left a mark. I stare at my reflection and pucker my lips. They look swollen, transformed.

ONE KISS AND SUDDENLY I'M UNA MUJER. NOT A NIÑA OR jovencita but a woman. I touch the mirror to understand how it happened without warning, but with the hot-pink dress on, the girl who had never been kissed is gone. I am Ana, about to be married and to travel to America. Juan Ruiz is expected before noon.

I look into the distorted mirror at the white lace ruffles around the neckline over and around my shoulders. The dress cinches at the waist and barely covers my knees. Juanita has blown out my hair and tied it back into a bun at the crown with ribbon upon curly ribbon, in white and pink. I put one hand on my waist, shift my hip to one side. Is that really me?

In New York I'll have a closet full of dresses and jewelry. All kinds of purses and shoes. And Juan will pay for me to go to the salon every week and get my nails done. And he'll take me to see shows and we'll go dancing with live bands. And our house will be full of his friends and family. Every day will feel like a party.

Mamá walks into the room carrying her pouch of makeup.

Come by the window. The light is better, she says.

I kneel on the floor and lean against her knees. Hold myself up nice and tall so she can study my face.

Look up, she says, and brushes mascara on my eyelashes, then blows into them to dry. She pulls the sides of my eyes and draws a line above them, leaning back for a better look.

I want to see, I want to see, I say, and jump over to the mirror. Surprise! My eyes are twice as big. My lashes twice as long.

Mamá pats pink cream on my cheeks and curses how dark my skin has become. Even darker after spending time with Gabriel in the pool.

What if Gabriel sees me now? He'd probably think I'm too much woman for him.

Mamá pats red lipstick on my lips and asks me to lick and spread.

But Juan won't like it, I say.

Just for the photo, she says. So your lips don't get lost on your face.

She takes a tissue to blot them. A trick she recently learned from a magazine. So it won't get on your teeth, she says.

I go back to the mirror, thinking of all those times Teresa stole my mother's makeup and put it on to sneak out at night to meet El Guardia. I smile to show Mamá that no lipstick got on my teeth. We all need some kind of mask.

Mamá makes me sit outside on a wooden bench, under the shade of an almond tree, where it's much cooler than our house—a real furnace. Teresa, Yohnny, Juanita, and Lenny are off to the beach.

Ana, get out of that dress, Teresa insists. El Guardia will be here any second.

She's in her bathing suit, a sausage casing, under the oversize men's shirt she uses for cover.

My little brother, Lenny, already in his cutoff shorts, slaps his sweaty arm against mine.

Gabriel will be there, Teresa eggs me on as if she knows about the kiss.

Oh the fun I will miss, I say, thinking about Mamá's warning. *Not a hair out of place. Not a speck on the dress or else.*

Ooh Gabriel, Lenny teases.

I try not to blush.

When he gave me a lift home on his bike, the feeling my mother calls the devil who steals reason came up between my legs. Without reason is how women make mistakes. Big ones, like Teresa, who got caught by the devil the day El Guardia stuck his cucumber inside her and gave her a baby Mamá has to care for.

Go, already, I tell them. Mamá'll kill me if I get up from this bench.

One time, Yohnny spoke back to her and she hit him with a broomstick so hard he lost consciousness. She did cry afterward for those three, maybe five minutes when we all thought he was dead.

You really want to go away with that old man? Teresa asks. Her tits sit on her chest like hand grenades.

It's true, Juan's old and hasn't married and has no children. This worries my mother, but he comes from hardworking people who can be trusted. And he's tall and fair, and his shoes are always polished. Besides, out of all the girls Juan could marry and take to America, he picked me.

Look, Teresa, I finally say, when one's hungry no bread is too hard to eat. I have no choice.

Teresa takes a small towel from her bag and pats the sweat from around my hairline and neck, her breath fresh from chewing on fennel.

You're a ghost with all this powder. And this ridiculous dress? Poor little thing.

I like the dress, I mumble. All my life I wore Teresa's hand-me-downs although she is wider and shorter than me. She's probably jealous. The dress smells new, all starchy and crisp.

C'mon, Ana, if the old man wants you he'll wait until we get back from the beach.

El Guardia's clunker pulls up. One of the doors has fallen off, but he has temporarily duct-taped it back to the car. Merengue blasts from his radio. He honks on the horn.

You don't have to marry him, Teresa says, extending her hands. As El Guardia revs the engine she reminds me that Gabriel is waiting for me at the beach.

I touch my lips. Underneath the lipstick, I can still taste his kiss.

Mamá, a real mind reader, rushes out of the house and swats Teresa away with a kitchen towel.

Get away from her. Why do you want to ruin Ana's life the way you ruined yours?

Mamá turns to me and asks, Do you want to stay here and end up with a good-for-nothing, pigeon-toed, backward man like El Guardia, who can't even feed his own child? Or do you want to go to New York with a respectable, hardworking man so you can make something out of yourself and help your family?

At least El Guardia loves me, Teresa shouts back, loud enough to cut through the music blasting from the car.

Ay, love, love, love. You children don't know anything about love or survival. You live in the clouds.

I can't look at either of them, so I stare at Yohnny, who's tying a goat to a tree. If he lets her loose she'll run. She looks at me with longing. I want to pet her.

Teresa's feet cut the ground, her nostrils flare, prepared to hold Mamá back so I can make a run for it.

I bite the inside of my cheek and breathe in the fresh-mown grass, the scent of lilacs and manure, of decayed mangoes fallen from the tree. I listen beyond the arguing and music for the hummingbirds that flap flap flap their wings, for the gravel under Lenny's feet, for Gabriel's breath in my ear. At least I kissed him when I had the chance.

El Guardia honks again. He knows not to step out of his car when Mamá's home. When she first caught his devil eyes on Teresa, she warned El Guardia, if he stuck it into her daughter she would chop off his dick. Everyone knows Mamá can carve a chicken blind.

C'mon, Ana, stand up for yourself.

Teresa pushes, although she knows my marriage agreement was sealed with hard liquor.

Leave her alone! Yohnny calls out to Teresa.

Bully me, and I transform into an ant. I'm not like Mamá and Teresa, who fight for every inch of land and man.

Yeah, leave her alone, Lenny says, and stands in front of me with his arms crossed high on his chest, knowing full well Teresa can flick him away with her pinkie.

Don't worry, I say. We'll all be together in New York one day. You'll see.

And we'll ride the subways? Yohnny chimes in.

And spickee inglis, Lenny says.

Over there you'll have no one, Teresa says. No family. No one to protect you. She presses her forehead against mine, our sweat gluing us to each other.

Yohnny karate-kicks the air and splits us apart.

I'll protect you, he says. I'll fly there and kick whoever's ass.

A man's heart in a child's body, that's Yohnny.

I hold back from laughing, to not upset Mamá. She counts on me to follow through on this.

Stop it, Teresa. I don't want to go to the beach, okay!

Teresa rolls her eyes and hugs me as if it's the last time I'll ever see her.

Mamá's so proud of me. Finally I've accepted what she knows is the only answer for me.

Enough already. Mamá waves them away. Leave now. I'd rather Juan not see you hooligans being such a bad influence on Ana, Mamá says.

Lenny and Yohnny whoop and holler their way back to El Guardia's car. They slide into the backseat through the open window and stick their arms out, waving good-bye.

You're just like Papá, Teresa says, who lets Mamá boss him around.

But even she knows this marriage is bigger than me. Juan is the ticket for all of us to eventually go to America.

The sun bites hard into one side of my face. I try to think of the beach, of the way the waves crash against the rocks, the fun to be had. Of Gabriel and the keys he carries in his pocket. The way he traced my body, his eyes like fingers. I had memorized the ends of his tight curls, his skin an orange-brown glow, as if someone had lit a candle inside of him.

All morning, my father rocks on his chair and smokes his pipe. My mother pokes her head out the kitchen window checking on me, smiling and waving. All her hopes and dreams tie into me. And as if to show me my good fortune—to sit, do nothing in my new dress—she bosses Juanita and Betty to fetch some yucca and batata out back, to wash the sheets, to feed the chickens, and to mop the floors, muddied from yesterday's thundershower.

You so lucky, they say. Unlike them, I've never fantasized about going to New York. They track every dollar bill mentioned in passing conversation and gossip about every American hair clip, pair of shoes, or dresses worn by girls in the area who tease men like Juan in exchange for gifts and opportunity. They all hope for a proper proposal to get to a place where even country girls like us become glamorous and rich.

If there was time Papá would've killed a goat and invited everyone in the area to celebrate my departure. Mamá would've piled the plátanos and chayote on one serving tray, yucca covered in red onions on another. Yohnny would've shared his brew of mamajuana to get everyone loose. The house would've been full with neighbors and family. One sip of mamajuana, and I'd be digging my feet into the dirt in my backyard to the beats of the drum and the scraping of the güira. And Gabriel would've tried to keep his distance out of respect for Juan. But Teresa would've made him dance with me.

What could a kid like Gabriel ever do for me?

And yet we would spin and spin around as if we could turn back time. Stop it somehow.

Oh, I want to be grateful for my fortune. But I don't want to leave our house in Los Guayacanes painted the color of buttercups by my late grandfather, the only house for miles that has survived all the hurricanes. Our house, the one I share with my parents, Yohnny, Lenny, Teresa, Juanita, and Betty, where there is everything I know and can imagine, for all of my life.

WHEN JUAN ARRIVES MY DRESS IS WRINKLED. MY HAIR A mess. All the makeup gone. I have dozed off in a sitting position, waiting because any minute now he's to arrive. I wish Teresa would've stayed with me and not gone away with El Guardia. That she would've given me, at the very least, her blessing.

Juan drives his car over the grass, close to the entrance of our house. A film of dust covers it.

He's here, he's here, Mamá squawks, worse than the chickens.

In the daylight, Juan looks even more pale than I remember him. Mamá says that's better for the children's sake. Dark children suffer too much. She gives me a paper bag containing a botella for me and Juan to drink every morning so the babies come fast. A man can't call himself a man if he doesn't have children.

Juan is in a hurry to leave because he borrowed a car to fetch me.

My brother reserved a room for us, he says, in El Hotel Embajador for the honeymoon.

Is that so? Mamá lights up with every word about my future life.

The nicest hotel in the country, Juan continues.

The last time I was alone with a boy it was with Gabriel. Juan is a man. A head taller, twice as wide. Gray hairs around his ears, thinning around his forehead. Soft, pillowy hands and cheeks. Inevitably, we'll be alone. My throat locks up, an emptiness fills my stomach.

To distract myself I run through the list my mother gave me before Juan's arrival. Go to America. Clean his house, cook him dinner, clip his nails. Send Mamá money, learn from Juan, learn from the brothers. Study hard in school and become a professional. Learn English. Send for Mamá and Yohnny first, so they can work. Send for Lenny so he can enroll in school, and then for Papá and for Teresa and the baby if she is ever willing to leave El

Guardia behind. I'll demand what I need from Juan, for myself and my family. I will make myself indispensible.

Mamá talks to Juan as if I'm not here. She doesn't know about Gabriel, who may still show up to the wedding and speak now or forever hold his peace although my life is no telenovela.

Don't worry, señora, says Juan, boisterous as a cowboy. I'll take good care of your daughter. His confidence is kind of charming. He obviously is capable of taking care of us all. He's not a weak man. And his power is even more pronounced by the surrounding wilderness—overgrown trees and bushes impossible to tame.

My ears pick up the howl of the siren miles away, the occasional motorcycle, the hawks sweeping close enough for us to flinch. I look away from our yellow house, a flower planted on the greenest of earths. I imagine myself inside the skyscrapers, in the snow, under all the bright lights.

WITH JUAN THERE ARE MANY FIRSTS. HE OPENS THE CAR door for me to sit in the front, on the passenger side. I always have to sit in the back with Yohnny, Juanita, Lenny, Teresa, and Betty: cramped. Just this, I'm sure, impresses Mamá. Marrying Juan is like going to the moon. Up front, I have the best view of the road, of the world passing me by as Juan accelerates the car, switching gears.

We stop at the Ruiz restaurant, which sits right outside the city on our way to the hotel. Of course, everyone knows Juan there. The women especially. He doesn't introduce me. He sits me at a table that reeks of Clorox. No tablecloths. No walls. Just a slab of cement on the ground and sheets of zinc held up by a few poles, to protect the few customers eating at the table or sitting at the makeshift bar if it rains. I wait. The lights make my hands and arms look green. The waitress serves me a morir soñando with a straw. I don't have to share it with anybody. I sip the shake with my eyes lowered, and listen to the familiar song playing on the radio. I remember the time I danced to that song with my brother Yohnny after the chores were done and dinner had been eaten.

Juan carries over a tray with two pressed sandwiches. Behind him, El Cojo, a funny-looking man, limps toward us, his shirt off by one button.

So you're the one, El Cojo says to me, then catches a fly with his index finger and thumb and flicks it to the floor as if wanting me to fear him.

So what do you think of the place?

I shrug. The restaurant?

You can call it that, El Cojo says.

Juan fake punches him and says, Don't worry, parajita, one day, people'll travel from all over to eat here. We're gonna make it real nice, you and me.

Really? I say. I had never thought I would own a restaurant before.

Don't get ahead of yourself, El Cojo says. You don't even have the papers for the land yet.

I stay quiet and pick at the sandwich.

Money. Papers. Always the main subject.

El Cojo pulls out papers for us to sign. He studies the series of two-by-two photos of different women and picks one.

She looks like you, right? El Cojo squints his eyes, to reconsider the photo from arm's distance.

Juan takes a look. I take a look.

It's perfect, Juan agrees, comparing my face against the woman in the photograph.

I bite my tongue. Mamá's right, men don't know anything.

El Cojo stands up. All right then, I'll be back.

He hobbles over behind the bar and acts as if all the work he has to do is one big favor, a real nuisance.

Juan takes a large bite of his sandwich. He catches all the drippings with his tongue. Eats quickly and voraciously. Mamá says you can read a man by the way he eats.

You not hungry?

Not really, I lie, too nervous to eat. The women at the counter stare at me or maybe at my lacy pink dress. They aren't much older, but nothing seems new to them.

Juan takes my sandwich and eats it too. He could've insisted I eat, as Mamá does when we have guests over. Even when they say they aren't hungry she sets a place at the table and makes them eat. And when their plate is empty she adds seconds, even if they claim to be full.

El Cojo returns and hands Juan a passport. Juan studies it. He looks through the papers. They shake hands and do small talk.

Congratulations, El Cojo says.

For what?

You're married!

Was that it? No ceremony? No guests or cake or you may kiss the bride or do you take this man? All this fuss Mamá made for a new dress and no party to go to?

Can I see?

I reach for the large yellow envelope filled with papers.

The woman in the photograph is an older version of me: Ana Ruiz-Canción born 25 December 1946.

I'm now nineteen years old?

The Original Certificate of Marriage hereby certifies that on the thirty-first of December, 1964, at the courthouse of Santo Domingo, Juan Ruiz and Ana Canción were married by an illegible signature.

Airline tickets: Pan Am, SDQ to JFK. 1 January 1965.

We are to arrive to New York City early early so the officers will be too tired to notice that I'm not the girl in the photo.

Teresa would call it bad luck to travel on the first day of the year, because it's like entering a room without going through a door.

By the restaurant's exit sign, I see some girls huddled over one another, whispering and giggling. Surely about me. My flaming pink dress feels brighter, more vulgar. The white lace barely covers my chest. Juan stares at the curled ribbons in my hair as if I am a present to be undone.

WE DRIVE TO THE HOTEL. JUAN TURNS ON THE RADIO. I have nothing to say. My dress hikes up when I sit in the car. He looks and tries not to look. His fingers shift gears inches away from my thigh. He reeks of rum and cigarettes. The brown paper bag Mamá gave me sits on my lap. Along with the botella, she packed an extra pair of underwear, a fragrant bar of jabón de cuaba, and a lipstick.

Ask Juan for new clothes. It's his duty. Men don't know their heads from their feet. Demand. Demand. Demand, she said.

At a stoplight he caresses my cheek. I try not to cringe. I don't want to disrespect. His hand drops on my lap like a dead rat.

You're too skinny, he says, that's got to change.

I cringe. He taps my nose and says, Don't worry. I'm a good man.

Always worry when someone says don't worry: my father's words.

He stops at a gas station and gets out of the car.

A panic enters my body. Worse than the day Lenny threw up tapeworms and his face turned red because some were caught in his throat. I thought he would die in front of me. Worse than the panic that entered me when I last saw Gabriel at the school and he had to save me from myself.

I'm all alone with Juan. And now I belong to him. In less than an hour, I've lost four years of my life. Ana Canción was fifteen. Ana Ruiz is nineteen. I clamp my legs together, ankles crossed, hands woven shut.

I check to see if the car door is locked. Two men are leaning back on crates against the wall outside of the tire shop that is now officially closed. It's dark outside. Beyond the dim streetlamp over the gas tanks there is just black. If I run I might be able to find my way back home. But Juan returns, locks my door, and flicks on the overhead light inside the car to get a better look at me. His mustache is a shadow over his lips.

You're so damn beautiful. You kill me, you know that?

He drives through the dark roads. We see only as far as the headlights. And far beyond, lights appear like fireflies.

La Capital? I ask.

He points, a real tourist guide. The house of Columbus is right over there. Have you been, Ana?

I have never visited the capital or any other part of the country besides San Pedro de Macorís.

He spews out names: the Fortress of Colón, the Ozama Fort. The greatest capital in the world: Santo Domingo, the heart of America, where it all started.

His talking overwhelms me. The honking of cars, the festive nighttime atmosphere, as if all the city is inside of a disco. Everyone's celebrating.

Do you want me to take you?

His proud voice pleads for adoration and gratitude. So I say nothing. Nothing at all.

JUAN PULLS INTO EL HOTEL EMBAJADOR'S PARKING LOT. I stick my head out of the window to get a better look, my eyes and mouth wide open. The fountains shoot water into the air. Flocks of flamingoes gather and disperse. Fancy cars line up in the parking lot.

You like it? Juan beams.

I step out of the car and spin around, taking in the shiny sequined dresses. Men in fitted suits, their hair greased and slicked back like movie stars. The large chandeliers, the buffed marble floors, the high ceilings, the arranged flowers, the lit-up pool, the air-conditioning, the cloth-covered sofas, the hundreds of people chatting, clinking glasses, smoking.

At the check-in counter, Juan orders champagne.

Send it to the room, he says to the bellboy. Fourth floor. There he goes with his charming confidence. All the world is there to serve him.

I hesitate before stepping into the elevator. He grips my hand and I close my eyes.

You better get used to it. There's an elevator in our building.

Our building? He lifts me up over his shoulder and laughs. I hesitantly kick open the door of our room, huge with a double bed. Large windows overlook the pool. The chill from the air conditioner wraps around my neck. I've never been inside a room so cold. I'm afraid to look at his face. It's all too much. Too much.

Someone's at the door. Champagne arrives. Juan pops the cork. I jump back when it shoots across the room. He hands me a glass.

Drink the first one fast, he says.

I don't drink.

It'll help relax you.

I gulp it like medicine. It goes straight to my head. I press my nose on the windowpane and look below. Women linger at the edge of the pool in string bikinis, men chase after them.

Come here. Juan lies on the bed. His shoes are already discarded on the floor. His blazer hangs on the chair. In minutes he's made himself at home as if he stays in hotels all the time. I pretend not to hear him, not to see his reflection off the window. I lean on it, the cold glass on my cheek.

He walks over, stands behind me. He unzips my dress. I'm not wearing a bra. Mamá says bras are to hold something up. I stand still, my back to him. He unties the ribbons from my hair, one by one, and lets them fall down my back. The hair around my neck makes me feel more protected, less cold.

He combs through it, his fingers catching inside the knots. He places his palm on my back, his hands clammy from holding the champagne bottle.

He slips the dress off my shoulders and it gathers around my ankles. He tries to get a look at my face. I resist. He pulls me toward him. I stiffen further, my stomach hard and tight.

Please don't, I want to say. Let's wait.

I see him see me, my naked body reflected on the window. He steps back for a better look.

What's so funny? I say.

Everything about you is so new.

He sticks his hands under my armpits.

So new. So soft.

He presses his bulge against my back. I cry. He turns me around so I face him.

I want to go home. Please.

This is your home. Me and you are a family now. Don't you see?

The crying comes faster and harder. It can't be true. I have a family. I have a home.

I want to go home, I repeat, my voice smaller, broken.

Your parents were the ones who called me so I could take you away.

I'll never love you, I say. I throw myself on the bed and curl up as small as possible. I no longer feel my body. I am no longer in the room.

I'm sorry, Ana. But we'll have to make this work.

Juan turns on the radio. He lies on the bed, next to me, my back away from him. He spoons me. The woolly fabric of his pants rubs against my bare skin, almost warm and comforting.

He says, Don't worry, little bird, I'm going to take care of you. He wraps his arm around me, still wearing his shirt, his tie undone.

Combs back my hair from my face and sings along with the radio.

Solamente una vez . . .

His voice thunders against my back. So warm, so rich, a glaze on my skin. Suddenly we're in my backyard. Ramón's on the guitar. Papá tends to the fire. Beer bottles clink, my brothers giggle. Mamá's full of dreams for me.

Una vez nada más
Se entrega el alma
Con la dulce y total
Renunciación

We listen to song after song, the words infused with loss and sadness. He turns me to face him. His eyes, bruised, tired, and hopeful. He grabs the champagne bottle from the nightstand, hands it to me, and says, Drink some more. It'll make it easier.

I hesitate, overwhelmed by the rancid flowery scent. I gulp it like the medicinal juices Mamá makes, straight from the bottle; the sour grape taste sits on my tongue.

I lie on the bed, stiff, turn my head, look toward the window. Watch the reflection of his legs and my legs, his clothed, mine naked.

He unbuttons his shirt. Exposes his plump hairy chest and stomach. Presses against mine, sticky but warm. He kisses my cheek, my ear, my neck, wet and lingering. His fingers feel like clothespins on my nipples. *Stop. It hurts.*

He unbuckles his pants. I don't look when he grabs it, hard and wide like a pestle. Chirping. Croaking. Screeching. The explosive mating song of frogs. The pain, short and sharp.

After, he gets out of bed and tucks in his shirt, zips his pants, puts on his vest.

Clean yourself up and try to sleep. We leave in a few hours. I'm out of cigarettes, he says, and walks out of the room.

The room is cold, so cold. I pull the starched white sheets over me. Move away from the wet spot on the bed. The airplane will be cold. New York will be cold too.

PART II

ARE YOU A MANATEE OR A SHARK?

Mamá asks this when she sees me idling by the bushes when I'm supposed to be doing chores.

When Mamá was a kid she saw lots of manatees. They'd show themselves up close to the shore, move slow slow across the beach. Large like cows, black and leathery. So close she could almost pet them.

Manatees have six teeth in each jaw—and not even in the front of their mouths, but in their cheeks. They move slow and mind their own business. Sharks, though, could have like fifty teeth in their mouth at a time.

But look at where that got manatees, she says. They're practically extinct. Sharks just have to show themselves and everyone steers clear.

IN NEW YORK IT SNOWS. SO MUCH SNOW. JUAN'S BROTHER
César welcomes us at the airport with winter coats. He's the only brother I had yet to meet. He emerges from a crowd of other men, waiting by the baggage claim. He's the youngest. And darkest. Tall and skinny, sparkling eyes, warm smile.

Not bad, he says, taking a good look at me, punching Juan in the arm. He covers my head with a large knitted hat, then grabs my bags from my hand. Juan pinches me under my arm.

Don't look at people, it attracts trouble. And close your mouth.

Am I staring?

Juan moves quickly, pushes me through the sliding doors. A big fat suction. The sharp cold air stings and bites. The city so loud I cover my ears.

What did you think of the plane? César asks. My first time, the plane was so shaky, I almost peed in my pants.

Everything good, I say. Like a dream.

Juan yanks me and all our luggage, stuffed with packages for his friends, his associates, his family, toward the parked car.

Inside my coat I can still feel myself, a residue of dried sweat all over my skin.

I stick out my tongue to catch a snowflake.

We don't have all day. Juan talks louder than everyone else.

Juan loads the trunk. César opens the back door for me. Welcome to New York, little lady, he says.

Oh. Thank you. My voice is alien to me. An ache in my chest.

Everything set for tomorrow? Juan asks César once we're settled in the musty car. Furry red rugs cover the front seats, and there are sheets of damp cardboard under our feet. A rosary and a picture of a naked lady dangle from the rearview mirror. I have the backseat all to myself. No Yohnny, Teresa, Lenny, Juanita, and Betty. No sweaty arms and thighs or bony elbows poking in my ribs. No talking over each other. I miss them so much.

All work and no play, César says, and laughs. He turns on the radio and sings along to a Dean Martin song full of static.

Juan shuts the radio off. The silence makes it as if someone died.

Snow mutes the city. The cars inch along the highway. The bridge spectacularly long. The river iced. The trees bare. Everything is gray.

You missed the exit! Juan yells at him, and slaps his head.

Trust me, César says, and drives right into midtown. I just want to give the little lady a taste of New York.

But now we'll hit traffic. Juan sucks his teeth.

I feel ant small among all the skyscrapers. We move through the city slowly, cars lined up, pushing up against each other like dominoes on cardboard. And the people, mummified, carrying so many packages in bright-colored bags, all in a hurry just like Juan, as if they have somewhere urgent to go.

My nose presses against the car window. My breath fogs the pane. A soft snow comes down. We're inside one of those snow globes I saw at the airport store.

All right, César, you had your fun. Can you get back on the highway now?

At the stoplight, César turns to me and says, Pretty cool, huh?

I nod yes. He's a troublemaker like my brother Yohnny. Like Gabriel, César seems to have secret keys to secret places. Nothing like Juan, all serious. All business.

After we drop Ana off, I need you to take me somewhere, Juan says to César.

At your command, jefe.

I pull away from the window. You're leaving me?

Just for a few hours. I've got some business to do.

But why can't I come with you?

Ana, don't even start. Your mother assured me you would know how to keep busy.

My teeth clench. I tremble. Manatee or shark? I show all my teeth but Juan has moved on. He turns on the radio and switches to the Spanish news station. Johnny Ventura's coming to town.

Civil unrest in Santo Domingo. Cuban exiles fired a bazooka at UN headquarters.

César speeds up on the highway, weaving in and out of cars. Outside the window the river glistens, the sky—early morning blue, but not like back home. New York's blue slices right through the skin.

JUAN'S APARTMENT SMELLS BAD. AT BEST, LIKE WET CARD-board, at worst, like something dead. I don't say anything, not to offend him. Suits, covered in plastic wrap, are piled on the furniture. Stuffed boxes. Bare mattresses lean against the wall.

How many of you live here? I ask.

César laughs. Depends on the day.

Don't worry, Juan says. My brother Hector moved out this morning. He got a job in Tarrytown and moved his family up there. It's us and César . . .

You're gonna live with us too? I try to hide my relief that I won't be living alone with Juan.

César's barely here, with all the trouble he gets into.

A man's got to use his gifts. César defends himself.

Juan shows me around the apartment. We climb over the clutter in the living room and walk into the kitchen, a long hallway of a room. A small red metallic table, a chair, and a white stove with four burners lined up against the wall. There's no place to cook over a fire, to stack the wood, to pile the coal.

A thin film of grease covers the stove and the walls surrounding it. I try not to focus on the large porcelain sink, yellowed and full of dishes as Juan speed-talks.

This is how you turn on the hot water, the cold water. This is how to turn on the stove.

Where do we get water and gas? I ask. Back home we fetched water from the well.

Juan, in a hurry to leave, doesn't bother to answer. The refrigerator's tucked all the way at the end. Only one person can enter the narrow kitchen at a time. The bedroom is on the other side of the apartment. The bed is unmade and more boxes are piled and stacked against the wall.

What's in them? I ask Juan.

Nothing that concerns you.

Next to the bedroom door is the entrance to the bathroom. A frayed brown towel hangs on a rack. The tiles, moldy and yellow. The sink and mirror are splotched with toothpaste and beard clippings. The shower curtain needs washing.

Make sure not to flush while someone's taking a shower, Juan says.

It'll freeze your tits off. César laughs.

Don't mind him, Juan apologizes.

At the door, before they leave, Juan hands me the brown paper bag I had seen César pull out from the car's trunk earlier. In it is something warm and alive. I drop it to the floor.

They laugh.

César picks it up and pulls out a chicken by its neck.

Welcome to America, he says.

He hands it to me. I look into its glassed-over eyes. The drop must have injured it. I've held plenty of chickens before, plucked, chopped, and cooked them too. But here, I want to save the chicken from its fate.

Juan jiggles his keys and wraps a red scarf around his neck.

Don't open the door for anyone. Don't leave the apartment until I explain how things work around here. Keep the doors locked.

Why? Do people break in?

Sometimes. But this is a good building. The people here keep to themselves and out of trouble. But don't be fooled, New York is dangerous. People here aren't like they are back home. They care only about themselves.

I must look scared and pathetic to him because he softens his eyes and picks up my chin.

Don't worry. I won't let anything bad happen to you. You're my pajarita.

Juan kisses me on my forehead.

Do you need anything while I'm out? he asks.

Demand, demand, demand, Mamá said. Underwear. Some

clothes. Food. Perfume would be nice. Nail polish. Money for my family back home. What to ask for first?

Ana, I don't have all day.

I'm good, I say. Not asking for anything might make him not ask anything from me.

César grabs Juan's collar and pulls him out of the apartment.

The apartment is a sad mess. Thank god I have the chicken as company. Dust covers everything. It all needs a wash.

I pull the chicken out of the bag. Prop it on the table. It quivers, barely moves. I'm sorry, I say, then twist its neck and stuff it back into the brown paper bag.

I take off my heavy coat, which is twice my size. Off goes the sweater Juan's sister-in-law gave me before I boarded the plane back in Santo Domingo. Off goes the flaming pink dress. After two days, it needs airing out. I put on a white undershirt I find in a drawer in the bedroom. The furniture is so filthy I fear something will crawl out from its cracks. And the smell, Mamá would know in a second. A mix of man funk? Cologne? Cigarette ashes? Dead rat.

Get to work, Ana! You're now a wife. You have duties.

I start with the kitchen. I mix vinegar with water in a bowl and scrub the grease from the walls and counters. I pull a hunk of ham, bottles of soda, a bag of bread, and a bunch of plátanos from the fridge and clean the shelves. I rearrange the condiments, making notes on a napkin, with a pencil I found by the saltshaker, of what Juan needs to buy at the supermarket. I place the dead chicken in the fridge for plucking, cleaning, chopping, and cooking later. I soak the sheets and scrub them clean. So soft. Like the sheets at the gringo's house Gabriel took care of. *Ay Gabriel, are you thinking about me?* I line the sheets to dry in the kitchen then make a clear path in the living room to walk through. I scrub the bathtub. Mamá and Teresa would love this bath. Just like in the movies, where you can fill it with bubbles. I find makeup, sunglasses, and earrings under the bath-room sink.

Women have been here? In this mess? No wonder Juan went looking for a wife.

Dusk falls, very quick. Juan hasn't returned.

I turn on the radio to drown out the clank-clank-hiss-hiss of the heater.

Gowing to da chapa, Ana go to get ma-a-areed, gowing to da chapa, Ana go to geet ma-areed.

I wrap a flannel robe I find in the bathroom tight around my body. The heater makes it hard to breathe. I open the window, to clear the air. I sit by it and wait for Juan. I place the ceramic doll Juan bought me at the airport in Santo Domingo on the table. She wears a blue dress and a yellow sash around her waist. My sweet, hollow Dominicana will keep all my secrets: she has no eyes, no lips, no mouth.

Down below, the streetlamps light up. In front of a showroom filled with cars, a young man shovels snow. He wipes fingerprints off the windows and stares into the storefront with longing. They're preparing to close. Above the store, the musicians in the building set up to play. Already a line forms. Everyone's dressed up.

Maybe Juan will take me one day.

IN THE SAME WAY HE SHOWED ME AROUND THE APART-
ment, Juan gives me a tour of the neighborhood. He's pleased that
I cleaned the place but annoyed he can't find anything. Before we
walk out of the building he lowers the knitted hat I'm wearing
over my ears and knots the itchy scarf around my face. I breathe
in and out of the woolly scarf. The bright white sky reflects off
the snow and blinds me. He wraps his arm around my shoulders
and together we fight the cold wind that pulls us away from the
street we're about to cross.

People wait for their turn, cars wait at the stoplight. All the
litter is stuffed into trash cans. So much order. Phone booths and
blue mailboxes on every other corner. Convenient. Efficient. No
green to speak of. Trees naked and gray like the cement of the
sidewalks. Across the street from our building is the parking lot
for Columbia Presbyterian Hospital.

One of the largest hospitals in the world, he says as we cross.
This is the Audubon Ballroom, where the Jews pray, the blacks
make trouble, and we can watch movies in Spanish and go dancing. Under the ballroom I can now see the car showroom up close.
Juan makes new fingerprints on the glass.

One day soon, we'll buy a new car, Juan says, tracing the silhouette of the Buick on display in the window. Across from us is
the German shop that sells sausages. Beside it, the Jewish photo
shop. The Cuban everything store displaying a life-size doll,
toilet paper, toy airplanes, packets of pencils and notebooks, cigarettes, shoe polish, a plastic bucket, a mop, extension cords.

If the Cuban doesn't have it, says Juan, it must not exist.

Down on 165th Street, we visit the post office. Inside, an
unsettling quiet, an antiseptic smell, a waiting area, an orderly
line. Nothing like back home where public offices have shouting
matches and vendors selling their fruits, pastelitos, and lottery
tickets to the crowds of people waiting.

Indoors, Juan makes his voice small and shows me the window where he orders stamps and buys money orders to send back home to Ramón, who administers their investments. All together there are four Ruiz brothers, three in New York now and one in Dominican Republic.

He points across the street to St. Rose of Lima Church; next to it is the rectory and a few steps away, the school. It looks like an apartment building, but Juan assures me it's a school. Soon, hundreds of children in plaid uniforms parade around the block led by two nuns. What a simple life they lead, with God at their beck and call.

Is that the school I'll attend? I ask.

No. In September, you'll go to a secretarial school so you can learn how to type. And then you'll work at my friend's agency. Don't you worry, everything's been decided.

Tell him you want to study to be a professional. To open your own business, to help your family. Typing is a good start, but that's not the only thing you'll do. Tell him. Tell him.

Juan walks quickly. He pulls my hand this way then that way, and finally we stop and enter La Bodeguita downstairs, under our building, next to the bar, Salt and Pepper.

A bell chimes when the door closes behind us. Loud merengue spreads out inside the cramped store, the burst of the drums, the scratch of the güira. At every turn I catch the tail of Teresa's skirt, Mamá's laugh, Lenny's knobby knees. My heart races, a sudden warmth. I pull off my hat and scarf, overwhelmed by the music, the little store, the shelves as tall as the ceiling. A young man watches me from behind the counter. He winks when I look his way.

Juan grabs my shoulders and tells him, Compadre, this is my wife.

You married? Congratulations, he says. Then to me, I'm Alex, at your service. If you ever need anything . . .

Before I can respond, or even smile back, Juan pushes me toward the wall of crates filled with plátanos, yucca, potatoes, lettuce. In my ear, he whispers, We don't buy vegetables here. This

Boricua sells them for twice as much as the supermarket. Then he picks items from the shelf and explains. This is for washing your teeth: Colgate. This is to wash the windows: Windex. This is to wash the dishes: Palmolive. This is to scrub the toilet: Comet. This is what you will eat for breakfast: Cornflakes. This is what you will eat for lunch: Chef-Boyardee. He piles ten cans of it on the counter.

Nutritious. Easy to make. You just heat and eat.

At the register, Juan grunts at each item as if the adding of numbers causes him pain. Alex smiles knowingly at me and says, Me and your husband go way back.

Weird to hear him say "husband." Alex winks at me and takes Juan's money. He pulls a Hershey's bar from a stack near the register and hands it to me.

American chocolate. It's good.

For me?

I'm not paying for that, Juan says.

It's on me, you stingy bastard.

Let's go, Ana, before this guy makes me spend more money.

Alex smiles with his mouth closed so I can't see any of his teeth.

Once inside our building Juan repeats, I don't want you to go into La Bodeguita without me. You don't know Alex. He's only trouble.

But he gave me free chocolate. He can't be that bad.

Be careful, Ana. I have eyes everywhere, you understand me?

Yes. I do. I do.

MAMÁ MADE US BELIEVE SHE HAD EYES ON THE BACK OF her head too. And yet we easily hid from her for hours on one of our almond trees. Yohnny had laid wooden planks across the branches and built a fortress armed with slingshots, a pile of rocks, and pointy wooden spears for the invasion.

The conquistadors are coming, Yohnny said. And we all looked for *La Pinta, La Niña,* and *La Santa María* to emerge far in the distance. We waved the ships over. We made piles of treasures ready to trade: coconuts, mangoes, sugar cane, and palms. The sea was thick with fish, the sky so full of birds we couldn't even see the sun.

What do they bring? Juanita asked.

Shiny glass beads to wear around our necks and bright red cotton scarves, said Betty.

Come, come, Teresa said, let me be your wife, your puta, your servant.

Oh, wait, I see a Marine ship, Lenny said.

I see it too, Yohnny said. Now the Yankees are here.

Get out the beer. Kill a chicken. A goat. Roast some of those sweet potatoes from our garden, said Juanita.

And what do we get? Lenny said.

They will show us their knives and guns and we will hurt ourselves with them.

Our stomachs hurt from laughing. We played until it got dark enough to see the stars and the spaceships. Lenny kept a log of them, date and time. What if one of those ships comes down and snatches one of us?

Do you believe in time travel, Yohnny? I asked.

You crazy, like traveling back to the past and into the future? asked Teresa.

Like why is today today and tomorrow tomorrow? What if tomorrow is today? Or yesterday tomorrow? Who decided the size of a minute or an hour? Why do some minutes feel so long and others so short? I mean, like the stars, how this book said that what we see is actually the past star, not the present star. Like right now, even if we can see them so bright, in their time, at their speed, they could've already been exploded. Gone. Poof.

What if right now you are here and somewhere else too? Yohnny said. Like you are Ana but there is another Ana, on another earth. Or in a future earth. And if we're like the stars, then maybe there is only a past earth, like a past Ana?

You think so? I asked. Could that really happen, you think?

ON MOST NIGHTS I TRY TO WAIT FOR JUAN BUT FALL
asleep on the sofa. I plate mangu and slices of ham and leave it
over the gas stove, in case he's hungry. I hear him peel off his
pants and fling them over a chair, undo his watch and toss it on
the dinner table. He relaxes his fat body against me as if I'm a
decorative cushion, smothers me with his smell of cigarettes and
whiskey. Slaps my ass in the same way Papá does to get cows
moving.

Dinner's ready, I say, then pop up to a sitting position. Dinner's ready, will always be ready, until death do us part.

Get me a drink. I'm thirsty.

Where's the bottle?

He sighs. You don't know anything, do you?

After cleaning and organizing for weeks, I have tried my best
to know where things are, but he keeps moving the bottle.

It's surely good to have a woman around here. My brothers
are pigs.

This makes me happy. When my brothers arrive I plan on
bossing them around. I'm a woman with her own house to tend
to, her own family to care for.

If I don't hide the good stuff, Juan blabs on, those pigs will
drink it all.

I fetch the bottle, this time hidden in the toilet tank, and pull
a glass from the cabinets. My hand shakes while I pour the whiskey. I want to do everything right, for him to be proud, to be
without regrets.

Are you sure you don't want to eat? I ask.

It's two in the goddamn morning. Get over here. Let me look
at you, he says, and stares long and hard at me. Usually he gives
me the *I-want-to-stick-it-in-you* look, and I close my eyes and just
let him stick it in. But today he has a new look, one I haven't seen
before.

You inspire me. You know that?

Me? What do you mean? The happiness must've shown all over my face. No one has ever said such a thing to me.

Me and my brothers been talking. We're gonna buy a Buick. Been eyeing it for a while, the one in the showroom downstairs. The Jews started a taxi business for their people, and I'm thinking if we get in on it early we can start with one car, then build the business, you know?

But don't you all already have a car?

We can't put that old car to work. We need a designated taxi car, a nice car, so I can drive people around in style, even you.

I don't need you to make a fuss over me.

Of course you do. You're my wife, my princess.

Really?

I thought of myself more as the flat-chested sister who had to do most of the chores.

And you, Princess Ana, are going to be our operator for the taxi business.

What do you mean 'operator'?

People'll call and tell you where they need to be picked up and we'll go get them. The Ruiz Taxi service will be run by Dominicans for Dominicans.

Juan's gruff voice cracks from exhaustion, from smoking. A spoonful of honey will fix it.

Juan, you're crazy. *Me asking people, What city, please? Name, please? One moment, please.*

His eyes light up.

You'll also learn to drive.

Could I really learn to drive?

And you can buy me a new coat with fur around the collar like the movie stars, I blurt out, and spin around swishing my flannel robe, the fabric rubbing together, sparking.

Yes, mi pajarita, you can have a new coat too.

Forgetting myself, I fling my arms around his neck and kiss him on the cheek.

So you love me? he asks.

My throat has to unlock. What do I know about loving a man?

Yes, I do, I say in a voice that sounds as if in between radio stations.

Nobody's gonna take care of you the way I take care of you. You know that?

Yes, Juan, I know.

Pretending, pretending. If I pretend enough maybe it'll feel true.

Both of us gonna have to make big sacrifices, to build us a house back home. Can I count on you?

Yes. Of course.

Juan wraps his arms around my head. If I turn it, he can break my neck like the poor chicken I put out of its misery over a month ago. I hold my body still. He props his head on his arms. I sink deeper into the plastic-covered sofa, his heaviness on top of me. He snores, soft then hard, an engine that needs fixing. No sex tonight. What a relief.

I listen to the cars honk outside, the hospital sirens wailing. A cold draft slides across my feet.

After he falls deep into sleep, I push him off just enough to slip from under him, to clear the plate on the stove. To turn off the lights. To make sure the doors are locked.

I'm a princess who's gonna drive a brand-new car. Ha!

CÉSAR AND JUAN COME IN AND OUT OF THE APARTMENT
to eat and shower. César often arrives rumpled, his hair shooting
in all directions, with bags under his eyes.

I saw an elephant walk down the street, he says.

Don't tell me.

That beast woke everyone up. Stopped all the traffic. His shit
the size of my head.

You're messing with me?

Elephants fall in love forever. Did you know that? So you
can't look them in the eyes or else.

Are you in love again?

César sits at the dining table with his sewing bag, the measuring tape around his neck. It's late, but he has to mend his shirt, the
one he plans to wear after work tomorrow to meet some woman
and go dancing.

Maybe this woman is making you see things, I say.

All women make me crazy, even you.

Don't stir me in that pot.

He sticks his tongue out at me and then threads a needle. So
quick. He places the ripped dress shirt under the lamplight, takes
his shot of coffee, and begins to weave in and out, making the
tiniest stitches, first vertically, then horizontally in line with the
cotton fabric. While he works I stand looking over his shoulder,
my eyes squinting to see better the tiny movements. When he is
done he makes me admire his work. It would take a magnifying
glass to see where it's ripped.

You want to learn how to sew and not leave a trace?

Just threading a needle takes me forever. Mamá had always
been disappointed in my hands.

Look at me. You need to hold the thread between the two fingertips. Go on, try it. Take the needle to the thread. Not the other
way around. That's the secret. Always yield to the needle because

it's inflexible. It's the secret with people too. If a person seems inflexible, yield, then slip in sideways and get what you want.

You sound like my mother!

He winks. Pulls out a pair of pants from the suit closet. Has me try it on. The waist dances low on my hips. He kneels to the floor and grabs my bare feet. The warmth of his hands surprises me.

Rule number one, always measure with shoes on.

I slip my shoes on. He pulls at the fabric, his hands patting down my leg.

This is how you pin.

His hands skim around my ankle like a critter.

Measure around the hem so it is even. Iron it before sewing. People skip the ironing, but it's a mistake.

I will teach you everything I know because in New York everyone needs a side hustle to survive. You can't just wait until someone finds you a job, you gotta have skills and get that cash.

Money, money, money. Is that all you brothers think about, César?

Don't you?

I SHOULDN'T HAVE OPENED THE DOOR. I WAS WARNED. BUT whenever the doorbell rings, I assume it's Juan. Except this time it's an old man with bushy eyebrows and missing fingers who wears war clothes and smells like an ashtray.

I'm your neighbor, he says. Mr. O'Brien.

Sorry, no inglis.

He shoves mail in my hand. I make out the name Juan Ruiz on top of an envelope.

Sorry, I say again, and take the mail and close the door. My heart bangs against my chest. Unsure whether I was right to take it, I place the mail on the kitchen table.

It's a long day waiting for Juan. I check the phone to make sure it's working. I anticipate Mamá's call. It's not easy for her to get to the phone in the center of town.

When Juan finally comes home I show him the letters. I tell him about Mr. O'Brien's visit in a childish tone that makes me upset at myself. I don't want to be scared of Juan like I am of my parents. But I am. When Mamá gets mad, her rage is loaded with fear and worry for me. When Juan gets mad, it's as if my dependence on him fuels the transformation in his body from concern, to anger, to fury. The veins in his neck swell, his eyes bulge, and he yells, You want trouble for us?

His voice always rips through me.

No, sir.

Juan slaps me across the face so hard, blood pools between my teeth.

That's so you remember, when I say not to do something, you have to respect it. You hear me?

I look at my feet. I hold back my tears, slump my shoulders, and retreat just enough to show deference. I have learned a lot from growing up with animals.

AFTER HE HITS ME, JUAN BRINGS HOME A TV AND INSTALLS it in the living room.

Happy? he says.

Oh my god, yes, I say.

Playing on the screen that day, in black and white:

Who
Loves
Ana?

Husband enters the apartment, slams his coat on the chair, crosses arms and yells for his wife. Bright-faced and excited, wife goes to hug husband. But when wife sees how mad husband is, she tries to escape. Husband signals for her to come back. Husband is quite handsome in his suit and slicked-back hair. And sometimes when husband gets mad husband speaks in Spanish.

I wait for those Spanish moments with bated breath.

Husband takes out a piece of paper from his pocket and waves piece of paper in wife's face. Wife cringes. Piece of paper is important. Wife's in trouble. Just like the time wife tried to sneak onto husband's show, where husband sings and plays bongos. Babaluuuu!

Husband tries to reason with wife but, but, but... husband yells and wife jumps back. Wife smiles and smiles. Husband is so loud the neighbors come to look but decide to let wife face her fate. Wife begs neighbors to stay. Wife hides behind her neighbors. Husband then yells at the neighbors. Wife and neighbors are all trapped now. [Laugh track]

Husband is now in kitchen wearing apron, whistling, happy. Surprise! Husband prepared food for wife. Wife reads newspaper as husband pops bread out of the toaster. Wife really likes food husband has prepared. Husband and wife make a big mess. Husband buys wife a box of candy. Wife faints. [Laugh track]

HAVE YOU HEARD FROM ANA? THIS IS WHAT GABRIEL ASKS
every time he sees Yohnny, Juanita, Betty, or Teresa. They lie on
the planks high in the tree and gaze up at the sky in the back of
the house, where Mamá won't come looking. On one side, the
dark sky threatens rain; on the other, the sun beams through the
wispy clouds, and the egrets fly low above them. Yohnny's supposed to be cutting back the grass to make a neat path to the
house. Teresa places on the ground a pile of whites to be washed
that have soaked all day in bleach.

What do you think Ana's doing right now? Yohnny asks Teresa.

She's not thinking about us, that's for sure. Teresa blocks the
sun with her hand. Ana's probably having a fancy meal right now,
eating a big hunk of meat she doesn't have to share with anybody.

Yohnny snorts. I bet Juan eats the meat and lets Ana suck on
the bones. Then Yohnny simulates steering a wheel. What if Juan
buys Ana a car, so when we get there she can drive us around?

Drive? Gabriel says. Have you seen her on a bike?

Yohnny! Teresa! Lenny! Mamá yells out. She begrudges how
Gabriel lingers, another mouth to feed.

Shhh, Lenny says, creeping below them, holding his knife,
aiming at a makeshift bull's-eye nearby.

If you cut me with that, Teresa growls, I'll tie you up on this
tree by your feet.

Why you gotta be like that? Yohnny tells her. Chill the fuck out.

Lenny aims, but the knife falls on his foot. Ay, ay!

Yohnny laughs. Next time, it will be your eye, you snot.

Lenny crouches, nursing his wound.

You go deal with her, Teresa says to Yohnny because she has
had enough of Mamá, who has doubled her chores after I left.
The unrest in the capital has Mamá and Papá on high alert, so
they fight all the time. There have been rumors that guerillas are
hiding in the valleys and mountains like they did in Cuba. If they

put a gun to Papá's head he'll have to choose between conspiring with the rebels or snitching on them.

Don't you want to go to New York too? Yohnny asks.

What, you think that you gonna go there and become some big-shot baseball player like Manny Mota? You don't even own a bat.

A guy can dream.

Teresa grabs a pigeon with both hands and blows into its ear: Ana, come home already. She lets it loose, pointing its beak in my direction.

THE PIGEONS APPEAR ALL AT ONCE. I FEED THEM EVEN IF Juan tells me not to.

They're the rats of the sky, Ana. They shit on the fire escape and feed on garbage. They're not like the pigeons back home that we plump up and cook on special occasions.

He says if we eat them they'll make us sick. Maybe even kill us. I have five of them that visit me regularly. I name them Yohnny, Juanita, Betty, Teresa, and Lenny. Sometimes they invite friends. If they don't eat the rice I put out for them, I stash away the plates before Juan arrives. Pigeon Betty likes to look at her reflection in the window. She bops her head and turns from side to side. Pigeons Yohnny and Juanita are inseparable. Sometimes Pigeon Yohnny pushes the others out of the way so Juanita has the plate all to herself. Pigeon Lenny is the smallest. And Pigeon Teresa, well, she takes up a lot of space, puffing her chest and poking her neck out as if she has a rooster complex. Sometimes I send the flock off to check in on my family and they disappear for days. When the pigeons return, letters appear in the mail. So many requests.

Teresa wants five dollars so she can take hair-cutting class.

The situation in Dominican Republic is out of control. Everyone's restless. None of the young men will be spared.

Can you send for Yohnny? Quick, before he gets himself killed.

Even Gabriel is walking around with a gun longer than his leg.

I caress the name Gabriel in Teresa's letter. The ink, the closest I am to the air he breathes.

Mamá asks:

> Did you get your papers?
> Are you in school?
> Are you keeping Juan happy?
> Can you send us money to fix A, to fix B, to fix C...?
> Poor Teresa works in a hole on the worst street of Macorís, where they steal the underwear off you if you walk too slow. She's skinny like you've never seen her because she can't recognize a cripple when he's sitting down.
> And El Guardia spends too much time in the capital, talking about the Yankees coming to save us and then selling himself to the rebels. He's coming back in a coffin.
> But Lenny, thank god for Lenny, who is going to school every day. But the ceiling's about to fall on us.
> Send money. Send money. Send money.

In between the lines:

> We miss you.
> We miss you.
> We miss you.
> Nothing is the same without you here.

WE LIVE IN A GOOD NEIGHBORHOOD, BUT BAD THINGS happen. Before I heard the gunshots I noticed the army of bow-tie-wearing black men enter the Audubon Ballroom, their families trailing behind them. Usually the cops hover nearby, but today there are none around. Not a single one. Maybe bigger trouble elsewhere?

Pop, pop, pop.

I crouch to the floor the same way I did when the military boys shot in the dark so that Papá would open the colmado after hours. I crawl over to César, who sleeps all day because it's Sunday. I clap in his ear but he's in deep.

Wake up! I tug at his pants. César curls into the sofa, his back to me.

César, please.

I duck my head.

What's happening? César says, half asleep. I pull him up from the sofa and stand behind him for protection. He opens the window. The city's volume turns up. A cold gust slaps my skin. A man pushing a gurney sprints across the street and slips into the Audubon.

César's head and chest now hang out the window. We watch a crowd of men rush out of the ballroom. One of them grabs a man and throws him to the ground, beating him, kicking him. Still no police? It's Sunday. Where are the police?

Finally, they arrive, clubs in hands. A man is wheeled out on a stretcher through the aluminum doors and across the street to the hospital. Cameras flash. People run out of the building screaming. Faces bury into shoulders. Hands flail. Who is dead? Someone's dead.

This is bad, César says.

What? What?

Another man is carried on a stretcher in the direction of the emergency room at the hospital.

This is really, really bad.

Maybe he or she will be okay?

Do you know how long I waited for this night? César says, fully awake now. Las Hermanas Milagros are performing at the Audubon, I even scored some new dancing shoes. I bet you anything the cops are gonna cancel the concert because of this shit!

Don't you care? Someone might be dead.

People get shot all the time, right? But getting a night off when there's something fun to do? That never happens.

Are you serious?

César moves throughout the apartment as if Las Hermanas Milagros is already playing. He steps from one corner of the living room to another, circling the coffee table, bumping into the dining table, the shelves, the sofa. He has a pile of records on the coffee table. He takes one from the top, pulls it out of its sleeve, and wipes it with the hem of his shirt.

El Pussy Cat . . . ay ay ay . . . Ana, this is the real good stuff!

El Pussy what? I ask as he pummels through the living room. I try to put things back in place. If only he stayed still.

Man, Mongo Santamaría channels God when he plays!

César screeches like a cat. His hand motions to scratch me. He bops his head and smiles. I flinch every time he bounces by me and reaches out, knees and elbows bent, head tucked in, teeth out, ready to pounce.

César sings and sings, out of tune, nothing like Juan.

Good, huh? His breath warms my face.

How can you dance right now? Look at those poor people.

Listen to this one. From me to you, he says.

César polishes a new record and places it carefully on the turntable, bends over to make sure the needle starts right at the beginning without slipping off. He throws himself on the sofa, puts his feet on the coffee table, and places his hands behind his head. He shuts his eyes to listen.

Isn't this the most beautiful song, Ana?

The phone rings. Let it be Mamá. Even if she'll only ask for money.

Mamá? I yell above the music and César singing and the noise outside the window.

But there's only a breath.

Juan?

The breath hangs up and a new creepiness invades.

Later, a still image of the Audubon Ballroom flashes on television.

Special Report! Especial! Special! Report! Reportaje!

A young man. A black man. Even handsome. Malcolm X.

The crowd on the street below amplifies the sound of the TV in the living room. Behind the dead man on the stretcher onscreen is the dental-supplies store and the small park where Juan and I sometimes sit on a bench and share an ice cream. There it is, our Broadway, making the news! The 168th Street subway entrance, the emergency room sign. Our building! The bright Salt and Pepper sign from the restaurant downstairs. The small rectangle in the midst of it all. Our red window curtains! There, a silhouette—is that me?

JUAN GIVES ME FIVE DOLLARS AND A SEALED ENVELOPE

that needs a stamp.

Go to the supermarket and buy eggs, he says. There's nothing in the fridge for me to eat, just oatmeal and cornflakes. Food for birds.

I have not yet left the apartment by myself. Always with César or Juan. Most days I don't leave the apartment at all. Between César and Juan, who come and go, from one job to the next, the wash has to be done every other day. The bathroom scrubbed. Meals made. Besides, I don't even have my own key. Juan says he hasn't had time to make a copy. Always an excuse.

Go already!

I feel like our chickens back home. Let in and out, at their owner's will.

I wear the wool dress from the bag full of used clothing given to Juan.

I don't yet own a wallet or purse, so I fold the five dollars and put it in my coat pocket. It swims in there. What if I lose it? I leave the building, relieved there's no cold wind to walk against. I cross the street toward the post office. It's on 165th Street, like our building. Across from the little park with benches facing the church. I stand in line with three other people. I try not to stare, so I look at the shiny black-and-red tiled floors, at the corkboard filled with notes. Everything is in English. Orderly and clean as a hospital. Soon I slide the envelope to the cashier after waiting on line. She talks as if her mouth is full and stamps the envelope. I nod, not knowing what I'm agreeing to. I give her the five dollars, damp with my sweat. She unfolds it and counts change. All these coins. Four dollar bills! I'm rich.

I must've been smiling, because she smiles back.

Once outside I high-five the sun. *Wepa! Mamá, look, a real New Yorker, doing my errands, a fistful of money.*

I turn on St. Nicholas to take a quick look at the school where the students wear uniforms. And then, straight straight I will go to Foodorama to buy eggs, milk, and maybe find apples and chocolate. Juan said the city is a grid.

Squares and rectangles, Ana. Numbers go up and down. The supermarket is on Broadway, off 161st. You can't miss it. But be careful. Don't talk to strangers. Don't go into any buildings that aren't stores. Don't look the police officers or drug addicts in the eye. Cross the street if necessary. And don't snail about. I have to get to work.

I look for signs of life inside the school, though the windows are shut tight. Nothing like my school back home, filled with interruptions and smart mouths. No Gabriel, who always snagged the desk next to mine. Maybe he still thinks of me?

I turn on 164th Street toward Broadway, but a police car is parked in the middle of the block. An officer writes up a ticket. I turn back on St. Nicholas, walk past the barbershop packed with men waiting for a buzz cut, wigs on display, a pawnshop with a window display of wedding rings, a camera, a gun. So much to discover. All I have to do is stay on St. Nicholas, parallel to Broadway, and then on 160th Street, walk up one block and there'll be the supermarket.

But 162nd Street is neverending. No more stores. No more 162nd Street. No more St. Nicholas. Edgecomb?

Nothing looks familiar. I turn around, looking for the George Washington Bridge. The Carvel Shop. The ground beneath me spins. The faces of strangers enlarge. Juan's waiting, he'll be late to work. A car slows down and rolls down his window. Words come out of a man's mouth. I run. My pockets, full of change, clink against my thigh. I run back in the direction I had come from but 162nd goes on and on. Then I see the pawnshop, St. Nicholas. I find Broadway. But I'm late. So late. I look around to make sure there are no witnesses. I go into La Bodeguita. The man Juan doesn't like isn't here. What a relief. It's another guy, much younger, who doesn't even greet me when I enter. I buy milk. Eggs. He calculates the sum. Not looking up from the cartoons he's reading in the newspaper. I give him a dollar. More coins!

The lobby door is already open. The elevator is already waiting. By the time I arrive to the apartment, I'm sweating inside my wool dress.

What took you so long?

Line at the . . . supermarket?

Really? At this hour?

I shrug. Juan is no idiot.

Now I don't even have time to eat, he says.

Of course you do. Sit, I say in a Mamá tone. I firmly place my hand on his shoulder, and like the animals on the farm, he calms down. Sit, Juan, sit.

He looks at my sweaty face. The wool of my dress makes me itchy everywhere.

If something happens to you, I'll never forgive myself, he says.

You see what a good man he is? Why did the streets of New York have to go and betray me that way?

BEFORE JUAN, BEFORE NEW YORK, MAMÁ, TERESA, JUANITA,
Betty, and I sat around the radio to listen to Jackie, the perfect
wife, so elegant, who was also married to a good man in America. The First Lady's breathy voice was difficult to hear under
radio celebrity Doña Alegria's loud scratchy voice translations.
After Kennedy was shot we listened to how much Jackie loved
her husband—so much so she put herself in danger when the
Russians threatened America. Thirteen days of worry, while little
old Cuba held the cards.

I want to die with you, Jackie cooed on air, and the children
do too, rather than live without you.

Learn from her, Mamá advised all her girls. She always says
exactly what people want to hear. She may be a widow, but a rich
one! That's why it's important to choose well.

And so we listened carefully to Jackie, who shared all her
womanly secrets.

The best thing a wife can do is to be a distraction, Jackie said.
A husband lives and breathes his work all day long. If he comes
home to more table thumping, how can the poor man ever relax?

It's true. When Juan comes home all he wants to do is relax.
He doesn't want to hear that the heater didn't come on until late
afternoon or that the drain in the sink is slow-moving.

Flick away your worries like a fly from a horse, was Kennedy's
advice.

One must not let oneself be overwhelmed by sadness.

Sex is a bad thing because it rumples the clothes.

Jackie's words made us giggle. Her dresses must cost more
than our house, more than our land, more than anything we will
ever own.

Maybe it's better to be not as rich and as important so we can
still have sex, Teresa whispered out of Mamá's earshot.

Oh, how I miss them. I wish they were sitting in my kitchen as

I wash the dishes. Maybe it's better to be a widow, I tell the empty chairs. What if Juan leaves the house and never comes back? A widow like Malcolm X's wife, Betty—oh, cousin Betty!—Shabazz, left to raise six daughters by herself. Like Jackie Kennedy, left with two children, but who's as elegant and fragile as a doll. Even my voice, like Jackie's, has grown breathy around Juan, as I hold my breath before each word.

WHEN THE DOORBELL RINGS I DON'T ANSWER. I GO TO the window. A man exits the building and looks up before I duck out of view. It's Antonio. The last time Antonio had visited he said Juan hadn't told him that he got married. Juan hadn't told him I was beautiful. Juan hadn't told him anything, despite the fact that they saw each other at work almost every day. They'd worked the tables at Yonkers Raceway since they first arrived in '60. On Antonio's last visit I served him whiskey on the rocks in our living room, but unlike other men, Antonio's soft-spoken. If I don't open the door it'll be worse, because we can't afford to turn away the business.

I buzz him in.

I tear off my housedress and brush the lint away from my wool skirt. Reapply my lipstick. Unravel the scarf holding my hair.

I turn on the radio and wait with my back against the door for Antonio's knock.

As always, Antonio is groomed: manicured nails and a trimmed mustache.

Started to think you had better things to do than see me, Antonio says, and waits for me to invite him inside. He carries a small bag stuffed with pink tissue paper, awkward in his large hands.

I'm sorry, I say, looking at my feet, then his shoes. I guess the radio was loud, I didn't hear the bell.

How does he keep his shoes so shiny even after walking in the snow? Juan's get snow stains and I have to rub the salt off every night. Antonio takes off his heavy leather jacket and hands it over to me. It's freezing outside! His jacket's cold. I assume his hands and cheeks must be too. He laughs as if I make him nervous. Older men are funny that way.

Do you want some water or anything else before we begin?

Antonio cocks his head.

Do you talk to all men this way?

My cheeks warm up. I usually offer water, which doesn't cost anything. Back home, I had to fetch water at the well, then boil it and drink it warm, because Papá doesn't permit us to take ice from the freezer. Ice is for customers. New York City water is so sweet, clean, and cold.

Can we begin? he says. I'm in a bit of a hurry today.

He places the pretty pink bag on a side table by the door.

Yes, yes, of course. I immediately open the closet door in the foyer and pull out two suits.

Juan used to keep the suits all over the living room in piles, bursting out of boxes. Boxes his associates had pulled off of trucks on their way to the department stores: Macy's. Gimbels. B. Altman and Company. But I organized them in the closet the same way they do in the stores. The hardest-to-sell suits most visible, right at the door opening. The newer shipments hidden in the back. I even grouped them by size for easier access.

Everything fits Antonio, his body like a hanger. I help him with the jacket. He smooths the lapels and straightens his back, examines himself in the mirror taped to the closet door. I suppress a giggle as he inflates his chest and arches his thick eyebrows.

You should try the pants on too. Juan won't allow returns.

Juan's a pain in my ass. If I hadn't known him for so long, I would've taken my business elsewhere.

I'll give you some privacy, I say.

I leave him to change in the foyer but spy on him through the crack between the wall and the door to the living room. His legs are muscular, skin brown like a man who doesn't fear the sun—Juan's skin is pasty, hairy, and dry—and Antonio's hair is sculpted a dark black, away from his face, shiny like his polished shoes.

The pants fit him well around the hips but need to be hemmed. Before he says anything, I pull from the shelf a metal tin filled with pins, needles, and thread given to me by César so I could start my side hustle.

It'll only take me a minute to fix them for you.

Juan didn't tell me you're a seamstress.

Don't be an exaggerator, Antonio. I just shorten pants. That's all. I can do it while you wait.

Juan doesn't know I sew and keep the money. Mamá would approve. Women must keep money on the side for when we need things, for our skin, hair, feet, for that special time of the month. But also to send money home. She expects Juan to help the family, but he counts every penny. When the price of toilet paper or milk goes down he rushes to the supermarket. In his mind, taking me off my parents' hands is enough. So I'm saving up to send Mamá money, crediting Juan of course.

My wife does my tailoring, Antonio says in a serious, almost scary voice. She doesn't appreciate other women handling my pants.

Oh. I don't mean to—

Don't worry, corazón. My wife's a smart woman, that's all.

So will you take both the suits?

Do I get a discount?

This part of the business makes me nervous.

I can't give you . . . I'm not supposed to . . .

Antonio doesn't insist. Other men become angry and demand to call Juan so they can speak to him directly. One man once yanked the suit from my hand, folded it over his arm, and threw the money at my feet, paying only what he thought was the right price.

Not Antonio.

For both the suits, he says, pulling money out of a silver clip. But next time, Ana, tell Juan I expect a discount.

His smoker's breath, laced with mint, reminds me of my father, who smokes a pipe. Antonio slings the suits over his shoulder so that their plastic covers won't drag.

He leaves the pink bag behind. I don't run after him. Recently, the old Jewish lady who lives right below us was robbed in the elevator. She's lived here for more than thirty-five years. Juan says no one's to be trusted, especially the blacks who sleep on the streets waiting for their next fix. Juan says *those blacks* as if he's skinning a goat.

They're like the Puerto Ricans, he says, wanting everything for nothing. Dominicans work hard for what they have. That's why there's always a job for a Dominican.

I've never met a man who works as hard as Juan. Every day, I warm water with salt for him to soak his feet. Every day, I have to brush his nails clean and spread cocoa butter on his calluses.

I slip two dollars from the sixty-two dollars Antonio gives me and I fold it inside my ceramic Dominicana. I jot the sale amount from the suit in Juan's notebook before adding it to his envelope. Juan only knows how to add, not subtract, jokes everyone who visits. Below the windowsill I log my earnings with a pencil. Each dollar inside the doll I add and each dollar spent I subtract. In six weeks I've already saved fifteen dollars to send and calm any worries about me.

When Mamá calls she talks and talks.

Aló, Ana, can you hear me? How's it going? Aló?

Great. I—

I knew it would be great. You'll spend your life thanking me.

But how is—

Is it cold there? I bet your closet is full with new dresses and shoes. Remember to keep all your jewelry organized so it doesn't get tangled up. So are you working? Did you start school yet?

It's not that easy. There's paperwork to be done, but I'm running Juan's business at home. He has lots of customers.

But does he pay you?

Well, no, but—

Tell him you want a job. You need to make your own money. You can't just stay home waiting. You learn English yet?

It's not that easy.

Don't forget to tell Juan to send us some money. Your father sprained his hand and the doctor's bill set us back. Well, you know how it is. Every little bit helps.

Wait, Papá what? Is he there? Can I—

Send Yohnny and Lenny some clothes when someone heads here. And deodorant and toothpaste for me. Teresa can use a bra.

Aló? Aló?

Aló? Ana? Tell him . . . Aló?

Oh, how I miss home, but who can I tell in person without so much static?

I open Antonio's pretty pink bag. Clearly a present for his wife. Or me? Why not me? Even a good man like Antonio has a dog's tail. In the bag, a small red box, heart shaped with ruffled fabric. Inside, four pieces of chocolate, thimble shaped. I put an entire piece in my mouth. I don't bite into it but hold it in my mouth, full and sweet.

I eat another chocolate thimble from the box. A burst of red cherry juice runs down my hand, onto my fingers. I suck them. My heart races. Tell him, tell him, Mamá says, as if it's so easy to talk to Juan. Of course I want to work. To learn English and have a closet full of clothes. I wrap the last piece in foil paper and toss it far back in the freezer. Carefully, I flatten the box and put it inside the plastic bag, inside the cabinet under the sink, filled with things I'd found while cleaning. Women things that don't belong to me. Like the makeup I try on and take off before Juan comes home.

JUAN ARRIVES LATE AND SKIPS DINNER. HE'S DRUNK, AND from the way his eyes weigh down his face, it's clear he's had a bad day.

Come here, he says, pants already on the floor, shirt unbuttoned.

I stand behind a chair, by now skilled at keeping my distance, knowing just how long it takes him to give up and how long before he will fall asleep. When he reaches for me, I edge around the coffee table, hoping he'll trip over himself. The last time I did that, I was the one to trip and bruise my leg.

But this time he manages to grab my hand and drags me into the bedroom. I know when not to fight, to allow things to happen so that time speeds up.

I sit on the bed, a pillow on my lap, legs crossed at my knees and ankles. I want to put the dinner away in the fridge before the roaches get to it.

Look at me.

But not even through my eyes will I allow him to enter.

I just wish he would say to me that I'm beautiful, whisper in my ear that I'm his only little bird and mean it. That he would cover the bed with flowers and look at me like a man in love, like Gabriel looked at me as if my curves were a riddle. I bite my bottom lip, hold back tears, and don't look at Juan because if I look I will only see his large pores, thick dark facial hair poking out of his chin and nose.

I place my hands over his sour breath.

And he charges at me, spreads my legs apart, grabs and pulls my breasts.

I clamp, as if through sheer force I can break his manhood in half. The more I tighten my muscles around him, the harder he thrusts. The harder he thrusts, the easier it becomes for him to enter. My thighs shake, my blood rushes to my sex. I want to die. *Finish me, finish me already!* I gyrate my hips. A wave of warmth comes to my cheeks. My insides contract in such a way that I fear I have urinated all over him. I cover my eyes with embarrassment. I try to push him off, but his hips push harder and deeper against me. He grabs my legs and pulls them over his shoulders, and again waves ripple over me, this time harder, faster. My eyes—my core—well up.

Yes, he whispers in my ear. Just like that, ay, Caridad. Cum with me. Cum.

He caresses my back, my arms, my legs, and his touch generates a shiver up and around me. Sweat trickles from his forehead onto my face. He buries his head between the pillows. His fingers are tangled in my hair, gently tugging at me, intensifying the unexpected sense of satisfaction.

Caridad. I'm relieved to finally hear the name spoken so out in the open. She is the breath who calls our house, whose makeup I found and stored in the bathroom cabinet.

When Juan is finished, I wrap the bedsheets around myself, ashamed. The soreness between my legs throbs, hungers, hurts. He lies on his stomach, his naked body a sleeping boar's. I stare at my reflection, at my flushed face, my hands still trembling. Something has happened to my body. Something inexplicable.

THE DAY THE BREATH STOPS CALLING, JUAN ASKS CÉSAR to join him to stand on line for a night shift at the Plaza Hotel, where Caridad now works. Yonkers Raceway shut down for a few days after the workers went on strike over wages.

César, although tired from his shift at the factory, can't ever say no to Juan so he throws on an extra sweater and they head downtown.

Caridad will hook us up, Juan says.

The same woman who almost cut your dick off when she found out about Ana? César says and shakes his head at the other men in the line, fresh-off-the-plane men in too-short pants exposing their ankles.

Why did I let you talk me into this?

Remember when that was us? Juan says. Hungry motherfuckers.

Caridad exits the side door and sees Juan and César on the line and waves them in. The other men sneer at them, unaware that for years Juan has been warming Caridad's bed.

I thought you guys were too good for the line, she says, now that you're big men in New York.

I wanted to see you, Juan says into her ear.

César, tell your brother, I don't mess with married men.

Can you believe her? She's the one who's married! Hypocrite.

Calm down, brother, maybe this was a bad idea.

Don't say I didn't try, Juan yells to Caridad, and walks away toward the rush-hour traffic and the droves of people getting out of work. The sky is already turning purple. The cold stings.

César can barely keep up with Juan, who is speeding down to the subway station, his face red, his teeth clenched. They ride the train in silence. Once they arrive to Washington Heights, Juan heads straight to the only gringo bar. It's Juan's type of bar, dark and quiet. Not like the Irish bar where fights break out, or like the black bar, where the music is too loud.

The bouncer at the door lets Juan inside but holds César back.

What the fuck, says César, pointing to Juan. Thas mi brotha.

Look, man, I don't want trouble. The bouncer turns his back on César.

Brotha. Mi brotha! This is not the first time a gringo won't let the darker-skinned César inside a bar. But this time, the bouncer also grabs Juan by the elbow and escorts him outside the bar.

Coño, carajo! Juan's arms flail, searching for something to punch. He turns deep red like a TV cartoon whose head blows up, and just like that Juan punches César on the side of his face and knocks him out, on the sidewalk.

The stink of old urine, the weeds bursting through the cracks, the sting from the cut on his hand when César tries to break his fall. This he will not let Juan forget later.

People stare as if César had been the one looking for trouble.

Don't you ever ask me for anything ever again! César yells out to Juan.

FINALLY, AFTER TWO AND A HALF MONTHS OF LIVING IN Juan's apartment, I've found a place for everything in our home. Even César has a designated corner for all his things. Although he hasn't come around lately. Maybe he found some woman. Maybe he got into a fight with Juan. It would explain why Juan has been so quick to anger.

I brush my hair away from my face, tie it into a large bun, and start to clean. I pour water on the floor, scrub the wood with a sponge by hand. As I fill the bucket, I laugh at how Mamá used to give me trouble when I missed a spot. I scrub the floors, satisfied, lost in the scent of pine soap in water. When the doorbell rings, my heart jumps to my throat.

I need to get in to check a leak! the super yells through the door.

Under no circumstances, even if the super knocks, am I to open the door when Juan isn't home. If it's so important, they'll come back.

The super rings again, this time pressing on the buzzer until my ears burn.

Maybe it's an emergency. I crack open the door, with the chain still attached, and look. The super's face, bright pink, full of red freckles, the same color of his hair. His pants, weighed down by his tool belt.

Miss, can I come in? We have a problem.

No problema.

Sí, problem. He urgently points to himself, then to the inside of the apartment.

I unlatch the chain.

On seeing the bucket, filled with soapy water, he picks it up and yells, in the same way he scolds his two granddaughters who run around the building on weekends.

No! No! No! Don't do this! He shakes his head and lifts his hands in the air.

I'm not stupid, I say in Spanish. What's wrong with cleaning the floor? Then I give him a piece of paper and I put a pen in his short, square-tipped fingers. Worker's hands.

No water on floor. Water leaks downstairs.

Once the super is gone, I take the worn, black leather-bound Spanish-English dictionary from the shelf.

When Juan comes home from his many errands, I show him the super's note.

I don't mean to get us into trouble, but how am I supposed to get rid of the dirt? I have to use water.

Did he see the bucket?

Of course, I was cleaning when he walked in.

Goddammit. This is the hospital's building. There are lists of people waiting to be tenants. Do you know what I had to do to get us on that list so we can live in a good building with decent people?

My mind races. *No, I don't know.*

But I only opened the door thinking it was a real emergency. I don't think he'll give us trouble. He seems like a nice man.

What do you mean he's a nice man?

The phone rings.

Leave it, he says.

What if it's Mamá?

Ana, you people are driving me crazy.

The phone continues to ring. Mamá has to go a great distance to call, I say.

He grabs the phone away from me, then clutches a fistful of my hair and jerks my head back so I look into his eyes.

I'm sorry, I didn't mean to—

His fist is directed at my face. I cringe. His face turns beet red, and it's as if he has been waiting all day to find something to hit, to hurt, to yell at. Instead, he flings me to the sofa. I slip from under him and jump on his back, and my fingers press on his eyeballs. Blinded, Juan swings his body around. I hold on like a tick. He trips over the coffee table, catches himself with his hands against the wall. I let go and run to the bathroom. But before I close the door he grabs me by the waist and carries me like a football, my legs kicking, my arms punching. He throws me on the bed.

Stay calm, a real woman knows how to manage a man, Mamá said.

Better to play dead than fight back.

Only a clever woman could make a man go from el burro to el subway.

A dutiful wife will be rewarded in time.

A well-placed rock in a river changes the current.

Juan grips my neck, his heavy weight over me making it even harder to breathe. No sound comes out of my mouth. I wish for the phone to ring again, for someone to knock on the door. My eyes blur, the room starts to spin, my body convulses, then nothing, a peace, an end.

I wake up to Juan slapping my face, calling me. His voice is distant, Ana, Ana. Then it booms into my ear, Ana, wake up. Please, wake up.

When I cough, when I open my eyes, he collapses on the bed and cries without stopping.

Go to hell! I cry with him.

After a few minutes, Juan disappears into the kitchen and serves himself his own dinner. Sits at the kitchen table, eats, smacking his lips after each bite. When he eats he shoves it in, past the tongue into the throat without even tasting.

What if I make a dramatic exit—arms open wide, one big leap out the window? How will he react then? Blame himself? Will Juan go to jail?

Then Juan washes his own dish and places it on the rack—his way of apologizing—but leaves all the pots uncovered. A bitter apology, if it is one.

The worst is over. Soon Juan will change his clothes to work at the raceway. In forty-five minutes his friend will give him a ride to Yonkers.

I go to wash socks. I scrub and scrub, not looking in the mirror, afraid to see whether Juan's hand bruised my cheek.

Ana?

Juan appears at the door. He's wearing the Mexican sombrero we hung up on the wall for decoration. Beyond pathetic.

Come here, pajarita.

His arms are raised, extended. His lips turn at the ends as if asking for forgiveness. In the softest of broken voices he sings:

Ese lunar que tienes,
cielito lindo
Junto a la boca,

I shake my head. A song won't fix us. No matter how beautiful his voice.

Ay, ay, ay, ay, canta y no llores

Just go away. Go.

Cielito lindo los corazones

He inches toward me and presses my head against his chest.

I'll come straight home tonight so we can be together.

He lifts my face and gently kisses my forehead.

After, I see that there are no marks on my face, nothing. Only a small cut on my bottom lip. Some redness around my neck.

THE NEXT DAY JUAN COMES HOME EARLY FROM WORK. HE finds me sitting quietly at the table.

I talked to the super, he says.

I look away. I'm not ready for him. Not yet.

You don't have to worry, Ana. There isn't much water damage, just a spot to cover on the ceiling downstairs.

One of my hands hugs the side of my bruised neck. I look out the window. It's still light out. For the first time in a long time, the people who gather to speak about the dead politician are gone. Only the police remain. Every day, a woman in a red hat places fresh flowers at the entrance so people won't forget what has happened to Mr. X. A lover? His wife, Betty? Mrs. X?

Ana X. I repeat in my head as Juan talks and talks.

The floors aren't concrete like back home, Juan says. These floors are like a basket: you pour water and it goes right through. Understand me?

He clumsily pours a glass of whiskey for himself. Good. He hasn't asked me to do it. Or about dinner. Good, because wife isn't planning to serve him. Today, I don't care if he throws me out the window.

Before you moved in, we had mice. Did you know that? They live between the floor and the walls. But you keep everything so nice, just like your mother said you would.

Juan taps on the floor with the heels of his shoes.

You hear that? It's hollow. Every time we move, the man who lives below hears us. When I first came to New York, I couldn't sleep because the people upstairs stampeded from one side of the apartment to the other. It drove me mad. So I searched and searched for a top floor.

Juan hands me a gift bag. When I don't reach for it he takes out a small black box.

Open it.

I don't want him to touch my hand, or my shoulder. Right then I decide I will leave him. If I stay he'll kill me. Tomorrow, Juan won't find me sitting at the table like a caged bird. At La Bodeguita I heard that a bus leaves daily from the terminal on 179th to JFK airport. Just twelve blocks away. Then a three-hour plane ride to Santo Domingo.

Your mother told me, You'll never meet another girl like Ana. She's got a heart the size of a watermelon. And you blushed. It was pitch-black out, but your cheeks—I saw they were red. Do you remember?

No, it had been too dark for Juan to even see the whites of my eyes, let alone the pink in my cheeks.

Juan laughs. He grabs my arm with unusual gentleness. He caresses my face. I focus on what I will take with me. The fifteen dollars inside the doll isn't enough. There's the envelope in Juan's safe; he has yet to put Antonio's money in the bank. I know the combination, which he'd given to me in case something happened to him.

From the moment I saw you, Ana, I knew you were the one for me. Open it!

I shake the black box and hear the clink inside. He takes the box and opens it. He holds up a pair of gold earrings with a translucent, tear-shaped stone: amber. I hold them. I decide to give them to Teresa, who dreams of princes on horses whisking her away to a castle but who has failed in Mamá's eyes for choosing a man with her heart.

You love me, Ana? Juan asks.

I bite my tongue and tuck in my lips. I focus on the tear-shaped stones. I clamp my legs together. I wish him dead.

Tell me you're happy with me.

My chest rips open, a fountain, tears soak through the sleeves of my sweater. My voice, an alarm, reaches far and wide. I want to go home, I say repeatedly. I wrap my arms around myself because I tremble like a boiling pot.

Goddammit! Juan slams his hands on the table, raises his fist to punch the wall, but holds himself back. He grabs his coat and stomps out, slamming the door behind him.

It's already dark outside. The apartment dark too. I have yet to turn on the lamps. I finger the stones, unclasp the earrings and try them on. I shake my head, catching my reflection on the television screen, lit up by moonlight. On this last night in New York City, I will clean all the windows and mirrors, finish mending Juan's shirts and ironing the rest of the clean laundry.

IF I LEAVE JUAN AND RETURN HOME, THIS IS THE WAY
Mamá will prepare for my arrival. On the table she'll have laid
out a plastic slipper, my father's leather belt, a sack of uncooked
rice, a ream from a tree, the fly swatter, and a wire hanger. Two
buckets filled with water and a brand-new bar of soap. Everyone
will attend my judgment. She'll make me choose from instruments and I will refuse. She'll spread the rice on the floor and say,
Kneel. I'll kneel without protest to keep her from getting angrier.
Either way, she won't get any satisfaction. I had the audacity to
throw away all her hard work. I killed her hope. She'll crucify
me by making me lift buckets full of water while kneeling on a
bed of rice. And I'll withstand the burn in my muscles and the
ache in my knees. I'll reverse time and go back to the way things
were before we even knew of the Ruiz brothers. My stony face
will make her hit my back, my legs, my arms with a slipper, or
belt, or hanger. And with each strike, she'll get angrier at herself,
make her fear she's gone too far like the day Yohnny almost died
from one of her beatings. She won't let me die. She'll just hit me
enough for me to remember what she's capable of. And after,
Teresa and Yohnny will take me down from the cross and rub
me with aloe and Tiger Balm and press packed ice where my skin
swells and say how happy they are that I am home and ask if I've
brought them anything from America. And through my fever,
I will overhear neighbors say, Ana's ugly for the photo; the girl
should learn how actions have consequences. What a pity, and
with such a bright future ahead of her in New York.

And for many nights I will hear Mamá lamenting that Juan
Ruiz can't be that bad and if she were in my shoes, she'd be bathing in the rivers full of gold.

I TAKE MY FIFTEEN DOLLARS FROM INSIDE MY DOMINICANA and seventy-five dollars from the safe. I wear all my clothing— wool dress under two shirts and skirt over pair of pants—instead of carrying a suitcase. The extras, I carry inside the Gimbel's shopping bag left behind by a suit customer. At 8 a.m., I make my way to the bus station on 179th Street. The sun has come up; and dawn's cold air presses against my cheeks though I'm sweating like a stewed onion under three layers of clothing.

Nobody knows me, but everybody seems to know Juan, so I keep my chin tucked into my chest. My scarf rubs against the bruise on my throat.

I locked the apartment door behind me. Without the keys, I can't ever go back. I left! I walk so fast I almost trip over a child holding his mother's hand. Twelve blocks, one avenue to the bus. If the ninety dollars in my purse aren't enough for an air ticket, I'll beg to be let on the plane. I can show the bruise around my neck. Someone has to have mercy on me.

I walk and walk, first up Broadway, past the entrance to the ballroom, where in a few hours the lady in the red hat will leave fresh flowers. A cluster of wig-wearing and long-skirted mothers push strollers the size of shopping carts near the subway stop. Past the triangle on 170th Street, where the trees light up at dusk and people sit watching their children play until the night takes over. I try not to look at the eyes of anyone, just at the fire hydrants, the bus stops, the iron lampposts, the uneven sidewalks cracked in parts that have imprints of hands and boot soles. Pigeons eat from the soil moistened by the recent rain. Is it true that the sewer houses the devil, and that if I get near it, it will suck me in? I know rats live in there. They zigzag from one side of the sidewalk to the other, too fast for a passerby to notice, but I have seen them on many nights from my window, slip in and out of people's feet. I walk and walk. What will Juan do when he returns from work?

He will show up with flowers or some other trinket, to no dinner or ironed shirts to wear to work tomorrow. He'll punch a wall or go out and punch somebody. I walk and walk. Sweat trickles down my back. A crazy lady under three layers of clothing. But I don't care. Let people think what they want, I'm going to the bus, to JFK, to the airport of Las Americas in Santo Domingo. Once there, I'll send word to Yohnny or Teresa. They'll find someone to fetch me.

At the terminal, buses are lined up between Broadway and Fort Washington Avenue. Long lines of people too. The numbers fly in my head: seven dollars one way. Twelve dollars round trip.

At 179th Street and Fort Washington Avenue, I turn away from the opening of the bridge, the roll of the cars thundering overhead, and I escape the noise through the glass doors. Afraid to go on the electric stairs, I climb the nonmoving ones beside them. I try not to look at the unwashed men who sleep on the floor. I try not to breathe in the dried urine stench and ignore the beggars. I clutch my purse and lift my bag at the terminal lobby, where crowds move with determination and certainty. Signs everywhere. Gates, numbers, blinking lights. My heart in my throat. What am I doing? Will Juan ever let me go? Will my mother even take me back? My mind locks.

A hand lands on my shoulder. I scream. That hand covers my mouth.

Shhh, Ana. You want to get me arrested?

César.

I bite him firmly so he lets go.

I'm going home, I say, turning around.

César shakes out his hand as if I hurt him. You got some teeth.

He pulls out a cigarette from his jacket pocket. You leaving without saying good-bye?

It's not like you're ever around, busy with all your girls. I say it in a voice I don't recognize. Why am I flirting? Now? And with César!

I change my tone quick and ask, Why aren't you at work?

It's been over a week since he came around the apartment.

Every time I asked Juan about him he would say, Don't meddle in family business.

I was looking for you, César says. When I step back, he laughs.

Relax, Ana! I'm joking. I was catching a van at the bus station to meet this woman who's hooking me up with a job.

I lightly punch his chest. His leather jacket is unbuttoned.

You're gonna get sick, I say. The cold doesn't bother you? Nothing you say or do will stop me from going home.

I start walking away, but he grabs my shopping bag and walks toward the terminal exit.

Give me my stuff back. I keep yelling, trailing behind him, past the glass doors, and then block after cold block. He finally settles at a park bench on the top of a rock on 175th Street and Fort Washington. He pushes aside some newspapers from the bench as I stop to catch my breath.

C'mon, César, I have a bus to catch. Please.

But if you go, who's gonna take care of us?

And that's the best you can do to convince me?

Still I sit beside him, too tired to fight. Lately, even when I sleep well, I am tired. He presses my head into his cuaba-soap-scented shirt, the same one I washed for him. He pats my back over the layers of dress, shirt, coat.

You know, Ana, on my first night in New York I was scared shitless. I couldn't sleep. The heater coughed like it had fur stuck down its throat. And there were these crazy people screaming right outside our window. I decided right then I was taking the first plane back home.

Let me guess, you stayed.

Never say you won't drink from a certain well.

It's different for men. You can do whatever you want.

I push César away and walk over to the iron fence separating us from the river. A strip of tall buildings. The cars zooming on the Hudson Parkway sound like the ocean. A push and pull. Birds chirp. A whiff of dried shit on the concrete nearby. In the distance, is the George Washington Bridge. When I first arrived to New York, the bridge lit up like a man-made constellation. I had thought the river to be narrower, bluer, more like the sea. Instead, it's gray and massive. A tugboat appears, then disappears. I feel the burn of César's eyes on my back.

Whatever it is that happened between you and Juan, I promise you, it'll get better. My brother can be an asshole, but he's not a bad guy.

You're always defending him.

He pisses me off too, but we're blood. Nothing can come between that. Even when I'm mad at him I remember in this shit of a life, we're all we got.

Blood is why I want to go home, too.

And go backward, Ana? What future do either of us have back there? Just like you I wanted to get the hell out of this city, but the next morning, the sun poured into our room, and Juan made me coffee and showed me how New York City cleans up real nice in the daytime. We walked downtown to the Empire State Building. Shit, it was all cream, no salt. King Kong holding his girl and banging his chest.

César kisses his fingers. Fucking beautiful. In twenty-four hours I saw more than in a lifetime back home.

The thought of having to return to Juan makes my breakfast come up my throat. I hover over a nearby garbage can and vomit, then wipe my lips with the sleeve of my coat. My head spins under the harsh wind as I reach for the iron fence.

I'M BLINDED BY THE FLUORESCENT LIGHTS OVERHEAD AT the hospital. Overwhelmed by the smell of antiseptic soap.

What happened?

My head throbs. I can barely lift it. I swing my legs to one side of the metal table. César sits in a chair beside me. He looks at me as if I'd died and he has witnessed a miracle.

Ana, you fainted.

I feel cold and naked in the thin gown, miss the security of my layers. Frantically, I survey the small room.

My bag—Juan's money!

And my clothes? My stuff? I ask.

César jolts out of his chair and opens a nearby cabinet where my clothes are folded and piled high.

It's okay. It's just us. Do you want me to get Juan?

I shake my head.

How long have I been here?

Not even an hour. The doctor says you should pee in this cup, and if everything is okay, we can go home.

I'm starving. I see the bowl of lollipops on the doctor's desk by the bed and reach for a yellow one.

A bright drawing of a giraffe for measuring a child's height hangs on the wall. I leave the bed and stand beside the giraffe—sixty-three inches.

Hey, little elf, the bathroom's over there, says César. The nurse says to leave the cup on the shelf out in the hallway.

I pee in the cup and take it out to the white shelf next. All of the cups have labels: New York–Presbyterian Morgan Stanley Children's Hospital.

Mine says: Ana X: DOB unknown.

I smile in relief at César, who knew not to tell anyone my real name. The hospital can't turn me away just because I have no money. I set my cup of urine among the others. Ana X: a woman without family. Maybe the price of being an American is to no longer have a family to claim you.

The doctor returns. His face, smooth as a water stone. His blond lashes, brows, and hair makes his blue eyes brighter and his words swirl in my ears.

If you sign here, you can go home. During pregnancy fainting is not uncommon, the doctor says.

I wait for César to translate.

Escú me . . . plis, sló, I hear César say.

The doctor makes the shape of a balloon over his stomach.

I cover my mouth with one hand, hold my belly with the other. It only takes one time. One time, and El Guardia got Teresa pregnant. Now everything makes sense. How the pudding I ate that morning got stuck in my chest. The many more times this month I needed to use the bathroom. The exhaustion in the middle of the day . . .

Congratulations! The doctor pats César on the back, hands him a white plastic bottle as if it were a cigar and shouts, Vitaminas!

I'm too embarrassed to explain to the men that I still bleed. Not too much, but enough. What if something's wrong?

Okey, okey! César shouts back, all smiles. He hands over the plastic white jar. I grab it. Whether he's excited or scared, I can't tell.

When the doctor leaves, César says, Now you can't go anywhere. You're going to have an American baby.

An American baby, I repeat. That's what Mamá wants. Juan wants. A blue-blooded baby with a blue passport and all its benefits. In that cold cold room, oh how I wish my family were with me so I could tell them the news. My mind and heart, a roller coaster. One minute set to leave, another minute flying with joy and fear. A baby! To love, to keep me company, yes, but with a baby there's no way Juan will let me return home for good. What if I never get to see my house in Los Guayacanes again? I burst into tears.

You should be happy, César says, and wraps his arms tight around me, and in that hospital I feel more than ever like a child who needs to be contained.

We walk back to the apartment, both too hungry to speak. He carries my bag. I loop my arm around his. The sun beams on us. The wind whips paper cups up from the corner garbage cans. I want to scream, sing, spin, laugh. I'm having a baby! And as if César can read my thoughts, he drags me across the street toward the pigeon park, in front of the Audubon Ballroom. With my bag still in hand, he climbs the large rock where kids sled in winter, and stands high up and bangs his hands into his bony chest and says my name, Ana-na-na-na! He shimmies down and startles the crowd of pigeons. They lift to the sky, blocking the sun. I have no choice but to dodge the falling bird shit and run along with him to find shelter under the movie theater awning, beside their Malcolm X memorial.

Did you get hit? he asks.

I examine my dress and my hair.

No, did you?

That's good luck.

I think it's the other way around.

He picks a bright red carnation from the ballroom memorial and gives it to me.

You can't do that, César.

I smell the flower before laying it back on the ground with the others.

He won't care, he's dead.

An altar is an altar wherever you go.

You still want to take that plane back home? he asks.

Don't tell Juan I'm pregnant.

What? You're gonna make Juan the happiest man alive.

I have this urge to dig my face into his chest, to feel his arms around me. I tuck my hand into his coat pocket and grab his key chain, then dart across the street in the direction of the apartment. The streetlights have turned, giving me time to cross, but leaving César stuck on the other side, behind the passing traffic. He runs in place, waving the cars to pass him by.

I reach the building door and rattle the keys of the apartment in the air. My cheeks burn from smiling so hard.

PART III

JUAN WAITS FOR ME TO LAY OUT HIS WORK CLOTHES. IT has been three days since I tried to leave him. Since, I've ignored him. A slap's one thing, a dent in the wall another, but choking? He could have killed me. Oh, and wait until he finds out that I'm pregnant. How bad will he feel then? How long can I keep this baby all to myself? César isn't the best at keeping secrets.

I climb onto the bed and touch up my toenails. My hands shake, smearing red nail polish around my cuticles, anticipating him to raise his voice, his fist, his anything. But this morning, he's an ocean without waves. Maybe because he knows he'd gone too far. Again.

Where is my new suit? he asks, almost nicely. Stop fooling around and pick out a tie for me. I can't afford to be late.

I look outside the window. After weeks of spring-like weather, New York City is under a freeze. Icicles hang off the window edges. Still, a growing crowd of people in front of the Audubon building hold signs and spill over into the park where the pigeons meet, toward the entrance of the subway station.

Damn hooligans, Juan says to fill the quiet, trying to take over our government.

Realizing he means the numerous politicians back home I turn away from the window.

We may lose everything, if Dominican Republic goes to war. We still don't have the land title.

I pick out a tie striped with different shades of blue and hand it to him, making the mistake of thinking aloud. Papá says, worry when you have to.

That's why he's poor like a mouse.

Juan pulls a folded dollar bill from his pocket and holds it under his nose.

This is what I believe in, he tells me. The way he looks at

money, like a child with candy, makes me sad. I leave the room to brew the coffee.

A woman will come by to drop off some money she owes me, he yells from the bedroom.

A woman?

Yeah. I lent her one hundred dollars. Her name is Marisela. As collateral she gave me her wedding ring to hold. It's in the safe. Every week, for six weeks, she'll pay back twenty-five dollars. The easiest money I'll ever make.

Do you want the coffee with milk?

He usually drinks his coffee black with a ton of sugar, but I always ask. If I don't, he'll call me lazy. Because what kind of wife won't bother to boil the milk for her husband?

Ana, I can't find my belt.

I leave the coffee to undo his belt from the pants he'd worn the night before. They hang over the chair in the living room and smell of kitchen grease and horse. I don't mind the smell. It reminds me of Los Guayacanes, of lazy horses grazing near our house while I fry dough over the pit. The smell also means Juan has extra cash in his pockets after the races, after catering in the stalls to the horse owners, who tip big. But what I find inside the pants is a folded paper—a letter?—that I tuck into my skirt pocket.

Dressed, Juan appears to be important: a successful American man. Not the child who'd once peddled lollipops on the streets without a pair of shoes of his own. I watch him finish his black coffee while standing. I watch him put on his tweed coat. Wrap the red scarf fragrant with the aroma of a woman's perfume around his neck.

Be good, pajarita.

He grabs me by the waist and mashes my lips with his mouth. He pats my cheeks three times as he would a baby's bottom.

You're finally gaining some weight, pajarita. I don't care for skinny women I can snap like a twig.

I lock the door behind him. When Juan leaves, a tangible calm comes over the apartment and also over me. From the window, I watch him walk quickly through a crowd thick as a pile of ants. People march with flowers, photos of Malcolm X, and poster boards.

BLACK AND WHITE TOGETHER!
JUSTICE!
GONE TOO SOON!

Juan keeps his head down when he passes the police. Inside the apartment, he is a bull. On the street, he looks small, vulnerable, even scared. As if I can blow him away like a speck of dust.

EVEN THE LETTER SMELLS LIKE HORSE MANURE.

Dear Caridad,

Please forgive me. I so desperately want to be with you but the situation is complicated. There comes a time in a man's life he must make sacrifices for the family. You know this more than anyone, with your husband at war, not knowing if he'll ever return home. And now with Vietnam.

You ask me to come to you but I can't just leave A alone. She doesn't know anyone. Her family entrusted her to me. She's my responsibility. You have no idea how difficult this has been for me.

Cari, my life, my heart. God, I miss you, or maybe it's better to say with the distance I'm remembering you, all of you, the way your lips curl up into a question mark, always suspicious that I am up to no good. Your eyes so brilliant, always glassy and curious. God, the smell of your skin, how soft it is. The way your naked body feels next to mine. The way the light falls on our bed in the morning. And how do you always, I mean always, wake up so beautiful?

I love you. I love you,
Your Juancho

THROUGH THE PEEPHOLE I WATCH MARISELA IN THE hallway looking at herself in a compact mirror. A perfect face: cat eyes, a pointy nose, pink-lined lips. Her straight hair is well behaved, ends flipped in a big curl. When I open the door I get the full layout: coat, bag, and boots all the color of emeralds. Standing a head taller than me, she's an ad for the happiest woman alive.

Marisela kisses me hello on both cheeks.

So, you're Anita, the wife of Juan?

I nod, an idiot with a wide-open mouth, plain and built like a young boy. I'm the girl who doesn't know anyone. I am now Anita, or just A, a big responsibility for Juan, not capable of having my own friends, my own life.

Cat got your tongue, Anita? Marisela invites herself in.

Her thin-lined eyebrows lift as she examines me, then the apartment. The pillows have been fluffed, and I wiped the dust off the large mirror above the sofa. The sun pours into the room through the dust-free windows. The apartment looks plain with her in it.

Do you want coffee? I ask, then kick myself. Never ask, just serve, Mamá would say.

It smells great in here. Is it lunch?

It's actually Juan's dinner, I say too quickly. I prepared it early because he stops home in between jobs. But please, sit. There's enough for both of us.

She nods and I take her coat. No need to tell her that for lunch I usually eat a can of Chef Boyardee. That it's soft and mushy, as if made for someone without teeth.

Marisela is my first female guest since my arrival to New York. So I set the table for two, using the nicer plates. Even her velvety voice belongs on a radio. I hum while I heat the corn oil to fry the last plátano in the fridge. Thank Santa Altagracia for my great judgment to have made pigeon peas with rice and stewed shredded beef today. I don't always make a full meal.

You're a doll, she says. You remind me of my sister. With the money Juan loaned me, I bought her a flight to New York. As soon as she gets here she'll get a job but also study. Ignorance is the worst thing in the world, especially for a woman. Don't you think?

I want to go to school too, I say.

You should go for those free English classes at the rectory, right down on 165th Street, next to the church's entrance. So you can get your GED. Everybody needs at least a GED.

A GED?

What are you, eighteen? Nineteen? Marisela asks.

Fifteen.

Oh? She looks at me as if for the first time then studies her nails, long and manicured.

I was fifteen, fifteen years ago. Imagine that. And you're already married. Are your people happy for you?

Yes. They're happy.

I was one of the first to get here in '61. I would cry, asking my husband to send me back home, but what life do we have there? It's not easy for us in this city. The only reason anyone calls me from home is for money. My hands are destroyed from cleaning after people. Look how dry they are. Do you have some cream?

She waves her hands at me. From the look of Marisela's palms, filled with dark lines, Teresa would say she's a woman who has lived many lives, a person to learn from.

I'm embarrassed to tell her I don't have cream. Every time I try to buy lotion, Juan hurries me, so I rub cooking oil on my skin. Marisela smiles as if she knows.

Oh, get it later, when we're done having lunch.

Does cleaning houses pay you well?

Better than working at a factory. I'm the best housekeeper you'll ever meet. I clean offices at night, downtown. That's not bad. The hard work is during the day, but it pays twice as much. I work for two ladies. One lady has two babies, so her house is a mess. And you can tell she don't lift a finger when I'm not there because when I arrive, food is glued to the plates. The refrigerator's a disaster, especially after the weekend. And the gringas always complain. Maria, please don't forget to clean under the sofa and beds. Or, remember to wash all the windows, it's been a while.

I laugh when Marisela imitates her bosses by lifting her pinkie and scrunching her nose.

And it drives me crazy when they have guests over and they sit to drink their tea and watch me work—or worse, when they stand behind me to see if I'm working right. If they have all that time to watch over me, why don't they do the cleaning themselves?

I laugh so much my stomach hurts.

Maria—because they call me that, no matter how many times I have to say Ma-ri-se-la—do you mind preparing me some coffee? I always like it better when you do it. And ay, Anita, these women act as if they're the first to have a baby. They carry them as if holding a bowl full of water, with such fear they'll drop them. They fall apart over the smallest thing.

I bend over the sink and almost piss my panties in laughter. What kind of a woman doesn't know how to hold a baby?

Maria, the baby won't stop crying. Maria, please take her, take her!

Marisela stands and extends her arms out to me, holding out one of my nice plates as if it's a stinky baby.

Ay ay ay, these gringas don't have to work, they don't have to clean their own houses, and when the babies cry they don't even know how to make them stop. One of the ladies wants me full-time. But she's the crazier one and I can only go there in manageable doses. If they only knew what my life is like. I've two little girls living in Puerto Plata with my mother. It's been two years without me being able to visit. If only I had a rich man who took care of me so I can stay home and watch my girls.

Marisela pauses to take a sip of water before launching back into her tirade.

Maria, did you let the coffee burn? Maria, next time, pour the water *over* the tea bag, it's the way it's done. Maria, remember to . . . Ay, girl, I bite my tongue because if I could I'd say, Go do something with yourself. Or give me the day off so I can do something.

The plátanos are ready. I serve Marisela a nice helping of rice and peas. I can't stop looking at her, at Juanita, at Betty, at Teresa, all of us, giggling and gossiping at the kitchen table.

I can't wait to start working, I say.

No. No. Don't be the same as those gringas who don't know how good they have it. You'll have double the work, working both outside and at home. And the cold out there? It kills me just to walk to the train station.

Marisela rubs her arms and shakes her face, anticipating the chill.

Ay, Anita, I spend my days watching that clock. Ay, how I love to be home.

I imagine how much nicer Marisela's house must be than ours, which is so drab and sparse. Juan doesn't want to spend on extras like curtains, bedspreads, and tablecloths. I bet hers is filled with portraits in gold frames. Chandeliers. Canopied beds. Crystal bowls. Doilies everywhere.

Ay, my house is a real sanctuary. One day you'll visit and see how lovely it is. A woman is defined by her home.

I try to hide my excitement over the invitation. It'll be so great to have a friend to visit.

Marisela savors the stewed beef, while I take small small bites to make sure there's enough for Juan. I pray she doesn't ask for seconds.

You're divine! What a gift you are. If I cooked as good as this, my husband would throw me a parade.

She laughs and I laugh too.

She eats everything off her plate, then looks at her watch.

I have to go. My shift tonight starts in two hours. Just enough time to change, prepare dinner for later, and get to work.

She pulls a bright pink nail polish out of her bag.

Here, a little something.

I grab it, delighted. The same color Marisela wears.

I watch her fingers button her coat then pull from her coat pocket a black knitted hat with emerald trim. She adjusts it so it covers part of her face.

Don't go! I want to say as we hug and my nose skims the length of her neck. Her floral perfume stays on me.

I keep the door open until Marisela is inside the elevator. She sticks her head out and yells: I only have to make it to the train! Wish me luck!

Moments after I shut the door, she rings again.

Sorry, Anita, it's me again!

When I open the door, she places the twenty-five dollars she owes Juan in my palm, folds my hand into a fist.

MAMÁ DOESN'T BELIEVE WOMEN CAN BE FRIENDS. BUT Marisela is different. And I'm a city girl now.

I try on some of my dressier clothes so when Marisela invites me over I'm ready. I own one pair of used heels from a neighbor whose daughter recently passed away. See if anything fits, Juan had said, and although the clothes are not special-looking, they do fit.

From Juan's closet, I also try on one of his bright white shirts. The hem skims my knees. His clothes smell of damp wool and Caridad's perfume: Rose? Lily? Vanilla? I look at myself in one mirror, then in another. The apartment's full of mirrors glued to closet doors.

I blow a kiss to myself, bending over like that photo of Marilyn Monroe. I expose my shoulder and shake my hips. I let the shirt fall to the floor and imagine Gabriel looking at my naked breasts. They're much bigger since I arrived.

I swim inside Juan's suit jacket. From a pocket, I pull out one of his handkerchiefs and pretend to sneeze as loud as Juan, whose full-body sneeze shakes the glasses off the shelves.

You can tell a lot by a man's sneeze. Ha, ha, ha.

I fall to the sofa, feet in the air.

Ana, go get me a drink! Hurry! Where's my dinner? What's taking you so long? Ana! Ana! Ana!

Oh, Juan, get your own stupid drink! I say to the hat on the table, then laugh.

I cross my legs like a movie star smoking an air cigarette, like my mother sitting on the ledge of Carmela's house. When she inhales, she lights up, her eyes, her smile, and I see the woman who once had to fend off many suitors—before marrying, before having children, before struggling to keep our farm, our family together.

I blow out a plume of nothing. My hands twirl in the air, imitating the flamenco dancers on the midday TV variety show.

I put my hands inside his suit pockets. *Men need so many pockets to keep their things!* Inside: a folded receipt for the raceway Juan works at. Unfolded: a phone number, a print of her lips in faded red.

The breath hasn't called in a while. Maybe she hasn't forgiven Juan yet?

Cari. Caridad. I mouth the names and swallow them. My stomach flutters. I copy the number in my notebook. I fold the receipt, make sure the front door is locked. In the bathroom—the only room I find privacy—I sit on the toilet to look at the numbers carefully, at the way she writes Cari, Juan's pet name for her. The edges of the paper are worn, the handwriting loose and big.

I try to imagine her face, her hair, her lips, the size of her body. Tall with melon-size breasts? Long hair with tsunami waves flowing down her back?

Caridad. Caridad. Caridad. I roll her name around on my tongue.

Maybe Caridad is lonely too. But at least she's truly loved by Juan. Why didn't I run away with you, Gabriel, with your soft eyes and pillow lips? My thighs tremble with a sudden and urgent desire to travel back in time, jump back in that pool, and have his hands on the small of my back while I float. That day, under the sun, was fully ours. Gabriel and I had all the keys to all the padlocks. Don't tell anyone, he said about the secret house. Don't tell anyone, Teresa said every time she snuck off.

Ana X, the holder of secrets.

Now I can call her and breathe into her ear.

CARIDAD AND JUAN FINALLY MAKE UP. I FIND THE CLUES, in his clothes, on receipts, and in his contradictions. I piece together how Juan sees Caridad between jobs and crawls into bed with her after work. How he sometimes falls asleep accidentally, unbeknownst to her children, who sleep in the other room. When she finally starts calling again, I listen in on their conversations from the phone in the kitchen, him locked in the bedroom, and at the phone by the bed.

Why me, Caridad?

What do you mean?

From a hundred guys standing in the cold looking for a job you chose me.

You seemed like the kind of guy who wouldn't ask too many questions.

Am I your first guy from the line?

Does it matter? You hardly ever sing anymore. I love when you sing.

What is there to sing about?

Ay Juancho, why don't you look at me anymore?

Juan won't look, not while her body is spread open. Arms above her head, palms up. Juan turns away the photo on the nightstand of Caridad's husband, who is in Vietnam and writes letters to say, Wait for me. Tell my children I love them.

Does your wife know about me? Caridad asks Juan.

Are you crazy?

Do you still love me?

Juan keeps saying his chest hurts but it's because he keeps holding his breath.

BECAUSE I WANT TO TELL HER EVERYTHING, THE NEXT TIME Marisela comes over, I blurt out, as soon as I open the door, I'm pregnant.

What happiness, she says, breezing through the door, throwing her coat on my arm, handing me a frosty pink lipstick from inside her purse all in one move. She spins me around and says,

Welcome, Anita, to the club of mothers. Only we know what it's like to carry another human being. At first it's the size of a pea, then a grape, an apple, an avocado, then it's as big as a papaya. To think something so big comes out of something so small. When I had my first one, ugh, I thought it would kill me, but I pushed and pushed, ready to die for the baby that I already loved like I've never loved anything else before. It's extraordinary to stand on the edge of life and death. You'll see. You'll see.

Let's see, I say with a quiet laugh, let's see.

I haven't thought about the reality of childbirth. The largeness of it, the smallness of me. The inevitable pain.

You're so lucky, she says, caressing my cheek. Your baby will be born American. We should celebrate.

Marisela turns on the radio and searches for a station with merengue. She grabs my hand and swishes her hips to the beat, leads me to the left and to the right.

Move that ass, shake those hips! she sings. Show me where you come from!

I try to undo my hips, loosen them. Marisela's hand drops to catch mine; then she gently pushes me away to turn me around and around and then my back to her, both of us facing the mirror on the wall.

Look at that face, she tells my reflection. Those big eyes of yours, so wise. They know more than you'll admit, even to yourself. That bone structure and fine Greek goddess nose.

If we were horses Marisela would stay close to me for eleven months until the baby was born. All the horses on our farm have female companions.

Just remember, Marisela says, women decide everything. My husband didn't want my sister to come but she's already on her way. And we'll open a salon. Not too big, something manageable. And people will come from all over the city, because nobody knows how to blow out hair like us Dominicanas. Who knows, maybe your sister can come to New York and work for me. Wouldn't that be divine? And you can bring us lunch. We'll pay you, of course.

It'll be nice to make my own money.

I notice the clock, 2:10. Marisela will have to leave in a few minutes to go to work.

Don't worry. Next time I visit, I'll trim your hair. The ocean would kill for such waves. A good haircut will help them cascade. Even the ocean needs a shore.

She points at herself. Do you think all this comes easily?

Marisela? Can I ask you a favor?

Yes, anything. We're comadres.

Don't tell Juan about the baby. I want to surprise him.

Ay sister, dear sister. Your secret is safe with me.

I DIDN'T MEAN TO FALL ASLEEP. EVEN AFTER A FEW CUPS of coffee, my body went heavy and my bones cold. The TV's all stripes. No more programming for the day.

Juan bursts into the apartment and turns on the overhead lights. I spring into sitting position.

Coño! Cabrones! Idiotas! he mumbles. Kicks a chair in his way.

What is it now? Did something happen at the raceway, where he's sometimes so busy he isn't given his fifteen-minute breaks, or allowed to go to the bathroom, where he can rest his feet to smoke a cigarette? Did he get into another fight with César, who hardly comes around anymore? Or is it Caridad?

He plows his way into the kitchen.

I realize I haven't cleared the plastic plate I leave out for the pigeons. What if he sees the rice wasted on the pigeons? What if Marisela or César told him about the baby?

I follow him.

Go, sit down, I say. Let me heat the food.

Under the brighter kitchen light, I can tell he's been drinking. Nose and cheeks flushed. Eyes droopy, which makes him seem sad. He picks up the pot lid and with his fingers scoops out a clump of white rice and stuffs it into his mouth.

I'm not hungry, he says.

Out on the fire escape the plate reflects moonlight and I shift to block it from his view. The cool draft from the slightly open window chills my back.

It's freezing in here!

When I don't move quick enough to shut the window, Juan nudges me aside. He pauses, then opens it, grabs the plate, and throws it on the floor. Rice scatters across the tiles in the kitchen and the wooden floors toward the living room.

Are you feeding the pigeons again?

No, I . . .

Don't lie to me!

No, I say. I mean yes.

I run to the living room where I ball up on the floor and turn my body toward a wall to protect my belly the way I've seen protestors do at the marches on TV.

What the fuck is wrong with you? Juan says, almost to himself. You think I'm some kind of monster?

We're having a baby, I'm ready to scream. But when I turn my head to look at him, he stands there and stares at me in disbelief. My hands block my face, my body trembles. Grains of rice poke into my legs and my arms.

Juan goes into the bedroom. I get off the floor, clean the mess, put away the food. Pigeon Teresa, the one with pink and green wings, pecks at my window, startling me.

Shoo. I whisper. What are you doing here so late?

You should've gone to the beach with us, Ana. You should've run away when you had the chance.

She taps, taps, taps. Inflates her body and lifts her wings. Fly, Ana, fly.

I extend my arms and stand on my tippy toes and stick my neck out.

WHEN I CAN'T ZIP UP MY DRESS, JUAN SAYS, LET'S GO TO El Basement.

Really? I say with excitement. El Basement?

El Basement is run by Giselle and Gino. It's where Marisela says she buys a lot of her name-brand clothes.

Hurry, or I'll change my mind. Then Juan holds up a finger. You can only buy one dress. Nothing more. You hear me?

Juan has a way to suck the air out of a tire.

We walk down to the building's back alley, then enter a side door and continue through a narrow corridor, past freshly painted bricks. I hold my breath, afraid of getting nauseous from the stink of the garbage collected behind the large metal doors—rotting food, dead rats, drying paint. I duck to keep from getting hit by the bare lightbulbs illuminating the windowless hallway.

We pass a few more doors before reaching one with a doorbell. Gino answers, waves us in, and I see Giselle with orange dyed hair, organizing boxes.

In front of them Juan says, Ana, you can get anything you want.

Look, Gino, a man after a woman's heart.

Oh, I just want one dress, I say, though I already want everything I see on the wall-to-wall racks.

Giselle sizes me up, arches an eyebrow, and goes back to unpacking a box that has recently fallen out of a truck.

But Juan keeps up the show. Ana, he says, you can have anything you want. He smacks a kiss on my forehead as if sending me off to the races.

I look through the racks, which are packed with clothing, covered in transparent plastic. Store tags dangle on the sleeves. I listen to Juan and Gino as they talk about prospective Dominican president Joaquin Balaguer.

He may just be able to bring order back to the country.

Better a devil we know.

But what about this guy Caamaño supposedly in cahoots with Fidel?

My knees knock with anticipation. How silky the sweaters! And the crosshatched threads on the suit jackets, the soft fur on the coat collars! I keep my hands clasped in restraint.

Why don't I show you some of my favorite pieces, Giselle says, when she sees me gazing at a bag studded with emerald sequins.

Please do, I say. It doesn't hurt to look.

I even have shoes to go with that bag, she says, ready to have some fun.

Juan taps his feet while I move on to carefully finger the piles of button-down sweaters in different colors on the tables. Then Giselle convinces me to try numerous dresses, with matching coats. Then I hunt for my size on the shoeboxes haphazardly stacked from floor to ceiling.

Pajarita, I have to go to work, Juan says with a forced smile.

One more minute.

Look how he spoils you, Giselle says.

Oh, yes, Juan's quite special, I say, and smile back at him.

I slip in and out of clothes behind a striped bedsheet that hangs off a cord in a corner. All the dresses are too big around the shoulders and tug my belly and hips. The pregnancy has become harder and harder to hide.

I finally choose a navy-blue dress, A-line, midthigh length.

Try on this matching coat, says Giselle and then shows me a pair of one-inch patent leather heels with large clasps. The cotton coat turns out to be two fingers longer than the dress. The shoes are a little big but perfect for when my feet swell. The blue-and-beige-plaid matching bag has a patent-leather buckle. I look at myself in the long mirror propped against the shoebox pile.

Wow, a real model! Giselle yells out to Juan.

How happy Mamá would be to see the woman in the reflection. Made and composed.

Juan nods. Can we leave now?

Demand. Demand. Demand.

So without a beat I nod back at Juan and say, Yes, I want all of it.

Juan waits until we are outside away from earshot of Gino and Giselle. He grabs my wrist. I drop the bag of purchases.

I told you, one dress! One dress! Do you think I'm made of money?

I don't flinch. I stare into him.

I dare you, I say, knowing he's too proud to do anything to me where everyone can see.

Wait until I get home later. You'll regret that smart mouth.

A LITTLE FOOD POISONING NEVER KILLED ANYONE.

So I climb onto the fire escape, sit on the steps, and wait for my pigeons. I grab Betty because she's always picking on Juanita. Clamp her with both hands. Duck back into the apartment. She coos in protest. The wooden board is on the kitchen table. On the stove, the pot of hot water. The bucket in the sink. It's okay, I tell her, calming her, looking her in the eye, and then I chop her head off. A clean slice. Her body quivers, then involuntarily spasms. I tie her feet with string and hang her from the faucet. While she bleeds out I work on the seasonings. Inside a bowl, I mash together a handful of cilantro, the juice of a lime, two cloves of garlic, some spices.

After, I scald her and pluck the feathers as if plucking the hair out of Juan's head. The naked pigeon on the wooden board waits to be marinated. The pigeon smell overwhelms. *Just like home.*

I chop her into six pieces and wash her in cold water. Rub the pigeon pieces into it. Toss in a small chopped onion and half a green pepper, placing the bowl inside a large plastic bag to seal everything in.

Meanwhile I heat the pot on the stove, add corn oil, a dash of sugar for color. When the sugar caramelizes I add the pigeon. Let it simmer over low heat and turn on the radio. Los Panchos are playing. I wipe the sink and double-bag the pigeon's head, guts, and feathers and throw them out in the incinerator in the hallway. When the meat is browned I stir in the rice and four cups of water. Add salt to taste. *Let's see who will pay, Juan?* Once the water evaporates, I cover the pot to simmer over low heat.

While the food cooks I take a long hot shower to get rid of the smell. By the time Juan walks in, an inviting aroma fills the apartment. He pauses at the door, eyes glued to the table I set with the special silverware and glasses he took from the raceway.

I serve him the rice and pigeon and a pile of fried plátanos. I pour cold beer in a glass.

This looks good, he says, and winks at me.

He seems famished after a long day at work. He arrived early, so he didn't go to Caridad's. Maybe he's not so angry about the dress.

Maybe I overreacted.

Wait, I say, and grab the dish before he can take a bite. He grabs it back, but the plate falls to the floor.

Now look what you've done! Those hands of yours. Sometimes you are a real chicken head, Ana.

But really fuck you, Juan.

Don't worry, I say. *There's plenty fucking more.*

I clean up the floor and serve him a hefty new plate.

He eats and eats.

Poor Pigeon Betty, what diseases did you carry?

It's delicious, Juan says.

You think so?

I'm beaming. It's the first compliment he has given me for my cooking in a long time. I serve him some water, and he looks at me. Really looks at me. My belly bulges through my clothes. My breasts are bigger.

I'll make you an appointment for a doctor, he says.

Yes, okay.

That's when I know he understands.

JUAN SURVIVES THE PIGEON DINNER WITHOUT EVEN A stomachache. He makes my doctor's appointment for April 15.

I wear my new dress.

Remember to say you're nineteen, like in your paperwork, not fifteen.

I don't tell Juan I've been to the hospital before. He waits outside for me.

The doctor tells me to take my top off and put a gown on.

I've never met a woman doctor before.

Her glasses slide to her nose tip. Her silver hair is cut short like a man's. The doctor's warm hand pats my arm gently. She leaves the room so I can undress.

Save for a poster of a family on the wall, signed by one Norman Rockwell, the room is a bright white. There's a sink, some glass containers filled with wooden sticks and cotton balls. I don't know whether to take off my bra, my shoes, so I take everything off and put on the gown, keeping my socks on.

I wait on the padded table. My belly, although small, it pushes out. Is the baby stretching? Is it a boy or a girl? Will the exam hurt?

The doctor knocks on the door, then enters before I can answer. She places her hand on my chest, tells me to lie down. She notes some bruises on my arm and neck from so many weeks ago—but they take forever to heal. She briefly looks me in the eye, and I look back as blankly as I can. She takes my temperature. My blood pressure. She places the cold stethoscope on my belly and listens.

Cwanto anyo too teeayness? Her voice echoes in the room.

Fif . . . I mean nineteen.

She presses all around my belly.

Looky good, she says cheerfully. Looky really bweno.

She shows me a laminated drawing from her desk of a baby inside of the uterus.

The doctor points to the paper and says, Kawbesa, and then points to her own head. She outlines the baby's head with her fingers on my belly. She takes my fingers and shows me how the head is near my pubic bone. I feel something hard and round.

She motions for me to get dressed and says, Bweno.

The doctor leaves. I sit there alone wishing more than ever Teresa could be here with me. Or Marisela, the only person I can call a friend. Or even Mamá, even if she may drive me crazy with her chatter. Oh, she'll be so happy when she finds out!

The doctor returns, this time with another woman, who carries a leather bag filled with files.

Hello, Señora Ruiz, the nurse says in crisp Spanish.

Ruiz-Canción, I correct her.

She sits beside me, extends her arm and holds both of my hands.

Your baby looks great, Señora Ruiz-Canción.

What a relief to finally understand, I say with a sigh.

And your family? Are they here with you?

No, they're in Dominican Republic. But soon maybe they come or I go. My husband says it's not easy to travel. You know, money. Papers.

Is your husband here?

Yes, he's outside, waiting.

Is everything okay at home?

Why were they asking so many questions?

Should I be worried about the baby? I ask the Spanish-speaking nurse but look at the doctor.

We just want to make sure that your home is safe for the baby.

The nurse hands me some glossy papers but I catch her sneaking glances at my neck and arms.

Here's some information, Señora Ruiz-Canción. Places you can go if you need help or have trouble.

I look down at one of the papers. A photograph of a woman with a busted lip and a black eye filled with panic.

No trouble! I say, then check my tone. No trouble.

I hand back the brochures and when she doesn't take it I stuff them in my purse.

Thank you, I say and smile back at the woman, ready to continue the exam.

I'll never be the woman in the photo. Juan isn't as terrible as that. He has loose hands when he gets angry. That's all. I hold my belly with both hands. They won't take my baby away from me.

The doctor turns to the nurse, who translates.

You should make an appointment to return in one month so we can follow your progress.

Thank you, I say, very much.

The doctor hands me the same bottle of vitamins the last one gave me. She calls it a sample, to get me started. I am almost done with the other bottle, which I hid from Juan under the sink. Now I can take them out in the open.

And here's some iron, the doctor says. She rattles the bottle like a maraca and the nurse informs me that I'm underweight. It's not unusual for pregnant women to become anemic.

So you must make sure to eat well, the nurse explains. Eat spinach, yams, red meat.

But I throw everything up.

It'll pass, the nurse says with compassion.

I don't want to let go of her hands, though she probably can't be trusted.

I stuff the vitamin and iron bottles inside my purse, which I hope they notice matches the coat and shoes. They need to see that my husband does take care of me.

Outside, I wish they could also see how Juan is already on his feet eagerly waiting for his wife. I feel oddly relieved when I see him. He's all that I can rely on at the moment.

So you have our baby in there? He sings and grabs my hand. Although he's late to work, there's a brand-new tenderness in his touch.

Doctor says everything's good.

Good.

He escorts me quickly across the street to our building. Inside the apartment, he picks me up off the floor and embraces me.

I'm so happy that we're going to really really be a family.

He pats my cheeks and says good-bye. And I feel even more re-lief when he leaves. From the window, I watch him walk toward the train station on Broadway. Will anything change between us now? I open the window in the kitchen to let in fresh air and spread rice on the plastic plate for the pigeons.

Sweet little birds.

MARISELA HAS WORK FOR ME TO DO. SHE COMES BY early, right after Juan has left for work. She carries two bags full of small ceramic dolls, thin ribbons, glue, and lace.

What's all this? I take one of the bags and place it on the sofa.

Marisela tears off her coat, revealing her outfit: fitted wool pants, a bright-colored sweater, and big furry boots. Her hair, in a French twist. She isn't wearing her usual face, but even without all the makeup she looks beautiful. I take a look at myself, my hair is still marked from sleep because I haven't been expecting anyone.

Listen carefully, comadre. You'll have to get this all done in three hours. I'll be back here to eat lunch and then take them with me. You'll get five cents apiece. They're souvenirs for a friend's wedding. There should be two hundred pieces in here. I told her I knew of a girl who could do it fast and for cheap.

Me?

Of course, you. Will you do it?

I finger the sample to follow: *Edwin Martinez and Andrea Thome forever 04/10/1965.*

Be careful with the glue—it's stronger than it looks and can peel your skin off. Make sure their names are facing out on the ribbons and that you don't cover the faces of the dolls. And the lace, you see how it folds on the back like a butterfly wing?

Before I can think of a question to ask, Marisela plants a wet kiss on my cheek and wraps herself again in her thick wool coat. She waves good-bye then closes the door behind her.

The phone rings.

I rush to it, always hoping for someone to call me from back home.

It's Juan. He wants to come home for lunch. Out of all days. His voice, a fist knocking on my door. He hardly ever comes home in the daytime, but now with the baby he keeps checking up on me.

Oh, you don't have to go through all that trouble. I mean, there's always food here waiting for you, I say, trying to sound indifferent. I glance at the bags filled with souvenirs on the sofa, wondering if Marisela will be able to pick everything up before Juan even arrives.

You miss me? he asks.

Um, the house feels . . . quiet without you here.

It's the absolute truth. When Juan is home he talks as if I'm deaf. He sucks his teeth and smacks his lips when he eats. On good days, he sings.

As soon as I hang up, I start on the souvenirs: five cents apiece, two hundred pieces—that's ten dollars to feed my Dominicana! I move the coffee table against the wall and organize all the pieces on the floor. I study a ceramic doll, smaller than my pinkie nail. It's of a bride and groom to be glued on a ribbon. In the sample, the glue is untraceable. I try to do the same. At first, I can't keep the glue off my fingers, but once I establish a system I work fast and make few mistakes.

The phone rings again. I rush to it. The damn breath again. She waits for me to say hello, to pause, and then she hangs up. She's called twice this morning. Between Juan wanting to return home for lunch and her calls, I figure they've fought. Maybe he told her about the baby.

I finish all two hundred souvenirs with more than enough time left over. I line them up on the kitchen table. I have them face the door so as to greet Marisela when she enters. I rush to prepare enough lunch for everyone.

When Marisela arrives she still is plain-faced, no makeup, as if we're not just friends but close friends, like sisters who see each other for what we are.

Marisela fingers the souvenirs and places them in the bags. She hands me the ten dollars as promised.

Doesn't it feel good to make your own money, Ana?

Well, it's good to be able to help my family back home. They always need. Do I have to tell Juan about the money? I say to change the subject.

What you do with it is your business.

Marisela eats everything on her plate. I want to offer her seconds, but there won't be enough for Juan. I want to share so many things with her, but Mamá—even if she's far away, all her warnings against friendships keep me from truly allowing myself to speak freely with Marisela. And yet she is doing more than anyone else has ever done for me, even when my house is plain, even when to her I must look like some naïve child. She's here, eating with me. Being with me. Helping me make money. It's impossible for me not to love her.

Marisela leans over and grabs both of my hands the same way the nurse at the hospital did. I don't know where to look, so I look at my nails, short from biting them.

You're so generous and good in the heart, Ana.

My eyes water. Not even my mother ever says such kind things. I realize then that one day, I'll be Marisela's age, and my daughter will be the age I am now. What fortune to have Marisela in my life, in my kitchen, filling the emptiness in my heart and in the apartment. My tongue is tied and I fear sounding idiotic. Instead I do something I've never done before, even with my own mother. I kneel on the cold linoleum floor, dig my head into Marisela's lap, and embrace her. For the first time, in a long time, I've found a true friend.

AFTER I KILLED PIGEON BETTY THE REST STOP VISITING.
They're not stupid. Now I can no longer count on them to deliver
secret messages to Teresa, who never makes the trip to call me. Now
she must get my news from Mamá. When I write Mamá telling her
I'm pregnant, I receive an envelope so thin and damp from the humidity, the black ink has bled. Most of it, impossible to read. I press
it against my nose to catch a trace of Los Guayacanes.

> Dearest Ana,
>   This pregnancy is gold in the bank. Don't wait for
> Juan to settle your papers. It's not in his best interest.
> You start on them right away so you can solicit us
> too. You can't have a baby without our help. I know
> Juan is in trouble because they dumped a pile of ce-
> ment after selling a chunk of our land for construc-
> tion, but nothing's happening here. So your father
> sold three acres and a horse to a woman in New
> York. She wants to grow cane, just like I've been
> telling your father we should do. But he doesn't like
> the cane business. It's gotten pretty bad here, a real
> tragedy. Guns are being handed out in parks in the
> capital to snot heads. So you can only imagine what a
> mess there is here. Lenny eats but doesn't grow. And
> Juanita and Betty just need to find someone to marry
> them so I don't need to feed them. Tell Juan to send
> money. Now he's obligated because you are carrying
> that baby. You better believe he will profit from it.
> Don't forget about us. No lights are too bright to for-
> get where you come from. Remember. Remember.
>   With love,
>   Your mother

ON SUNDAYS THE RUIZ BROTHERS GATHER. THIS SUNDAY we will visit Hector, all the way in Tarrytown, to discuss the possible invasion of Americans in Dominican Republic. Finally I get to meet Yrene, Hector's wife, who's always left at home with the baby. It's also nice to have César back after his short disappearance. What woman's bed was he keeping warm this time?

Even if Juan can drive, César drives the car.

He prefers to be driven, César says, like a big man.

Juan laughs it off but César is right, Juan does walk about with an air of being better than his other brothers. Because he's lighter skinned. Because he has straight hair. And taller too, by comparison.

César's dark skinned, with tight-curled hair and a flatter nose. Unlike Juan, who cares very much what everyone thinks, César doesn't seem to care. His eyes are filled with trouble and fun. No matter what he wears, it all seems put-together. And he acts as if the whole world should take care of him. When César turned five, both of his parents died, one after the other, and he was too young to remember them. His three older brothers basically raised him.

Hector and Yrene moved into a house—not an apartment—in Tarrytown. Their home isn't piled up high like ours. They live on their own earth, with their own plants, in their own yard. They have one boy. Yrene isn't Dominican.

I don't trust Puerto Rican women, says Juan. They might as well be American—cold and only out for themselves.

He says it in a wounded way, clearly tied to some personal experience with Caridad.

Juan turns on the radio. I sit in the backseat like a child. But it's better so that his heavy hand doesn't rest on my thigh. His eyebrows pull into a V. The radio broadcasts the Mets vs. Giants game in San Francisco. Pitching for the Giants is Juan Marichal, who Juan bets big money on.

One day Dominicans will take over baseball, Juan says. Even if Marichal is one of a handful of Dominicans in the major leagues and doesn't get the attention he deserves, when he lifts his leg and sneaks his killer pitch nobody can deny that the white boys have nothing on him.

The drive goes fast, not even an hour. But Washington Heights and Tarrytown can't be more different. In Tarrytown there are birds chirping, dogs barking, the faint laughter of children playing in the backyards. Front yards with white fences and flags waving hello. Flowers in terra-cotta pots.

Hector waits outside for us on a plastic chair on his porch, chain-smoking cigarettes. A pile of stubs on an ashtray on the floor. His hairline receded, his freckled forehead pronounced. He isn't the handsomest of brothers, but the peppered day-old beard and the softness in his eyes make it clear he is harmless, a good man.

My brothers, he calls out, even before César parks the car in his driveway.

Hector grabs both my shoulders, takes a good look at me, and pats me hard on my back. Then he pushes me away to grab Juan's neck and pull him into his house, César close behind them. They are like a centipede, one organism, lots of arms and legs.

Hector makes us enter from the backyard. The ground, all cement. A rusted wire fence marks his land. Their large short-haired dog is tied to a post and barks incessantly at Juan, who hides behind me.

Sit, Hector commands. High five! Soon the dog sits and gives Hector its paw.

I must've been smiling, because Hector winks at Juan and then asks me, You want to try?

Stay away, Ana, Juan says, as if I'm the one with fear.

I crouch down and let the dog smell my hand. Hi fi, I say, in my strongest voice.

The dog lifts his paw into mine. His soft fur warms my cold hands.

That's enough! Juan says, terrified.

Calm down, brother, César says.

We look back at each other, tickled. Juan's scared of a sweet dog. Juan, a real city man.

Let's go inside, Hector says.

Once inside, Juan relaxes. The living room is full of brown. We sink into the chocolaty-brown sofa, with tan cushions so soft, the coils of the mattress underneath poke at our bottoms. The floors are covered in a pale beige rug. Toys scattered all about. No one has cleaned the rug in months. Crusted food snagged here, dried soil there. The small television, full of fingerprints. A loud banging of pots draws me toward the kitchen.

I stand in the nearby hallway waiting for Yrene to greet me. The faucet's on. The radio's on. She pokes her head out and startles me.

What doing, in dark? she says, in mangled Spanish. Her voice is strange, as if she doesn't know all the words.

I'm Ana, Juan's wife.

She looks me up and down and sucks her teeth. I stare back with a smile, showing all my teeth as if I can break her. She has just pulled rollers from her hair; large round curls bounce around on the top of her head. A barrette holds it in a twist the same way Teresa does her hair. I miss Teresa so much it hurts. Yrene's much darker than Teresa but with high cheekbones, a pinched nose. The bones around her neck poke out. Teresa's round and soft everywhere. Yrene's eyebrows are plucked in a thin line, a perfect arch as if she spent hours on her face and her hair. But not a stitch of makeup. She's wearing a housedress and flip-flops. I am overdressed in my church clothes. I will have to work hard to earn her favor.

I creep into the kitchen. She hands me a plátano and a knife. Her fingernails are cut short and square like a man's. She moves about in a way that makes it difficult for me to look at her face.

Okay, Ana, help, she says.

I peel back the skin of the plátano and slice it diagonally one inch thick.

She heats oil on the stove and purses her full lips, lifting her chin, signaling for me to keep helping. The men are hungry, her son napping. Yrene doesn't make small talk. I'm glad. She's older than me, maybe thirty. Her body, pear shaped. Voluptuous motherly hips.

In the kitchen she moves about like an octopus, swatting flies, slicing, cutting, washing. The kitchen is cluttered and small, everything piled on shelves—the dishes, the pots, the baby food jars, bottles. I start to wash the dishes. Carefully, not using too much soap, making sure water doesn't stray from the sink. Yrene's nervousness makes me nervous, as if I'm doing something wrong. I drop a dish. It slips and shatters by my feet.

Yrene breathes loudly, exasperated.

I quickly go to pick up the pieces. Six, maybe seven pieces.

I'm so sorry.

Because the floor needs a good sweeping and mopping, I take the broom from inside a small closet not wider than my hand, and sweep the entire kitchen.

Where's your mop? I ask, ready to help her. She obviously needs help.

Away! Go! Her voice strains. Her eyes fill. Her barrette has come loose, her hair in disarray.

Now, baby wake, she scolds, and leaves me in the kitchen. All the burners are on. I quickly fry the plátanos and stir the rice. All the food looks pretty done. I turn off the burners.

I peek into the living room. The men drink whiskey. Hector calls out for Yrene in English.

You speak English? I ask Hector.

All the men laugh.

What's there to laugh about?

Hector had to learn the hard way, César says, he married a gringa.

The brothers all look at each other as if the secret between them is too big to tell.

To us Yrene is without a mother tongue. Her father had moved from Puerto Rico to fight in World War II. She is one-hundred-percent Americana, something I will never be. How lucky she speaks English so well. How strange for her to look like us but be one of them.

Come here, Juan says, and pats the space next to him on the sofa.

I sit next to him and he rubs my head, smoothing my hair down.

Ana's gonna make a beautiful mother, he says. She really knows how to take care of me.

You're a lucky man, Hector says, already drunk in the eyes.

César lifts his beer, winks at me, and says, Let's make a cheer for Juan.

I'm going to be a father! Juan says.

Hector leaps to his feet.

Yrene, get some glasses. We have so much to celebrate.

Let it be a boy! Juan salutes.

With brains, Hector adds, pouring rum and Coke in every-one's glass once Yrene arrives with a tray.

She cuts her eyes at Hector when he says they should try again, as if their thirteen-month-old son doesn't count. They had lost their first child a few days before he was born, and their sec-ond son was born retarded.

And let's hope the kid gets his mother's face, says César. Yrene smiles then frowns when he walks over to clink my glass and plops himself in the chair next to me. His thigh touches and lin-gers on my thigh in an act of solidarity.

They all look over as if waiting for me to smile.

I extend my arm to turn on the radio. The Giants lost three to four.

Son of a bitch! Juan says, then comes over and grabs my shoul-der and rubs my head some more. I slip from under Juan and excuse myself. I need fresh air, so I exit to the front of the house.

I sit on the plastic chair. Wrap my coat tighter around me. The cold is trapped inside my bones. This is all so different from Los Guayacanes. Each house with uniform lawns. No animals. Just pigeons and squirrels. No smells of fruit or flowers. The cottony clouds dot the blue sky. To look at the bright sun, you'd think it's hot like back home. Why are the clouds so dotted here? What makes them that way? The cold air? Are Mamá, Papá, Lenny, Betty, Juanita, and Yohnny outside now, looking at the same sky, the same sun?

FROM THE MOMENT I GREET MARISELA AT THE DOOR I CAN tell she bears bad news. Despite the cheeriness of her bright pink knitted pants and matching sweater, her face betrays her.

Please sit, Marisela says almost immediately, and holds both of my hands on her lap. I imagine the worst: She's dying. Her sister's dying. Her husband has left her.

I'm in big trouble, she says.

What?

My husband came back from D.R. last night, and he noticed I'm not wearing my wedding ring.

I don't know exactly what she's about to ask, but I sense it.

Are you hungry? I say, I made sancocho.

On the days Marisela is due to make payments on her loan I always cook a full meal. Rationing the ingredients just so. Faithfully eating the Chef Boyardee when I am alone to stretch our groceries.

I go to the kitchen; Marisela follows.

He thinks I took it off to be with another man, she says, watching me pour a bag of beans into a bowl. Anita, can you believe that? As if with all the things I have to do, I would have time for that.

I tell her how I can't even tell Juan a man was nice to me without him getting upset.

Ay, Anita, my sister, my friend. I knew you'd understand.

I carry the bowl with me to the table, for protection, for assurance, and sift through the beans looking for pebbles.

Marisela places her hand over the bowl and says, Listen to me, Anita.

She makes me face her. For the first time, I notice the gray in Marisela's hair, the two small lines between her eyebrows—a number 11. Her body slumps toward me, pleading.

Women don't beg, I remind Marisela, hoping to lighten the heavy mood.

Look, kid, jokes aside. I need my ring back.

Now it's you who's joking, Maris—

Anita, listen! I promise to pay back the money the same way as I always have. Juan doesn't need my ring. He has my word. You have my word.

No, Juan won't allow it.

He doesn't have to know.

But Marisela, I can't get into Juan's things. I don't even know where to look.

She may look hurt, but I'm not about to give a dog a leash made out of sausage links. Juan drilled me more than once on the combination of our safe. He gave me detailed directions on how to handle his papers if he were to die. Marisela's ring is in the safe inside a small yellow envelope. But how can Marisela ask this of me?

Please, Ana. I'm always on time with payments. I won't disappoint you. I promise.

Marisela, you're asking for the impossible.

Haven't I been a good friend to you? Did I tell Juan about the money you made from the souvenirs? Did I tell him about your pregnancy?

It's my neck on the line.

She grabs my wrist.

Girl, if I don't have the ring on my finger when my husband comes home tonight I'll be as dead as all those boys in Vietnam. He thinks it's at the jeweler. He didn't even want my sister to come. I told him I had saved all that money by doing my own nails and hair.

I recognize the fear in her eyes. Maybe Marisela's husband hits her too. She's never said as much—but neither have I. When she noticed the redness on my neck weeks ago, I told her it was a rash. If we're such friends, why don't we both just tell the truth?

Please, Ana, if my husband finds out about this, he'll never forgive me. He and Juan already have a complicated relationship.

Complicated how?

Marisela's face pales. She bites her bottom lip and lowers her eyes in contemplation.

Look, Anita, there are things you can't understand. Better you don't even think about. You're so innocent. Ay Anita, if I could be your age and start over!

Her head bends onto my sleeve. Ay, she cries. I scratch her arms and back, feeling the contours of her body, her tears dampening my blouse.

I'll get that ring for you, I say without thinking.

I leave Marisela sniffling alone in the living room with a roll of toilet paper. The safe, the size of two shoeboxes, is hidden inside the closet, behind the rack of clothing. The combination is the date his mother died. I take a deep breath, almost regretting my decision. Even with my head inside the closet, I can hear the sobs out in the living room. They are getting louder. Don't exaggerate, is what Mamá would say because she doesn't trust anyone. Especially not family. But I don't want to be like Mamá. Besides, Juan'll never know—as long as Marisela continues to pay every week.

I return to the living room and put the ring on her finger.

I missed you, Marisela says, admiring it. On her hand, the ring comes to life. The small diamond appears brighter, bigger. She embraces me.

Thank you! Thank you!

Will you stay for lunch?

Ay no, I can't today.

It'll only take me a minute to prepare, I say.

My sister's home alone.

Sadness bathes me. I had even added fresh tomatoes to the rice and grated carrots into it for color.

You know how it is when we first arrive. Everything's so confusing. But next week, I promise I'll come. I'll even bring my sister. You'll love her. She's a few years older than you are.

Marisela embraces me good-bye. She looks back as if forgetting something. I try not to think about it. Next week we'll have
lunch. I'll wear my new dress, coat, shoes, and purse Juan bought
at El Basement. Maybe Marisela and I will finally take a walk in
the park together.

YESTERDAY JUAN ARRIVED FROM WORK DRUNK. HE FELL onto our bed without talking. He waved me away. Asleep before I could ask him if he wanted something to eat, before I could peel off his socks. When he's drunk, he sometimes rolls over onto me, his dead weight suffocating me. Does he know how heavy he is? How the stench of a day's work at the raceway is buried deep inside his skin, his hair? How my stomach turns when he comes near me with his work-drink smells?

I let him sleep late because for once he has a day off. I'm also relieved he's too tired to ask about Marisela's visit.

I keep myself busy organizing the glasses in the cupboard until he calls me from the bedroom. I have become skilled at telling his voices apart.

Ana!

My mind races. Marisela's missing ring. The money I'm saving to send to Mamá. A bad day at work. Some trouble in Dominican Republic. A fight with Caridad or a fight with one of his brothers.

Ana! His voice grows louder.

It's a bad day at work. His voice as if he has hair caught in his throat.

I tuck my knees to my chin, my feet flat on the cushions. I hug my legs and rock my body as if I'm on a rocking chair. I wait. Sometimes Juan calls me and falls back to sleep.

Ana!

I stand by the bedroom door, open it a crack and watch him sit at the edge of the bed. The sun fills the room.

Come here. He pats the empty space on the bed next to him.

I'm here. I stand under the doorframe like one is supposed to do during earthquakes. I hold on to the moldings and plant my feet, feeling each of my bare toes on the wooden floor.

He waves me over, pulling away the comforter as if it's

bedtime. I inch closer, and before I know what is happening, he pulls me to sit beside him. In his fist he holds one of the brochures the doctor gave me.

What the fuck is this?

I don't know.

I look toward the door, twisting around as much as I can so that he can't see my face; my arm over my stomach, ready for the worst.

Who gave you this shit?

He shoves the paper in my face. In my mind I see the list of phone numbers and the map of the island of Manhattan, with red dots and arrows pointing to places where women like me can get help.

The lady at the hospital. She gave them to me.

That brochure was in my purse. What is he doing looking through my things?

What did you tell them?

The photograph of the woman with a busted lip stares at us, at me.

Nothing, I swear, Juan. They give it to everybody, I say in a calm voice.

Juan takes a deep breath again.

They gave me many papers about nutrition and the baby too. Didn't you find those? I say, sneaking in an accusation.

He reads through another brochure. On it is a tadpole inside a womb. His back slumps, his head a wilted flower. When his knees widen, he pushes against my leg. One of his thighs is the width of both of mine. He turns to me and picks up my chin so my eyes look into his.

Tell me you love me, he says.

You know I do.

Tell me you're happy to be with me.

I'm happy. I am happy.

With me. Tell me you're happy with me.

I just nod.

Juan takes my hand, unwraps my arms, lifts my shirt so that my belly is exposed. I'm afraid he'll punch it.

You got a piece of me in you now. You know what that means?

My throat hurts from holding back tears, words.

Me and you are connected forever.

His large clammy hands rub my belly as if I'm his ball of fortune. He pushes me onto the bed. He lays his head on my belly, presses his ears against it. His head slithers up between my breasts, and he grabs them. Grabs my hair, tugs my ear, his hot morning breath on my face. He slaps my face, hard and fast. My skin sticks to his palm.

You better not be going around telling people our business. Don't you know how much I love you? You want someone to come and take our baby? Take you away from me? You think they won't do that? This is America. You hear me?

I study the lines on my hands for assurance. Back home an old woman told me I will live a long life. He kneels, exhausted, dark circles under his eyes. He needs to shave.

Ay my little one, please don't cry. Not today, okay?

His arms envelop me. I tuck my chin into my chest, hold my breath against his sour stench. The sheets have to be changed. There is the laundry to do, plátanos to boil for lunch.

What would I do without you, Ana?

You'd go to Caridad and make her happy, I want to say. Just go to her, already.

I'm nothing without you, my Ana.

He pulls me onto the bed, my back to his body. He falls asleep again.

I focus on my breath. On the baby growing in complete darkness, incubating in a similar heat to Los Guayacanes. My daughter and me, one day running along the water, over the rocks, picking up large pink shells and listening to the call of vendors selling fresh fish off their carts and to the women fighting for the pesos in my pocket, everyone saying their fish is freshest, everyone claiming they have the best sauce. My bare feet making footprints, ash-white from the saltwater. My baby's thick curls, her big Canción eyes asking me to name the palm trees, the bougainvillea, the flamboyán seeds, the clouds, the hummingbirds, the wild cats, the small islands in the distance. And for once, I will know all the answers.

ALTHOUGH IT'S BEEN A WEEK SINCE I'VE SEEN MARISELA, it feels more like a month. I prepare extra food for her sister. The small roasted chicken, marinated overnight in Mamá's special sauce: lemon, rosemary, parsley, and garlic. I turn up the radio to listen to Johnny Ventura, who César says is going to sing at Happy Hills on 157th Street. Even Juan wants to see him perform live.

We'll dance 'til our feet hurt, César promises.

On most days, I twirl myself and my belly to the music on the radio.

What's holding up Marisela? Outside my window, the trees are green, and the tulips planted around them are upright in full bloom. Women show off their new spring coats in bright colors and matching hats. The Jewish women walk in groups of two and three, pushing strollers, while the older children grab at their mothers' coats. One day, I will have my own to push down the busy streets.

Ventura's voice fills the apartment with fast merengue beats. I sing along, shaking my hips in the same way he does so the audience goes wild with my performance. Is Marisela's sister as different to her as my sister is to me? I sing into the broom and giggle to myself while sweeping the living room for the thousandth time. The smell of chicken makes my stomach growl. I open the stove and pour the juices over the meat to keep myself from looking at the clock over the refrigerator. I look out the window, admire all the cherry blossoms that line the small islands between the cars going north and south. Tarrytown is north. The Empire State Building is south. The river is west and east. West and north are safe because the Jews live there. East and south are unsafe because the blacks live there—they burn cars and garbage cans and throw themselves to the street for no good reason. Self-destructive, is what Juan calls them.

He never mentions the black woman in the red hat who still appears to refresh the flowers for Malcolm X in front of the Audubon. With her children. Why had this X man been so loved? Did he sing to huge audiences like Johnny Ventura? It's hard not to love a man who can sing well. Even when I'm angry at Juan, when he sings my anger breaks.

I press my forehead on the windowpane and search for Marisela's bounce in every woman on Broadway. When I understand that Marisela is no longer coming—probably already on her way to her other job—I go ahead and eat. And after, I light a white candle for Marisela, asking God to protect her. I take twenty-five dollars from my ceramic doll to pay towards Marisela's seventy-five-dollar debt. Juan will ask for the money. He will ask if she is well. I will say yes.

Now Dominicana only has five dollars left.

Marisela will surely give me the money in the next few days as promised. I should've asked for her phone number. Friends should have each other's numbers.

I don't want Juan to arrive home and see I have cooked so much food. So I make a generous plate for the old lady downstairs who walks her small white dog in the mornings and greets me whenever our eyes meet in the lobby.

I stand outside the old lady's door, afraid to knock. Just as I turn away from the door the old lady suddenly opens it as if expecting me. She takes the plate from my hand and says, Thank you, then waves for me to enter. The dog sticks its nose out from between her legs. I purse my lips—how strange to keep a dog inside an apartment.

Thenk you, I say.

She points to herself and says, Rose. My name is Rose.

Mi nem Ana, I say.

Come in, dear.

This I understand because she keeps waving her arm toward the apartment. As soon as she shuts the door behind me I smell dried flowers and menthol. Her sofa is a bright green, her walls filled with paintings of bright circles and lines. I don't know how to stand, where to stand. She moves slowly toward her kitchen, square-shaped and tidy. You can tell she never cooks.

Do you want some tea? she asks.

I smile at her words. What can be behind all the closed doors? A closet? A bedroom? A patchwork quilt is draped over a tall chair. Her floors and shelves are dusty, and the walls a grayish white. They could use a fresh coat of paint. I follow her to the kitchen. Because her windows face the back of the building, onto other people's windows, she needs to keep all the lights on in the apartment for brightness even during the day.

She places the plate I brought her in the refrigerator without even looking at what's inside. I want to say, It's fresh. Ready to eat. A real shame to have to reheat it later. Do other people bring her food? The thought makes me inexplicably jealous.

She puts a short, fat pot on the stove. And does the old lady talk! I nod and smile and nod. She places two teacups on a tray. She pulls some thick, plain-looking cookies out of a tin can. I jolt when the pot of water whistles. This makes her laugh. She picks it up, shaky hands carefully pouring the hot water over small bags full of herbs. I fear she will drop the pot. And why such a strange pot for boiling water? Does she have a different pot for everything she makes? She says more words while placing the tray near me. Floating inside my teacup is the little bag. Not a cinnamon stick and cloves. I watch her take the bag out with her spoon. I do the same. Plop a sugar cube into the cup. I do the same. Stir. Stir. Then she sips. I sip. The plain cookie is delicious. Buttery, sweet, crumbly. I make note of the tin can, the blue can with big white lettering. When I'm done with my tea, the old lady slaps both her hands on her thighs and walks toward the door. I understand I should leave. We are done. No fuss, no hugs, no anything.

Tenk you, I say, nodding my head and smiling. She waves good-bye, simultaneously waving me away, as if she's relieved our visit's over. I rush back upstairs, hold my belly to keep it from bouncing. My thighs burn from climbing the steep staircase. My heart beats fast and hard. I lock the door behind me. The candle on the windowsill continues to flicker over Broadway where the

Audubon building is breathing people in and out. I also watch people emerge from the train station, getting on and off buses, walking in and out of buildings. Will Rose return the plate? All day I wonder if she ate the food I made her. I imagine her sitting in her kitchen looking out at the brick walls and other windows. Does she eat my food cold, straight from the refrigerator? Does she even eat chicken?

TWO WEEKS HAVE PASSED SINCE I LAST SAW MARISELA.
The ache in my body, the heaviness in my chest is so bad I fear my heart will stop, that the baby will die of sadness. Marisela has one payment left, according to Juan. Mamá will be disappointed. I trusted someone. I lost my secret stash for my necessities. Now I can't help the family. All my hard work is gone just like that. Gone. For this last payment, I borrow from Juan's emergency stash, which I recently discovered rolled tightly and stuffed inside a pill bottle. If I don't replace the money Juan will definitely kill me.

I wake up with a headache coming, a chill in my bones. The stillness inside terrifies me. The newspapers only bear bad news. Dominican Republic is at war. The United States Marines have landed in full to stop the rebels from taking over. Santo Domingo is on lock-down. What about my land, my restaurant? Juan says, more anxious than ever. Those bastards!

He forgets where he left his keys, his wallet. He double-checks his pockets, a sure sign he's preoccupied. I understand him. Marisela has taken everything I had. Ay, the messes we make. Only we know what they are. I look out of the bedroom window toward the cathedral and see people dressed for church. Marisela goes to church. Maybe I will find her there.

Juan slumbers, half-naked, reeking of restaurant kitchen and rum. He's hungover from a long Saturday night. I crack the window open so the air in the room will circulate. He watches me while I do my hair and adjust the clasp of my earrings.

Where do you think you're going? Juan calls out to me.

To church, I say. We aren't heathens. We believe in God.

Back home, to go to church was a trip, only for the holidays. But in New York City it's just down the street. I've waited enough.

My voice shakes in anticipation of his reaction, but Juan buries himself further in the sheets and lies in bed, his gaze half asleep.

I wear my A-line dress and the gold earrings with amber teardrops he bought me. I color my lips with the pink lipstick Marisela gave me, hoping it will conjure her. I slip on my shoes.

Juan stares at me, not in a menacing way, almost tender. He has new gray hairs near his temples, probably because of the troubles in Santo Domingo.

Wait, wait, I can walk you there. He pushes himself to sit.

Not necessary. I'll be fine.

Okay, woman. Just don't linger out there.

He turns his back to me as if he doesn't want to see me leave. As of late, he only talks about the small patch of land the restaurant is on. Even with all the bribes, still no title. Pan Am has canceled all flights. He feels trapped. I understand.

Outside, I breathe in the spring air. Four months ago the snow piled up so high; now the trees are showing off new buds. People shed layers of clothing. As I walk to church, Rose catches my arm. I want to thank her for returning the dish a week before— inside a plastic bag on my doorknob, squeaky clean and empty as a licked bone—but I can't find the English words. I want to ask her about the chicken. Was it good? Does she have any family? I hope she didn't feed the chicken to the dog. Every time I see her, the poor lady is alone. Back home, even the crazy women are fed and visited by someone.

The light through the stained windows bathes my skin red, blue, and yellow. The church is five times the size of the one in San Pedro de Macorís. Rose and I sit together toward the front, close to the altar. I regret our seating choice immediately because I can't see everyone who walks in. How am I to find Marisela? The priests talk about God in English. I breathe in the frankincense and appreciate the people's calm, listening to the sound of the organ, the singing of the choir. The benches wobble and creak when the people stand, sit, kneel. I follow. The children in front of me tug at each other's hair. When one sticks out his tongue at me the mother turns around to excuse them.

I smile. One day, I whisper to my belly, you'll explain to me what people are saying.

I pray for my mother, father, and brothers and sister. I pray for Juanita and Betty. I pray for my baby inside me.

If you're listening, God, bring me Marisela.

When Mass finishes, the priest parades down the aisle followed by a train of altar boys, the choir, and finally the congregation. The front of the church exits first. I search the pews for Marisela's face. No Marisela. Maybe something bad happened to her. Maybe she was taken away. How many women back home have disappeared from one day to another? Too many to count. Maybe Marisela is trapped. How many women get to choose who to marry and can truly dictate their own life? As God is my witness, my daughter will have choices. I pray she'll be stubborn and free like Teresa.

Outside the church I stand at the top of the steps. The well-dressed crowd multiplies. The priest shakes the hands of people as they exit. I wait in line. When I reach him, he grabs my hand; his are padded and soft, not worker's hands, and his eyes are gray, his smile kind. The sun draws a halo over his light brown hair as he speaks. Not understanding I just hug him, wrap my arms around his back, grab the heavy fabric of his long robe and hold it inside my fist. I breathe in his church smell and he lets me cling to him, pats my head, gently pushes me away.

Bless me, I say in Spanish.

God bless you.

He turns to greet another person.

I stand among all the people and fight back tears. I miss my father. I miss my mother. Bless me, I whisper to myself. Every morning Papá and Mamá, I ask them and they bless me.

God bless you, Ana, and may he give you wisdom.

I can't move my feet. Walk, I tell them, walk. An arm tugs mine; Rose gestures for me to escort her home. And suddenly I feel my legs again.

Rose holds my arm until we are inside our building, until we arrive to the second floor, where Rose's dog barks before we even exit the elevator. I climb the four more flights to get home.

When I arrive, Juan waits in the living room, already dressed, smoking a cigarette.

So. What does God have to say?

All I can think about is Marisela.

That betrayers don't deserve forgiveness, I say flatly.

He looks bewildered, almost delighted that God would say such a thing. In his mind, God is for the unlucky, the poor, and the desperate. Juan thinks he is none of these things.

JUAN AND HIS BROTHERS NOW TUNE IN TO THE RADIO AT
all hours and scour the papers to figure out what all of the politi-
cal business will mean for them. They invested more money than
they actually had, borrowing here to pay there, a real gamble.
After years of making friends in the courts, in the government,
in the banks, to get around the endless bureaucracy, they're in
a panic. Nothing in Dominican Republic can be done without
knowing someone. If the country goes left, they want to be ready,
but if it goes right, they want to be ready too.

On April 24, 1965, José Francisco Peña Gómez, the only black
man in recent history to have a chance for the presidency, took
control of the government and Radio Santo Domingo. The an-
nouncement was timed for two in the afternoon, strategically post
lunch, when most citizens would be waking from the siesta and
listening to the radio. Peña Gómez announced the overthrow of
Donald Reid Cabral's provisional, American-backed government
and rallied the people out into the streets.

Forget the curfew, Peña Gómez told them, it won't be en-
forced. And so all over the country people overflowed the street corners and the avenues, celebrating. Even Juan, who'd never trusted
a black man, admired Peña Gómez.

It takes some real cojones to seize the radio station, Juan says.

Juan, César, and Hector sit around the dining table hedging
their bets while I feed them. I don't want to worry about Mamá,
Papá, and everyone back home, but it's impossible not to worry
with all the Ruiz brother talk.

Ramón's wife's brother's cousin's sister, who is a housekeeper
at the Palace, has been feeding Ramón firsthand accounts of what
is happening on the ground. She's the one who makes the military
generals' beds and scrubs their toilets. What housekeeper doesn't
keep an archive of her boss's invaluable trash? Ramón mentions
documents dating back since 1963 that prove the United States

has been meddling in the Dominican Republic's affairs, stashed underneath mattresses just in case a poor devil needs a favor.

Just like they went into Vietnam, says Ramón, the Americans are now in Dominican Republic. Punto y basta.

Even if Donald Reid Cabral was not elected by the people, he rules the military. He may not be a dictator like Trujillo, but he too would not think twice before having us all at best kneel on rice. So Ramón bets his money on Cabral.

There's no way any Dominican leader will win without America's guns.

Juan Bosch won once, he will win again, César says.

That's because he had Kennedy's ear, says Juan. But look where Kennedy is now. Dead. Dreaming is good to do when you're sleeping. But as long as we're awake, nobody wants to go hungry.

JUAN SITS AT THE LIVING ROOM TABLE ON A WOBBLY chair.

We have to talk, pajarita, he says.

His tone brings a chill to the back of my neck. He only calls me little bird when he has bad news. I don't want to hear what might be wrong now. For the first time in three months, I haven't woken with nausea. My pregnancy has finally settled in my body, my hair thick and my skin clear, tight and luminescent as a hard-boiled egg.

Let me make you some coffee, I say, and spring from the chair. Is there any whiskey left in the bottle? I better serve it as well.

No, Ana, sit. He clamps his hand around my wrist.

Marisela! He must've seen her. I look at my freshly painted pink toenails, waiting for the bomb to stop ticking.

Juan, it'll only take me a few minutes to get the coffee.

In that time I can make a run for it to the door. And my purse? Dominicana is on the windowsill but without a dollar to speak of. My shoes are in the closet in the bedroom. I will have to run away barefoot.

Pajarita, he says, I have to leave you.

You're leaving me? I say, feeling a mix of joy and fear.

Just to Santo Domingo. Relax. I'll be gone for a few weeks, maybe a month, hopefully not more. You know how things are there, everything takes longer than it should.

Under his steady gaze I take a deep breath to contain my excitement.

Don't worry. I tried to fix it so I didn't have to travel. But if I don't go, everything we worked for will be lost. Pan Am has started flights again from Puerto Rico. I'm already on a waitlist to travel from New York so I'm the first to go.

But I don't understand, I say, and mean it.

Given the opportunity to flex his role in world affairs Juan launches into a lecture. I'm more than happy to listen this time, knowing I'll soon be left alone to do as I please, with no one to wait for or to look after.

See the Americans have occupied Santo Domingo, siding with the military to prevent another Cuba where Juan's land would have been taken and redistributed to the people. It was Juan's idea—his idea, not Ramón's!—to invest in the land to open a restaurant next to La Reyna, the motel for politicians and rich boys doing their business in secret. Before the Ruiz brothers laid the slab of cement, the plot of land had been overgrown with fruit trees and weeds. Now it's a restaurant with a limited menu but a full bar. But one day, he says, one day the waitresses will wear uniforms and Juan will install a jukebox.

César promised me he'll watch over you, Juan says, now standing and walking in circles.

Whatever needs to be done, I say with the sigh of a bad actress. Inside, I'm screaming. Yes! César! I can start the English classes, and go on long walks, and César will take me dancing. For sure, I will also be able to track down Marisela. She couldn't have broken her promise unless she had to.

Juan circles the coffee table, goes on and on and on about Dominican politics, how he knows a few people with enough influence who may still be able to protect his assets. Without the title he could lose the land. Mamá and Papá don't have a title either. Who could remember when Mamá's family began squatting there?

And whatever happened to the coffee you offered me? Juan asks.

I head to the kitchen to my new life. Already I'm off checking in on my neighbor downstairs, helping her cross the street and doing her errands. I'm off to Woolworth's just a few blocks away, browsing each and every item on the shelf, intoxicated by the smell of pancakes and syrup. Adios, Juan, I'm off to see a movie with César and later to try the hot dogs sold by the man below my window.

Black and sweet, just the way you like it, I say, handing Juan coffee.

After traveling the world I sit and listen to Juan still talking about papers and money, papers and money, and how much we stand to lose.

BEFORE JUAN LEAVES FOR THE AIRPORT HE SHOWS ME how to close and open the door and how to lock the windows.

Remember to carry your keys inside your fist. Do not talk to strangers, and don't open the door for anyone unless I've called you. Do you understand? You must be smart and careful.

My eyes wander to his two suitcases. I spent last night and this morning carefully stuffing them with gifts, used clothing for the family, letters for everyone, and all the favors for Juan's friends to take to their family members. I'm too overjoyed to listen.

Go for the eyes. Juan lifts his fist with the keys between his fingers and fake-punches me in the eye.

Yes, yes, don't worry, I say without flinching—and smile the way I used to when my brothers play-fought with me.

Maybe all this time Juan has been truly afraid for me. Not too long ago a twelve-year-old girl stabbed an elderly woman on the subway. And then there was that fourteen-year-old boy who stabbed a man in the chest for a nickel. Every other day there is a story of a rape, a robbery, a purse snatched. But Juan is more than afraid. He feels like any misstep on his part can make the cops take him away. You'd think Trujillo is still alive, his spies reaching as far as New York City. So many people disappeared after just looking at El Jefe the wrong way. But how does the secret police work in America? What does the American President Johnson do when his people misbehave?

Juan kneels on one knee to kiss my belly. His forced jolly tone scares me, but I try to keep the lightness in the air. He almost looks as handsome as Ricky Ricardo in his suit.

Ay, Juan, you act as if you're never coming back. I'll take care of everything.

I surprise myself and hug him for the *Ana Loves Juan* show.

No. No. It's my job to worry, Ana.

A laugh track fills my head.

Now look, Lucy, we're not going to go over all this again. You cannot be in the show.

Give me one good reason.

You have no talent.

Give me another good reason.

Juan kisses me on the top of my head.

When we hear Hector's car honking downstairs, Juan picks up his bulging suitcases.

Once he's out the door, I rush over to the window and wait. Soon I watch as Hector and Juan share a cigarette by the car. Then Hector opens the trunk and places his luggage inside. They enter the car. It drives to the corner. It stops at the red light. And finally, finally, finally, the light turns green.

PART IV

THE MOMENT JUAN IS GONE, THE DRONE OF THE REFRIG-
erator amplifies and the wailing sirens outside pierce through the
apartment. Soon night will fall. The storefront gates will come
down; the streetlights will come on. I turn on the radio and the
television. I turn on all the lamps too. I prepare dinner.

César's supposed to come straight after work. Not meander
as he usually does, often spending the night with one of his girls.
César works in a dress factory downtown, in the 30s, where he
says the fabrics cram the store windows and trucks block traffic. He works with Jews who pay on time in cash and don't talk
bullshit the way we Dominicans talk. After work, he often gets
caught at a bar with some woman who feeds him.

But not like me, I think while stirring the rice. I'll feed you so
good you'll run home to keep me company every day.

I rub my belly, because the baby especially knows how good
I cook. Ay my baby, my conspirator, my compañera, my everything.

Juan left the fridge and cupboards full, so I have lots to choose
from. He insisted I stock up on Chef Boyardee because it never
goes bad, but the smell makes me sick, the mushiness sicker. I
pull two slices of kingfish from the fridge, a can of coconut water,
and dried coconut still in its bark shell. Juan complained that the
coconut was expensive, but I crave it, and even the stupidest men
know you can't deny a pregnant woman.

I grate the white meat onto the cutting board. The darker
it becomes outside, the more I check for César walking down
Broadway toward me. I peel then chop a green plátano into
thick wedges, fry them, and place them on a paper towel. All
of César's favorites. I set the table in the living room. Take a
shower.

Where's César already? I wait to eat until we can sit together, but he's taking so long. The last person to sit at the table with me was Marisela. I ache thinking of her. At least Juan never said anything about the missing money.

Just like a man, that César. I stand over the stove and turn the rice over, then let it sit a little longer over the flame so the bottom hardens to a concón. All along, my ears stay tuned to the telenovela *Corona de Lágrimas* that is playing in the other room.

I love you . . . I hate you . . . Come here.

Trumpets on the radio blare over the dialogue.

Crown of Tears—the telenovela title alone gets me to think of the crown of curls on César's head. I worry about him wandering Harlem by himself after work. Juan has fought him on this. Harlem is hot, and trouble will find him there. Harlem is where César got the crazy idea to let his hair grow and pick it out into a puff. But César says he feels at home in Harlem, where the women don't clutch their purses or cross the street when he walks by them. No one stops him at the door when he walks into a bar. And then there are the white girls, who go to the Harlem bars to dance, to drink, to shoot up, to have sex, and stumble out into their taxi with empty wallets. Yes, he likes those girls who have a desperation about them, who want to be forgotten. Who're not thinking about the future. Speak to me in Spanish, they beg him. Please, pretty please.

Stupid man. César's probably eating food from the streets when I made him a feast with so much love and care.

I close my eyes—the heat from the stove, the competing sounds, the smell of sauce, the hot corn oil, the fish, and suddenly Yohnny sneaks up behind me, digs his hands in my ribs. Ana! Mamá calls out for me. Lenny pulls at my skirt and asks me to join him in some game he invented. Juanita, Betty, and Teresa giggle over some boy. They never did include me in those conversations. *Ana's too little to know such things. Look at her now, playing at woman with that belly, cooking for her brother-in-law who doesn't even bother to show up.*

Ana-na-na, I hear Mamá and the radio and the television all call my name.

I poke a fork into the fish and eat it from the pan.

When César finally arrives to eat dinner, all the food is cold. Three hours late! He's looking at me funny. He smells of wet wool and old sweat.

It wasn't work or the bar that delayed César. It was the airport. He went last minute with Hector to drop off Juan.

What's going on in here? He turns off the overhead lights, the television, and lowers the radio.

I was cooking?

Surprised the neighbors haven't complained, he says.

It's just so quiet when no one's here.

I take a deep breath of relief. At least he's home.

What took you so long? I ask and make a fuss relighting the stove. César sits at the table, sighs, and wipes his face with the tablecloth.

Juan gave me some trouble.

What do you mean?

When we got to the terminal, after I carried his heavy-ass luggage to the check-in for him, he accused me of stealing his money. So I tell him, You're crazier than a dollar watch. But he keeps asking, why I'd steal his money, yelling it in front of everyone.

César has at least a few drinks in him. I fight the urge to pick the lint from the factory, caught all over his hair, and comb his thick eyebrows.

Instead, I say, Why don't you eat? I made coconut fish. I'll finish frying the plátanos.

Ana, he says, looking dead at me, did you take Juan's money?

My mouth drops. Ah, so now you're accusing me of being some kind of vividora?

You said it, Ana, not me.

His face turns hard, angry, protective of Juan.

He looks at my belly and puckers his lips to one side of his face. Then he walks around me like some cop, his hands clasped behind his back. I focus on serving the food.

I bet it was Antonio, I tell him calmly. He's locked himself in our bedroom to try on suits. It could've been any of the men that come and go doing business with Juan.

César shakes an index finger at me and says, Juan wouldn't think twice to chop off Antonio's hand so you be careful who you point fingers at.

Really? I say and give him my Lucy Ricardo face. Would my husband do that?

César lets my question hang in the air. He sits back down and savors the fish. Then he laughs. Why you scared? You in some kind of trouble?

Really, César. Why would I need to take Juan's money? He gives me everything I need.

Instead of stealing Juan's money you should be selling your cooking. Damn, this fish is good.

Just eat and leave me alone.

I head to the kitchen to hide my face.

I'm serious, though, you would make good money selling food to the guys at work. They'd kill for a home-cooked meal.

Who knows. Maybe one day.

Isn't that why you married Juan? Why you came here? You don't have to pretend you don't care about money around me.

He's poking with his words. Poking and poking. I snatch the dish from him.

Hey, I'm not finished.

Why are you being so mean to me?

He takes back the dish and eats the last of it.

He gets up and drums a salsa beat and sings with the song on the radio, *Esa mujer fue mala* . . .

He rolls onto the sofa, covers his face with a pillow, his bare feet hanging off the edge. A black leather cord with a peace sign dangling from his neck.

You can't just go to sleep after insulting me, I say, clearing the plates. Offer to wash the dishes, at least.

Ha! César says under his pillow. You play the dead fly, Ana, but, unlike Juan, I see you, loud and clear.

Mamá says all animals have to defend themselves. Goats stamp and charge their attackers, fish swim away for cover, but flies play dead.

JUAN CALLS ME EVERY FEW DAYS, USUALLY IN THE MORNING.

Everything's fine, Juan.

Do you miss me?

Of course I do.

From a distance, those words slip out of my mouth as easily as saying hello, good-bye, please, and thank you in both Spanish and English.

Have you seen Mamá yet?

I'm not here on vacation, you know.

Mamá will soon see I didn't put any money in the letters. All the money I saved went to Marisela's debt.

I'll head to the campo next week, Juan says when I don't answer.

Make sure to give Mamá everything I sent them.

I try to sound authoritative, but my voice is small even on the phone.

The list is long. A box of pancake mix for Lenny. Yohnny's cornflakes. Underwear for both boys. Cans of Chef Boyardee. Deodorants, toothpaste, bars of American-smelling soap for my parents. And the letters telling Mamá and Papá that I'm well. That everything's going as planned. That even with the baby I'll study and become a professional. I tell them I'm saving money to bring them to New York. First Mamá and Yohnny, so they can work. Then Lenny, who'll study and learn English as he's still young enough. And oh, how happy I am. How everything worked out for the best, thanks to Mamá's judgment. How great the weather is. Not a drop of rain or snow! I tell Yohnny not to waste his time messing with politics and to stay out of trouble and to focus on preparing for New York. Don't let Mamá hoard everything, I tell Teresa. You know how she is. And though Teresa can't admit that El Guardia has a bad temper I tell her she should read the brochure I included in the envelope that the doctor gave me about how to protect oneself from danger. Point at your assailant. Show your teeth. Yell no repeatedly. In America everyone is expected to fight like a goat. I kept the brochure with the maps and sent her the other. It's in English, but there are two photographs. One of the women in the photographs looks like Teresa: dark curly hair, thick eyebrows, full lips. And hey, is it true what Juan says, that people are killing each other for no good reason? That Americans are throwing a lot of fire at Dominican Republic just like Vietnam? Is it really just a fight about whether to turn mansions into schools or make the beaches public? Speaking of beaches, how is Gabriel? Send him my hello. And Juanita and Betty, I sent them perfume samples.

I forget I'm on the phone with Juan until he asks, And César? Is he taking care of you?

Yes, he is fine, I say, glad that, as far as I can tell, Juan is not suspicious of me at all.

THERE'S A PRICE TO PAY WHEN MESSING WITH THE PRETTY flowers. This Mamá says after Lenny gets stung and hops on one foot in pain.

When a bee stings she pops her own heart. Did you know this Lenny? At least you're alive to tell the story, Mamá laughs while Lenny cries.

That's not true, Teresa says. It's only when the bee tries to escape that its ass rips off and it dies.

Do they know they're going to die? I ask.

Ay, Ana, haven't you figured it out already? All girls have to make sacrifices for the good of the colony. They sting to protect their sisters and brothers. And they will do anything to protect the queen. Every colony needs a queen. That's why they feed her all that jelly, so she gets big and fat and lays all the eggs.

Mamá rocks on her chair rubbing her stomach while we all sit on the grass by her feet.

CÉSAR IS THE TYPE TO TRAP WITH HONEY AND NOT WITH vinegar. So he pretends all is good with us. His thick, overgrown curls are wrapped by a halo of smoke, a cigarette dangling from his lips. And when he stretches his arms above his head, hipbones sticking out, I have to fight myself from sticking my hand in his armpit so I can hold his smell of cloves. His bedroom eyes linger on me after dinner. The bigger my belly grows, the shorter my skirts have become. I throw the dishtowel at him and serve him coffee.

Let's go to a movie, he says.

Across the street?

No. This Boricua I know works security at Radio City. Where the rich go.

So you're not mad at me?

Should I be? Put on a dress and fix up your face.

César puts on a shirt, dyed in streaks of blue and yellow.

My girlfriend designs this fabric.

Always a girlfriend.

Of course. She takes a plain color, twists it, and dyes it into another color and then another color. She got the idea while traveling in India. What do you think? Cool, no?

With that shirt he looks like one of those guys who protests on the streets and holds signs against the war. All this spring, President Johnson has been bombing Vietnam as if his ego was hurt when they killed some Americans. Now thousands and thousands are being sent to die. I just hope no Dominican is stupid enough to kill an American.

César combs his hair out into a big puffball. I adjust the beaded choker, admiring his skin, taut and smooth. He looks ridiculous but so unique. What would Marisela think of César's colorful outfit? Futuristic! she might say. Individual! She'd be impressed that César works in fashion and dates the gringas who model the dresses in the showroom. Who he says eat sugar packets for lunch, and live on cigarettes and coffee.

I feel plain, fat, and boring.

Wait, César! I run off to outline my eyes with thick black eyeliner and add another layer of mascara. I pull my hair away from my face with a bright pink scarf. I strike a pose like Twiggy. What do you think now?

Diablo. If Juan saw you, he'd throw *us* to the lions.

There is an Us. It's undeniable. An us that can't exist when Juan is around.

César links his arm around mine and I don't let go, not for one minute. Not on the subway platform, where we wait and watch the pigeons fly from one side of the platform to the other, where the roar of the train makes me cover only one of my ears. Even inside the subway car, where the fluorescent lights make my hands look yellow, I hold on to him.

At Radio City Music Hall the marquee lights above us flash the words *Sound of Music* across his face. The smell of roasted peanuts from the vendor fills the air. As people wait to enter the theater the protestors across the street cry out '*Nam! 'Nam! 'Nam!* and *Dom. Rep.! Dom. Rep.!*

Is it always like this out here?

But César can't hear me as he pumps his fists and joins the chanting—*Dom. Rep.! Dom. Rep.!* In his excitement he pulls us away from the theater and toward the crowd. I lose my grip on his arm and gasp as a taxi driver honks for him to move out of the way. The crowd of protestors swells into traffic, and the nearby police extend their arms, building a human wall to push them back.

For a minute I lose César.

César! César!

I feel him yank me backward, back onto the sidewalk, then

through the line of people to the theater and around the corner until we reach the side door.

Employees only, he says, out of breath, and puts his fingers to his lips. He knocks and waits.

I feel in over my head. I want to tell him I want to go back home.

The door opens.

Boricua! César grabs the guy's hand and pulls him into a half-hug. The guy wears thick beads, bright sandals, one long braid. Both look like they come from another planet.

Peace, my brother, the guy tells César. Enjoy the show.

I hold my belly with one arm and César with the other as he moves us through a dark hallway. We peek into the main entrance, where a large chandelier hovers over us, sparkling. The hours it must take to keep it free of dust. And the large auditorium, with tall arches, and shimmering gold curtains. We make it to the front row, where the seats are covered in burgundy velvet that matches with the rug. Everything matches! Even in the audience I see somber-colored suit jackets and monochromatic dresses, with matching bags and shoes.

What if we get caught without tickets? I say, now embarrassed by César's strange shirt and big hair.

You worry too much. The movie's about to start, he says, and looks around as if he's expecting to see someone he knows.

Radio City Music Hall is cold. Our theater in San Pedro de Macorís is an oven. The movies shown are almost always in black and white. Nothing shiny in the theater except the candy wrappers given out to the children by the owner, who's known us all our lives. Here in Radio City Music Hall no one smiles at me. No one talks. Lenny, with his ashy elbows, isn't on my lap. Yohnny isn't telling me stupid jokes. Teresa isn't curling the ends of my hair. No one throws popcorn at the screen.

The camera sweeps across iridescent grass, snow-capped mountains, and blue-blue vast skies. So much color! Such a big screen! My eyes are too used to our black-and-white TV screen, smaller than a cereal box. But now I am Maria and I live in a big house with all that land. And when Maria sings, my eyes well up. I've finally fallen in love? I'm finally free?

We exit the theater. The protestors are gone, the city suddenly quiet and deserted. César grabs my arm.

Let's walk to the next train station, he says, and lights a cigarette.

The streets downtown are brighter than they are in Washington Heights. He skillfully weaves from block to block, avoiding the XXX signs and the men on corners dressed like birds.

You enjoyed the movie?

Yes, and spending time with you.

As soon as I say it, I regret it. But what else is Maria supposed to say?

We walk in silence. I try to remember streets and the building numbers: 53rd and 55th, Sixth Avenue, and this different Broadway. Every few blocks another limb, each neighborhood with its secrets. This is the city, big and complicated. How easy it is to lose oneself. I hold on to César until we arrive home.

He throws himself on the sofa in the living room. He covers his body with his coat and salutes me: Until tomorrow, beautiful raccoon.

I only understand once I'm in front of the bathroom mirror that my eyeliner has bled under my eyes.

I lie in bed, restless. I stay on my side, though Juan is far away. I rub my belly thinking of Marisela, Juan, and my family. Of César, who is in the other room. I wonder how Maria would solve a problem like mine.

WITH JUAN GONE I ATTEND THE FREE ESL LESSONS AT THE rectory next to the church. I squeeze into a heavy wool skirt that covers my knees—too warm for the weather, but it still fits. I lock the door behind me, go to the elevator, then return to my apartment door to make sure it's locked. The rectory is only two blocks away, but knowing no one will be waiting for me makes me feel vulnerable. What if immigration grabs me and takes me away like they did the sister of Giselle from El Basement, who went to the police after some guy stole her pocketbook, and somehow they understood she didn't have papers. Off she went.

On second thought, I should've left César a note in the apartment, but the elevator arrives and I don't want to be late to the 10 a.m. lesson.

I walk with my keys in my hand, to punch someone in the eye if they accost me. I know to introduce myself to the teacher—in English. *Alo. Elooo.* I'm no longer the child my mother shipped. I'm about to become a mother. There's no reason to be afraid. People walk the city streets every day and survive. I just need to mind my own business and when I see trouble walk the other way.

I secure the floral scarf around my head that I found under the sink, redolent with what is surely Caridad's perfume. It's all over the scarf.

Bob, the building porter who sweeps the front entrance, points to the sky and makes the gesture of opening an umbrella. No, I won't turn back even if the sky threatens rain. The air thickens with the humidity, and a strong wind pushes me across the street, away from the church. Is this a sign to turn back? People smile at me, nodding hello when I walk past them, the way city people only do with children and the elderly.

I grip the keys in my hand.

Today the concrete sidewalk feels harder under my feet. So

much cement! Back home cement means progress. In New York City, it's the trees and grass that make it feel rich.

The rectory smells of frankincense and bread baking. I'm the first to arrive. Images of the Virgin Mary, lit candles, and Jesus cover the dark wood panels. Folding metal chairs surround a conference table. On the table, a stack of magazines, scissors, and glue. The large blackboard hasn't been eaten away by salt or stained with past lessons. It looks brand-new.

Excuse me, can I help you?

I whip my head around and step back when I find a woman covered from head to toe in a black habit towering over me. My belly flutters.

Inglis? I point to the sign.

The nun's skin glows and her eyes brighten.

Welcome! Yes, here we learn English. You're early, but take a seat.

Bafroom? I ask. The baby, the size of a small banana, is heavy on my bladder—when I need to go, I need to go!

The nun points down the long, narrow hall. The walls are paneled with dark and shiny wooden cabinets. Stacks of Bibles and other books bound in leather fill the shelves. At the end of the hall, light filters through a stained-glass window and lands onto a table off the kitchen piled with transparent bags filled with wafers. Jesus's body! I pick one bag up and press it against my nose. When I hear the nun coming down the hall I shove the bag into my purse. I fumble to open the door, slip in, and lock myself inside.

She's waiting for me when I exit the bathroom. Her tendrils of hair look like cooked spaghetti. Even without any makeup, she's pretty. Though I planned to put the bag of wafers back I follow her to the main room. What if the priest already blessed the wafers? If nuns have direct communication with God, what if Jesus whispers into the nun's ear that I'm carrying him inside my purse?

At the table, we find six other students. I search for Marisela's sister among the strange faces. No one fits her description. The nun hands everyone a piece of blank white paper. She tapes a piece of paper on the board and writes: My name is Marta Lucía.

She points at herself and asks, What is your name?

I write: My name is Ana.

A woman with wild red hair and a hairy lip lifts her sign and shows it to Sister Lucía.

Very good, says Sister Lucía.

When asked something in Spanish, she responds only in English. I'm lost, so I watch the other students and follow them. An older lady speaks in yet another language I don't understand. No one else speaks Spanish except for Sister Lucía. How confusing.

She walks by my chair and bumps my purse off the back.

It's okay, Ana.

Sister Lucía picks up the purse and carries it away with her.

But Miss . . .

I'm ready to drop to my knees and confess. But everyone's too busy trying to understand Sister Lucía, who speaks too fast, to see my panic.

Please, I mumble to the nun, to Jesus, my feet stuck to the floor, my eyes on the brink of tears.

I watch her hang the purse on a hook beside some jackets and other things. I watch her make sure the rectory door is locked, reassuring me my purse is safe. I watch her return to the table.

Thank you, God, I say as Sister Lucía places a blank sheet of paper and a marker in front of me. She tapes her own paper on the board and on it she writes: I was born in Chile.

Where were you born? she asks the class, takes one of the magazines, cuts out a photograph of a house, and glues it to her paper. She asks everyone to do the same and we grab magazines as if there are fewer magazines than people.

I love horses, so I cut out a horse. Unlike Marisela, mares take care of their pregnant friends. There are few apples in D.R. so I cut out apples. Only at Christmas would I be allowed one bite, except for the year Yohnny stole it and hid it under the bed, where a mouse ate it. Then no one ate apples.

For when the heat doesn't work in the apartment, I cut out a fireplace. And because a fortune-teller told me I will have a long life and two children, I cut out two, a girl and a boy, both blond with big blue eyes, wearing matching clothes, beautiful and rich.

Sister Lucía tapes my paper on the board beside her own and the others.

I was born in Greece.

I born in China.

I was born in Russia.

She repeats everyone's sentences then asks us to repeat after her, Born.

Boln . . .

Bon . . .

Bone.

Born! Born!

When she reads my sentence aloud, Sister Lucía says, I was born, and writes Dominican Republic over my República Dominicana.

Do-mi-ni-can Re-pu-blic, she says.

I repeat.

Very good, Ana, very good! Sister Lucía claps her hands.

My name is Marta Lucía. I was born in Chile. And you, Ana? She points to me.

My name is Ana. I bon in Dominican Republic.

No, Ana, say, My name is Ana. I *was* born in Dominican Republic.

I repeat.

Very, very good, Ana. You can now say you speak English.

Sister Lucía gives me a big hug after class. When she hands over the purse to me, she accidentally drops it.

No! I dash for it and yank it from her.

It's heavier than it looks, she says.

I play the crazy goat and say, Thank you, Sister Lucía.

I walk as fast as I can, afraid to look back and turn into salt. The purse weighs heavier than the lipstick, mirror, and wallet. Though my feet are heavy like bricks, I fly down the street.

Miss, miss! I hear a man yell behind me.

I turn, gripping the keys in my hand.

A young black man is waving Caridad's scarf. He's dressed in one of those tailored suits I often admired standing before the Audubon on Sunday afternoons. I press my purse against my body, thinking about all the things Juan has told me. I walk as fast as I can, the baby pushing against a rib, and no one is there to save me. I trip. The man rushes to my side, grabs my arm, and when I look up, all I see is floral fabric.

Miss, you okay?

Juan! I scream and put my arm in front of my face and curl my body around my stomach and my bag.

The man comes closer.

Me nem is Ana, I say again and again. I bon in Dominicana República.

He chuckles. I admire his bright teeth. My fear evaporates and I feel silly. I allow his hand to help pull me up.

Tenk you.

You're welcome, miss, says the man, walking away and shaking his head.

I place the scarf around my neck, mouthing, You welcome, over and over in my head. I cross the street and enter the building. Bob the porter holds the door for me, and I say, Tenk you, and he says, You're welcome. I go into the elevator and say, You welcome, and then I finally lock the apartment door behind me.

I sit on the sofa. The apartment grows dark as large black clouds hover over the city. From my purse, I pull out the bag of unleavened bread. I place Jesus in my mouth and let him melt on my tongue. I eat one piece after another. Maybe he can protect me from the inside; maybe now he can't ignore me like he did the day I asked him to bring back Marisela. I eat him until I'm full. I lie back on the sofa and breathe softly because I don't want to throw him up.

Jesus, bless my baby.

IN ORDER TO LEARN ENGLISH, SISTER LUCÍA SAYS I NEED to practice every day. Every morning, I walk César downstairs on his way to work and borrow a newspaper delivered to the lobby. So it's not stealing. I give myself the job of collecting all the bubble gum wrappers, cigarette butts, and other litter my neighbors and their visitors leave behind.

You're going to put the porter out of a job, César says.

Bob comes between 4 p.m. and 10 p.m., six days a week, I say, picking up a paper coffee cup from the elevator floor, and there's still trash. It's our building too. Who knows, maybe if I take care of the building it will one day take care of me.

I also take books people leave on the table by the mail, even if they're in English. One day I will read them: *To Kill a Mockingbird, Anne Frank, One Flew over the Cuckoo's Nest.*

I study some graffiti on the elevator wall written in pencil: Victor & Emily inside of a heart. Should I leave it or wash it off? I don't mind helping gray-haired Bob, whose eyes have a film over them. He makes me feel safe, always opening and closing the door for everyone, guarding the building.

Upstairs, I sit with the newspaper and a fresh cup of coffee.

Why is English so hard? I ask my Dominicana, who watches faceless from the windowsill. I place a dictionary nearby and start my lessons. Education is the key to becoming independent and making something of myself. I glance over the newspaper, looking for familiar words. *Dominican Republic* splattered all over it like confetti. Our little country makes the news a lot.

A José Xavier Castillo dies. Shot in the head. Playing. Where is José from? No clues. Just that he's dead.

The rain comes down harder, as if it's mad at those who dare to walk in it. Colorful umbrellas dot Broadway.

Army shoots Oscar Alida Pérez, seventeen years old. Poison GI.

Poison? I look the word up. GI. Accused of poisoning. I look up accused.

No more Cuban travel.

Colonel Francisco Caamaño says, U.S. go home. Fighting continues.

Forty-three die in San Salvador earthquake.

Too much. Why don't they have anything good to say?

I pick up the telephone to see if it's working. No Mamá. Not even the breath. I should be relieved Caridad no longer calls. Does Juan call her often from Dominican Republic?

I blast the radio. César has changed the usual station so rock music now shouts through the speakers. *I can't get no, satisfaction!* Sister Lucía says that listening to English music is a good way to learn the language. I jump onto the sofa and dance, shake my head and hips, scream, *Ay con gue no satifason!* I play air guitar, bang on drums, wave my guitar, leap from the coffee table to the sofa, shaking my fists in the air.

Bang! Bang! Bang! When the song finishes and commercials come on, I turn off the radio and hear a banging from below. I press my ear to the floor. The neighbor's broomstick.

So sorry, Mr. O'Brien! Don't worry, okay? English lesson over! I say through the floor cracks at the man who has a missing finger and wears war clothes. I will make extra lunch to share with him. So many people living all alone in the city. I bet no one is visiting him.

I pick up the phone and dial Caridad's number I had copied in my notebook. It rings and rings. Then finally, Hello. Hello. She listens. I breathe.

My dear Caridad,

The days are long in Santo Domingo. I smoke cigars to make the wait bearable. I'm exhausted. Everything's damp. The humidity, a bitch. I press the pen lightly or else I puncture the paper. We take turns staying up to watch the front door of the house. Ramón makes me hold a gun while we guard. All of it makes me nervous. The dog especially. Ramón insists on having a dog. It barks incessantly and I'm not kidding you, it hates me. Yesterday, while everyone slept, in the pitch dark, only a candle to keep me company, I heard a whimper, like a kitten, but it was a boy, trapped in a web of wire Ramón installed all around our property. He was trying to climb over. Wires, broken bottles, nothing keeps anyone from climbing into our backyard and trying to break in. Poor kid. Starving kid. Lost kid. The dog was going to eat him if I didn't go out there, so I shot the dog. Fucking dog. He just kept barking. The kid's hair turned white.

I don't remember your smell. Send me something with your smell on it? Soon I'll come home. This war can't go on for too much longer. Remember when I visited you in your bed and everything was so easy. I have so many regrets. We should have had more courage, you and I.

I love you,
Juancho

WHILE CÉSAR WORKS, I TAKE LONG WALKS AROUND THE neighborhood. I go into Woolworth and study all the bottles of lotions and hair products. Write down the names and the ingredients so I can later look up the translations. I want to join the people sitting at the counter. The smell of pancakes, hot dogs, and sweet syrup is tempting, but the man behind the counter looks at me as if he doesn't want me there. So much of the city belongs to other people. Not wanting trouble, I leave.

I go by the park near the river and watch the children play. I look into the restaurants on Broadway and watch how carefully the waiters carry large trays filled with elaborate dishes, moving like dancers in the crowded rooms.

I stop in front of a redbrick building that occupies an entire block. A purple-haired woman carrying a parrot on her shoulder. She tosses a candy wrapper on the floor. Then I throw it in the trash for her. I notice someone wearing large sunglasses and rollers under a scarf. She enters the building across the street. The determined walk—Marisela?

Marisela! I call out. The traffic light is red and the cars won't give me a break. Marisela! I recognize the pink pants. She enters the building. I follow her in. But she's no longer in the lobby. I watch the numbers on the elevator go, 2, 3, 4, 5. It stops at 5. The lobby reeks of urine. The walls are in the midst of being replastered. The lamp is missing a bulb. Maybe she's visiting someone. This can't be her building. Her sanctuary. Not the Marisela I know.

I should've gone home. No one knows where I am. The building doesn't feel safe. What if it isn't her? But I can't stop myself. For weeks I've been waiting, hoping to see her. I want to punch her, kiss her, hug her. Ask her.

I get on the elevator, and press the number 5. A roach the size of my thumb accompanies me, along with the smell of dead rat. The long and narrow hallway on the fifth floor has countless doors on either side, each marked with a letter of the alphabet. Each door has its own sound, music, voices, barks. The twitching lights overhead create a disorienting strobe effect. I press my ear on each door, for a clue, for her voice. But even if I find her, what will I say? My body tenses up, my lips clamp. I order my feet to run. Run! Down the stairs, through the lobby, and back home. But I can't move. I wait.

A door opens and a girl with a bag of trash heads out. She seems a few years older than me, with tube socks up to her knees, staring right at me. Her hair wrapped tight around her head in a dubi. I must've scared her, because she yells into the apartment, Marisela!

My eyes burning into the girl's slippers, the hem of her frilly dress.

Are you her sister? I ask. She looks like her, except younger.

Do I know you?

Who's at the door? Marisela yells.

Tongue-tied, I freeze in position and stare.

You a crazy person? the girl asks.

Marisela appears at the door without her face, sweaty and disheveled. She pushes her sister aside, it's as if a ghost stands before me.

Ana? You have no business being here.

I glance into her apartment, cluttered with boxes and large black garbage bags. It reminds me of the mess I found in Juan's apartment when I first arrived. But Marisela? I expected more from her.

But who is she? I hear the sister ask.

No one, no one at all.

My heart pounds, throat locks. I find my feet and run down the hall holding my belly, praying the elevator will be waiting. The door is heavy and sticky. I pull hard. I stomp on the elevator floor, my arms crossed high on my chest in disgust.

I am no one. No one!

The ache in my chest is unbearable. My breath short. My

strength gone. Every step home, an effort. In this city nothing is what it appears to be. No one is to be trusted. Juan has always said this. Mamá has always said this. What a fool I've been to think Marisela's fancy clothes were honest. What a liar. A thief!

I cross the street to Broadway toward my building where Bob opens the door with warm arms, where the lamps are not broken and the floors are mopped clean.

THAT NIGHT, WHEN CÉSAR ARRIVES, I'M CURLED UP IN BED,
with the last of the sun making a thin stripe on the bedsheets.

César rushes to me.

Are you okay?

I have cried for most of the day. My eyes are pink and glassy, my hair in knots from tossing and turning.

Dinner's on the stove, I say from under the pillow that covers my face. I don't want him to see me all blotchy and puffed up. The bean soup is oversalted from all the tears.

César takes off his shoes and lies on the bed with me. He spoons me from behind and combs my hair back. I don't cringe.

Tell me everything, he says in a high-pitched voice as if he knows that what I need is my sister, Teresa.

I welcome his warmth. I want to grab his arm and tuck it into me, to pull him closer and fall asleep with his body the same way I used to do with my sister on those nights Mamá would beat us both and send us to bed. Instead, I flip my body toward him, grab his hand, and stare into his eyes.

I'm all alone in New York, I say. I don't have any friends. No one to trust.

You have me. Have I not been here for you?

But you belong to Juan. If you had to choose, you would choose him. Tell me I'm wrong.

César thinks about it.

You called me a vividora. Is that really what you think?

Why won't you just admit you stole Juan's money?

I did it because of Marisela, I say, and burst out into tears.

Wait. Wait. Don't cry.

Now you'll tell Juan I'm a thief. You've already taken his side.

That's not true, Ana.

Please, don't lie to me like everybody else does. I know about

Caridad. I know Juan only married me so Ramón and all you brothers can build on our land.

Who told you about Caridad?

You see, you see. You're probably her friend and sit with her and laugh at how stupid I am. You're all so calculating. Only thinking business and money.

But Ramón is only trying to help your father. It has nothing to do with you.

Maybe you're the stupid one.

I take the pillow and pound César with it.

Wait, wait, I didn't do anything.

César jumps off the bed. I throw the pillow at him, then another one. He dodges them. I look around for something else to throw.

Believe me, you don't have to worry about Caridad. I mean Juan won't ever love her like he loves you. She's Puerto Rican.

What are you saying? All your brothers have married Puerto Ricans!

I pick up the radio and aim at him.

No, not the radio! he says, and widens his eyes and fake-smiles.

I hate you.

We can get the money back from Marisela, I swear. I know where she works.

Of course you do!

He sits back on the bed. He gives me a tissue from the box I keep on the nightstand.

Why don't you splash some water on your face and sit at the table with me while I eat, he says. Please.

I just want to go back home, I say, and really mean it.

I'll always choose you, he says, I swear, I will.

Like all men who don't want to see a woman cry, César lies. But hearing it does bring me comfort.

JUAN'S OUT OF BREATH, OVER THE PHONE. FROM THE moment Juan arrived to Dominican Republic he tells me, he's been hustling to keep up. Juan's needed someone to draw up the title to his land, but he's no longer Dominican enough to work the maze of authorities who would happily look the other way for a fee. Even his brother Ramón, who remained in Dominican Republic to stay on top of things, can't find a way to bring down the absurd asking price to make securing a title worth it.

At night, Juan locks himself in the house, because he says only fools get involved with the guns being given out on the streets to fight Reid Cabral's firepower. With the United States behind him, a democratic election is doomed. No one can be trusted. Not even family, he says.

For years Juan and his brothers have sent money to Dominican Republic to invest in land, the restaurant, and the building above it with enough apartments for each brother. They all plan to return one day and live in them or give an apartment to one of their children. With money like a leaky faucet, Ramón is the one trusted to manage the money in the Ruiz bank account. Otherwise, one digs into the savings—ten dollars here, twenty dollars there—to resolve a problem, then another. Ramón is the serious brother, who always asks for everything in writing, who logs the purchase of every nail, can of paint, roll of toilet paper. For a good number of years Juan, Hector, and César have all worked two, even three jobs, sending a percentage back home so Ramón can lay the cement, add the walls, install some windows. But while in Dominican Republic with Ramón, to secure their investments, Juan understood something was wrong. Between Juan, César, and Hector, who make frantic phone calls in disbelief, I learn that Ramón has done the unforgivable.

At first Juan finds everything as expected. The restaurant has a proper bathroom, three walls, and a rooftop built strong enough to support two more floors for four two-bedroom apartments. The engineer and Ramón meet with Juan, and they share all the drawings for the larger project. The engineer says that Rome wasn't built overnight and that they could build one floor at a time.

Then on the morning the banks are finally open after being shut down for security reasons during the insurrection, Juan says to Ramón, I want to go to the bank to see our account.

It'll be a nightmare, says Ramón, with everyone rushing to pull out their money. People are scared. But we mustn't be scared. The United States won't let Dominican Republic collapse. It needs us.

Juan insists, Give me the information and I'll look through our paperwork. What if something happens to you, Ramón? My name should also be on there.

They won't let you in without me.

So come with me.

I can't, Dolores has me doing errands. She's been too afraid to even go to the supermarket, so she gave me a shopping list.

So drop me off at the bank. While I stand on line, you can do the errands and then meet me after.

You don't trust me? You're insulting me, Juanito. Be careful where you step.

Ramón stands up and hovers over Juan. This is how he resembles their father, with a face that smacks you with a look.

Juan stands up though his eyes only meet Ramón's shoulders. Juan's body is twice as wide. They're alone in the house and both have been locked up inside for too long.

No disrespect, brother. I just want to see everything with my own eyes.

Have I ever steered you wrong? All I do is think about you. Make sure you succeed in this shit of life. Wasn't it me who told you to marry Ana? You were wasting your time with stupid women who were just trouble for you. If it wasn't for me—

Don't start, Juan says, holding his fists close to his sides. I want to go to the bank.

And then he grabs the glass on the coffee table and throws it against the wall. It shatters everywhere in tiny pieces that sparkle in the morning light all over the ceramic floor.

Unlike Juan, Ramón never loses his cool. He leaves the house and without telling anyone goes on a long trip to the other side of the island. Not even his wife, Dolores, who he fell for the moment he saw her scratching the sole of her foot on Calle Vicioso, knew where he went.

That's when Juan learns there's no money in the bank. Ramón has made a bad investment elsewhere. No money to start the first apartments over the restaurant. No money for Papá's land.

I listen, wishing I could change channels.

Poor husband. First husband thinks younger brother stole his money, which was really taken by wife after so-called friend stole it. Now husband is betrayed by older trusted brother. So when wife asks husband if he's had time to visit in-laws, husband inhales and says, Ana, please, I'm doing the best I can, I understand.

MAMÁ SAYS IT'S BETTER TO KNOW THE ENEMY AND HIS
price. The United States backed Trujillo and now backs Reid
Cabral. Even if they don't fully agree, the U.S. knows they can
be bought.

Marisela knew my price. When I needed a true friend, she
called me her sister. When I needed a role model, she flashed her
clothing and her smile, told me I should do this and that. Always
full of advice. When I was most afraid of Juan, she fed my own
sob story back to me.

So when César comes home after work I decide to set my own
price.

Were you really serious about me selling food to your
friends?

Hello to you too.

He sits on a chair at the table, ready for me to serve him dinner. Because he isn't taking me seriously, I sit on the place mat,
facing him, one foot on each of his thighs. I grab him by the collar
with my two hands and make him look me in the eyes.

What's with you, Ana? He's dying to laugh.

What is life, César? Why am I here? Why do we suffer?

César's not like Yohnny, who can talk for hours and hours and
together we would fall into a hole of questions.

Ana, can I eat first?

Don't give me Juan's sure-one-day talk, I say. I want to make
some money so I can take care of myself, bring my family to New
York. C'mon, are you going to help me or not?

César digs his hand in his front pocket and pulls out a train
token.

You'll need this token to get on the train. Start with food for
thirty customers. Better to sell out than to bring too much.

I hold the golden token with a Y cut out, the size of a quarter, that can take me to the beach, to the Statue of Liberty, to anywhere in New York City.

Now, can I eat in peace?

After dinner he gives me step-by-step directions to his factory in the clothing district. I write them in neat handwriting in my notebook, already full of new English words.

Just remember, always act as if you know where you're going so no one will mess with you. Chin up and no eye contact.

He places a map on the table.

The city's an island. Rivers on both sides. It's a grid. Streets go up and down, avenues east to west. Remember, country girl, if you get lost, just follow the sun.

THE FIRST DAY I TRAVEL DOWNTOWN TO SELL FOOD, THE sun makes the sidewalk glisten. Sweat beads pearl on my chest and forehead. I carry a tote full of fried pastelitos stuffed with ground meat and raisins, wrapped in tin foil. César says I can sell them for ten cents each. I've made fifty pastelitos. I quickly calculate my profit, factoring in travel and ingredients: over a hundred dollars in two months.

The hot weather keeps the pastelitos warm. César told me to wait outside of his building at noon sharp, ready to grab the lunch crowd before they find something else to eat in the thirty-minute break.

I walk quickly toward the subway. I put the token in the turnstile and think ahead to the elevator I will take. To the downtown platform. To the stop on 28th and Seventh. Then the four blocks up to 32nd to César's jobsite, a tall skinny building next to two wide ones—the Oven, he calls the factory, with a smell of fabric and worker sweat that can easily kill a person.

I stand outside. People rush past me, pushing carts crammed with colorful dresses covered in plastic. Men yell out of trucks, load and unload boxes, some of which might eventually end up on sale at El Basement. Cars honk. I don't know where to stand and stay out of the way.

César grabs me before I even see him. Behind him stands a pack of men, all with lint in their hair and beards, all taking in deep breaths of fresh air as if they've come out of a cave.

Hey, guys, this is my little sister.

She's a looker, one says.

Keep it in your pants, César scolds.

Suddenly, a crowd surrounds me.

One at a time, fellas.

I hand over two pastelitos at a time, while César collects the money and manages the crowd.

Two for twenty-five, have your money ready!

I go with César's price, though at ten cents each I was ready to haggle. But the food goes faster than I'm able to remember their faces. In minutes, my pastelitos sell out.

Sorry, fellas, another day, César says, holding the last two for himself.

He takes me to a small bench by a building and points, This is FIT, the university for fashion.

Efayti, I say. I want to go to the university.

Why? You're a rich woman now.

Where's my money, then?

César transfers all the coins from his different pockets to my bag.

Six whole dollars, I say, swishing the coins around.

What you going to do with all your fortune? He bites into a pastelito and licks his lips.

Send my sister a money order so she starts beauty school.

What you gonna make us tomorrow?

Will I get in trouble for this?

He seems to forget that until we have our papers we have to be extra careful. My tourist visa expired months ago. When the baby's born I will apply for permanent residence; so will Juan. Then I can solicit my mother. And Juan can solicit César. And I Lenny and Yohnny.

It's America. You supply, people buy. Next thing you know, we have a chain like McDonald's.

You live in the clouds, César. It's not so easy. Look how hard you have it with the restaurant in Dominican Republic. It's loss and more loss.

Ah, my brothers eat with their eyes and not their stomach. You start slow by making us lunch. Then you get a cart. Then a store. Then a bunch of stores. Small steps lead to big steps.

A rush of people in suits run to lunch, carrying briefcases. I suck in my cheeks like the wiry models with big hats who point their noses in the air. Goddesses. Must be strange to see the top of people's heads first, before eyes or even smiles. How cool, to hold a briefcase filled with important papers and speak English perfectly.

My name is Ana. . . . I like watch television. . . . I like learn Efayti. . . . I like sit in sun with César.

What time will you be home tonight? I ask, not caring if I sound possessive.

Why? Miss me already?

Should I make dinner or not?

If he only knew how I counted the minutes until he arrived so we can sit at the table, eat together and talk about our day, what I'd learned from Sister Lucía, what happened in the latest *Corona de Lágrimas*.

I gotta go. Time's up. Add more raisins next time. Gonna call your pastelitos Mini Anas—sweet and salty all at the same time. When you look at them, you wonder what's hiding under the golden crust and—bam!—there it is, the surprise. So much goodness.

I giggle with embarrassment.

See ju later, alligator, he says.

What?

It's what Americans say.

CÉSAR AND I DECIDE NOT TO TELL JUAN ABOUT OUR FOOD business.

When Juan calls, of course, we laugh and almost give ourselves away. I snap the kitchen rag on César's hands so he stays quiet. I turn my back on him and twirl the springy phone cord in my fingers, trying to sound composed and uninteresting.

What's so funny between you two? Juan asks. He isn't stupid.

Nothing, I say. Some stupid TV show. The phone has a delay and our conversation echoes.

How are things over there? Over there?

I don't know. Everything moves slow here, he says. The gun-crazies running about at night. Offices open one day, close another. And the noise is outrageous: helicopters and bullhorns, people politicking and selling crap. People'll sell you their own mother to get in with the government, and no one except the Americans know what direction it'll go. I'm trying to make sure we don't lose the little we have.

Papers. Papers. Papers. Juan has many papers to set straight.

Tell me you love me, he says before hanging up.

I love love you you, I say, and wink at César.

We eat dinner. César moans when he eats.

You're a noisy eater.

It's 'cause you cook so damn good, he says.

César wipes his mouth, gets up from the table, and sits on the sofa with his legs spread wide apart. He leans forward to get a better look at me. My legs are crossed, my bare feet under my thighs.

Come sit by me, he says.

Oh, I've got so much to do.

I spring up and gather the dishes, turn my back on him.

Put the dishes down and come over here.

I search for something urgent to do, a moment to breathe. Something between us is shifting fast.

Sit on the chair.

César points to the one across from the sofa where he sits.

I want to trust him. I tug at the hemline of my skirt and sit with my legs clamped shut.

Please don't disappoint me, César. I beg him with my eyes.

He drags the chair by the legs so our knees almost touch. He picks up one of my feet and says, Relax, sister.

That's right, I say, relieved. We're family.

Both his hands encircle my foot, his thumbs pressing on my sole, kneading.

It tickles, I say, confused, curious, scared.

He pulls on my toes gently and massages my calf around my knee. His touch is firm. His fingertips glide up and down my legs. Goose bumps emerge as if there's a cool breeze in the room. I hold my breath. The baby presses against my lower belly. Dampness between my legs. So nice to be touched.

Don't pregnant women love foot massages?

He props my massaged feet on his thighs and leans back on the sofa. He lights the cigarette tucked behind his ear and stares at the ceiling.

You're different than all your brothers, I say, studying the triangle of skin exposed above his low-slung jeans every time he lifts his arms to take a drag.

In what way?

For one, you don't seem to care what anyone thinks.

Is that a good thing?

He sits up, leans toward me as if to kiss me. Fills his mouth with smoke and blows into my face. I cough.

Idiot, I say, waving the smoke away.

Wanna see a Bruce Lee movie?

Now?

After I clean up we can go watch some cool karate moves at the San Juan.

I jump up, grateful for the wooden slabs, firm and warm under my feet. I rush to the window. The movie crowd, filled with squeals and laughter, already assembles outside the San Juan Theater. Women's heads on boyfriends' shoulders. The long kisses between teenagers. Mothers holding on to their children. So much happiness on the ticket line. And to think that just a few months ago, above the San Juan Theater, inside the Audubon Ballroom, a man had died. The building, a large altar. That's how the world is, everything's forgotten.

César stands behind me, his breath on my neck as he looks to the Audubon. A rise in my chest, a softening at my knees. He grabs my arm, his fingers accidentally caressing the side of my breast. César, my brother, also the closest of friends. I try to halt the throb between my legs, the lump in my throat.

WHAT DOES IT FEEL LIKE? I ASK YOHNNY THIS AFTER I caught him on his knees. Juanita was standing up, her back pressed against the cement walls. His mouth was pressed up between her legs. Her eyes closed, her chin up, her hands directing his head. They hid behind a cluster of palm trees, on a large bedsheet by the beach shore, after swimming, at a distance from the others, who lie lazily out of sight.

We're at the beach in Los Guayacanes. We've hauled a big pot of spaghetti. We're a large pack that day because even Juanita, who Mamá tries to keep away from Yohnny, was allowed to join us.

Yohnny hands me a peach.

Bite into it, he says.

The skin pops and the fleshy juicy parts explode in my mouth.

Now press your lips in there.

He points into the fleshy parts of my peach.

Go on, press your lips and rub against it softly.

Are you crazy?

Don't you want to know?

My lips are covered in sweetness; the fleshiness slips away and into my mouth. I lick it, touch the seed with my tongue. I pull away.

Now you know why I love peaches, he says, winking the way he does.

Salty, sweaty peaches.

You have to stop with Juanita, I say, or you'll get in trouble with Mamá.

Don't worry, little sister, I have a plan.

You do?

You think I'm gonna spend my life around here waiting for someone to save me from this hole? I'm not as pretty as you, he says.

I don't need anyone to save me.

I'm just saying that soon soon I'm going to take that road and never look back. Try my luck in a city like New York. Make some real money. Drink that New York City water straight from a faucet. You know what I mean?

BECAUSE THE FOOD SALES ARE GOING SO WELL, CÉSAR can't sleep. All he thinks about is expansion.

The sun hasn't even come up. Wake up. Wake up! He calls for me in the dark.

What happened?

He turns on the lamp. My eyes hurt. My head spins from a dream: Yohnny running onto a road away from our house—except the road is more like a stream with large rocks, and he hops from one to another carrying some kind of object. Mamá yelling, Come back!

César wears a red scarf around his neck, and a long white skirt is draped over his shoulder. I finger the gauzy cotton, unwind the tape measure from César's neck, then roll out of bed to follow him to the living room. The living room lamps are still on, the sewing machine out, and the Dominican flag, which Juan keeps folded in the closet among the suits, is splayed on the coffee table.

Is it Carnival?

We're going to be rich, he says. It's a side of César I've never seen before.

Calm down. You're scaring me.

The World's Fair is two dollars a ticket. We need four dollars to enter. Every day, half a million people visit, and I bet none of them have ever tasted pastelitos.

I pull my hair into a knot over my head. I splash water on my face to wash away the image of Yohnny in the stream. Where was he going? I try to focus on what César is saying, but Yohnny's eyes haunt me—his but not his. Back home, young men have been throwing themselves onto the streets. But I hope Yohnny knows better.

Still half asleep, I drag myself to the kitchen where I fill the percolator with water—there was so much water in that stream. I press down the coffee.

Last year, César is saying, the food lines at the fair were outrageous. Everyone complained about it.

You think those white people would want to eat pastelitos?

César strips off his pajamas to try on a pair of white cotton pants and a white shirt. The red scarf pops out of it. He turns on the record player, plays an old perico ripiao, and starts to move. Like a dancer from another time, his hands fold behind his back, his feet dig into the floor.

Oh, Mr. O'Brien will complain. It's too early.

He brings down the straw hat from high on the shelf, with a miniature flag poked into it, and places it on his head.

And at the Dominican Pavilion, they're only serving rum.

Dominican Republic has a pavilion?

I search through the cabinets for a new container of oatmeal. I sniff some cinnamon sticks and pour out a few cloves onto a paper towel. With a knife, I poke open a can of evaporated milk.

Look at this. He dangles a dress as if it's on a hanger. The dress has white ruffles along the neckline and a stretchy elastic band at the waist with a full long skirt.

Wow, so pretty! I tear it from him, skip to the mirror in the hallway, and hold the dress in front of me.

But look at Miss Dominican Republic, I say to my reflection. I do the fake wave and smile. César opens his palm, invites me to the small floor space between the coffee table and sofa, and with knees bent slightly and his shoulder scrunched he starts to move like the country old-timers do, and I follow along, swishing the skirt and shaking my shoulders.

The percolater whistles.

The coffee! I jump to catch it before it spills over—but it's too late.

Now look what you made me do! I call out to César. Now Miss Dominican Republic has to clean the stove.

Don't worry about that. At the World's Fair she'll sell half a million pastelitos!

He takes the fake rose from the vase on the shelf and places it between his teeth.

WE WAKE UP AT FOUR IN THE MORNING TO FRY PASTELI-
tos to sell at the fair. César has ten dollars saved, enough to make
three hundred pastelitos. If we sell them all, together we will
make seventy-five dollars. We have to use the same oil at least
five times, way more than I am comfortable with, but if we want
to make a profit, sacrifices have to be made. I separate the layers
of pastelitos with paper towels. How long will they keep before
they go soggy? Will people buy them?

César, don't you think twenty-five cents is too much?

Ana Banana, my boss told me so, a frankfurter cost twenty-
five cents at the fair. And that's dog meat. And we'll have to dress
the part. Pretend we're part of the exhibition.

Can we get in trouble?

With your panza and my smile?

I've seen the World's Fair advertised on the television. A man
in a spacesuit flying over people's heads. Africans wearing masks,
playing drums and dancing. A ride with dinosaurs; exhibitions of
fancy cars from all over the globe. The world and the future are
visiting Queens, from Spain to India, Italy to Hong Kong!

What if the police get us? I ask, I don't have my papers.

Don't worry, Ana Dominicana. Trust me.

We ride the train downtown and then transfer to the fancy number 7. Painted a sea-blue and steel-gray, it looks like a bluebird.
There is a policeman in every car. In every station. People on the
subway stare at us in a way that makes me tuck in my feet. Juan
found these nursing shoes in the garbage, but I gave them a good
scrub so they look new. Thank goodness the skirt skims the floor.
I hope the rose César has tucked in my hair distracts people from
looking at my ugly feet. They're the only shoes I tolerate when
my feet and ankles swell as thick as an elephant's. Between the

frying and wiping the grease off the walls, I've already done lots of standing.

Look at the Dominican princess! he says.

Playing dress-up with him is fun. He too now, from another time, our parents' time, visiting the future.

At the entrance of the World's Fair protestors slip us flyers and more flyers.

STOP THE WAR!
NO WORLD'S FAIR UNLESS FAIR WORLD.
END JIM CROW.

So many people! Still we stand out in our costumes, and the ticket collector does a double take at our heavy cloth-covered baskets. Knowing the line is too long for anyone to hold us back, César says, Dominican Republic, as if it works like a key to a door.

At the entrance, our eyes widen at the sight of an enormous globe. Taller than the building we live in, high enough to be seen from all the corners of the park. Where is Dominican Republic on that globe? The fountains shoot up foamy water. Flags, from all the countries represented, flap wildly.

C'mon! César tugs on my shirt. We will sell more near the food pavilion.

He's tied our flag around his neck like a cape and placed one of the smaller baskets of pastelitos on my head. He carries the bigger basket.

A horse-drawn carriage passes us. Children point at us. A tourist takes a photograph of us.

César urges me to smile.

I'm not some doll! I whisper, annoyed.

Pastelitos! Pastelitos! César sings in the tone of the farmers from back home who sell fruits and vegetables from their carts. He flashes his smile, moving his head to the left and right as if he is riding on a float in a parade.

Twenty-five cents! Pastelitos!

People walk by us without taking César's bait.

I'm already getting tired. The last time I carried something on my head, it was a water pail from the well. But it was half the size and I wasn't almost six months pregnant. I no longer feel like playing Country Girl or Folkloric Ana in an America heading to the future—a future growing in my own belly.

I put down the heavy basket, stretch out my neck, and search for a patch of grass to stretch my legs on.

But we just got here, Ana—gimme that.

César sucks his teeth and takes my basket.

Just wave and smile to people. We have to keep moving. We're not that far from the food pavilion where we will catch all those hungry people who don't want to wait on lines.

I stroll alongside the Japanese geishas, the Chinese drummers, the Indian fakirs, the Spanish guitarists, and hundreds of other people.

I lift my chin and wave at everyone, putting on the same smile I've practiced with Juan, with Marisela, at the ESL classes, with my neighbors, the super, in my letters back home.

Pastelitos, twenty-five cents! César calls out.

We stop to rest and stand there like show monkeys.

Over here! someone says in Spanish.

We walk a few feet over to the man and his family.

Where you from? The man speaks in a funny accent.

Dominican Republic, sir. César lifts the cloth draped over the basket.

Give me five for a dollar.

I look toward a patch of grass. Finally a place to sit. I also need a bathroom.

Where you from? César asks the man.

Spain. But I've got a house on your island. We visit every summer, but with this stupid war . . .

César hands over five pastelitos and takes the dollar. He quickly covers the basket to save them from the flies. The man's children jump to snatch the food from their father, who suddenly looks teary-eyed.

The Spanish pavilion is the jewel of the fair, you know?

Of course, says César.

We fled Spain because of Franco. And yet, here we are visiting his pavilion, to ease the homesickness.

César, can we sit for a minute? I ask.

Excuse me, sir, he says, tips his hat to the man and then comes over to me.

We have to keep moving, Ana, I can't do this by myself.

César's annoyed. He's spent fourteen dollars and we still have to make it back. I owe him that much. But the unforgiving sun beats on us, without a breeze.

Pastelitos, I say weakly. But we find a few takers.

Miss, miss! Can I take a picture with you?

An older white woman walks over to me. She touches the rose on my hair.

Boy! she calls out to César, gesturing that he stand next to me and turn around so his back faces the camera and they can see the flag better.

Instead, César places the basket in front of him and rolls back the towel to show her the pastelitos. I'm embarrassed for César, for how submissive he acts before this woman.

Miss, twenty-five cents.

When she understands he doesn't want to take the photograph, the woman turns to her husband and says, Those thieves. All they want is money. She says it loud enough for me to recognize Juan's tone when talking about blacks and Puerto Ricans and Jews and Americans and anyone not Dominican.

César, please let the lady take our picture.

He stands so that we're now the centerpieces of a wedding cake. A crowd gathers around us.

The lady hands over a dollar bill to me, then tells us to smile for her camera.

I smile and try to stay still, try not to pay attention to the crowd of tourists taking my photo. Why do they want our photo? What will they do with it? What if Juan sees—

The flashes blind me.

I place the basket back on my head. From the slump on César's shoulder it's clear we've both lost something.

Pastelitos! I sing in a loud voice to make up for César's sudden silence. I smile wider than before, when handing customers pastelitos, and especially when collecting the money in the pouch César sewed into my skirt.

When we've sold seventeen dollars' worth, I ask César if we can sit on the green lawn across the International Pavilion where the thick grass looks untouched. Why is no one else sitting on this beautiful stretch under the trees, this sanctuary from the sun? I need to rest my feet. To reorganize the pastelitos, eat some myself, and have César fetch me some water. Maybe I can even go to the bathroom. Holding it in hurts. My ankles must be the size of my knees. I'm only six months along—imagine my feet at nine months?

César undoes the flag from around his neck and lays it on the grass.

Sit here, he says. Are you okay?

In his gaze, I see my own glassy eyes and dark circles, my parched lips, and the sweat beads all over my forehead.

Yes. Water. I force a smile again.

I watch him run to a frankfurter cart and buy a Coca-Cola.

I don't know where to get water, he says. He twists the cap off and places it in my mouth. The cold and sweet instantly energize me.

Bathroom. Need bathroom, I say after a long gulp.

Maybe someone will let you skip the long line. Wait here.

He runs off. I watch him dash in and out of the crowd, searching for a kind person who'd do me a favor. I step off the flag, slip off my shoes, and walk barefoot on the grass. I squat to relieve my back, to spread the weight of the baby across my thighs. I'm so tired. I cover myself with my skirt and as if I can become invisible by closing my eyes, look to God, toward the beam of the sun, and pee through my panties and into the grass like a dog marking its territory. A wave of relief; my body unclenches for the first time in hours. Free. I ask God for his protection and am grateful for the width of the skirt. Grateful for the anxious crowds rushing to and from the pavilion paying me no mind. Grateful for my invisibility.

When I open my eyes, I'm startled by the sight of the man with the jetpack flying overhead. Like the one on TV.

Will we really all be flying soon?

I search for César's bright white shirt and pants. Far off, I hear drumming. An accordion. A steel drum. I listen to the competing sounds of the shooting fountains, the golf cart backing-up beeps, the squeals of children. I stand up. The heaviness of the cotton skirt drapes over my legs. I arrange the two baskets close to me. Using the baskets as a shield, I pull off my underwear and ball it into a small plastic bag to be placed in the trash. I go to the edge of the fountain nearby and wash my hands.

Pastelitos, I sing to the people who pass me by while I enjoy the fruits of my own recipe. It has been two and a half hours. Lunchtime has already passed. Will we be able to sell all of this food?

Miss! A large wooden stick taps me on my back.

I flinch. A policeman. A gun on his belt.

My name is—

Ana! César yells from a few feet behind him.

César! I cry as he comes over and takes me by the shoulders.

All right, kids, off the lawn, says the cop. Nobody on the grass.

César and I grab our baskets and scurry toward the cement paths.

The policeman turns his back on us to scold another couple nearby.

We walk up and down the paths in the park and take breaks on benches.

They're too soft now. We should just give them away, I say. My inner thighs are raw from rubbing against each other. The heat has made me delirious. Can't we go home and take a shower?

We can't give up now. César pushes away a paper cup from

a bench and wipes the seat so I can sit. He places the baskets by my feet.

I can't anymore, I say, afraid to disappoint him. If I take another step I will die.

We have made thirty-six dollars and fifty cents minus the fourteen dollars spent so far.

We did good, no? I say, then burst into tears.

César crouches between my legs, kneels on both knees, and places his hands on my cheeks.

Why are you crying? What happened? He uses the sleeve of his shirt to wipe my tears.

I am, I'm . . . so tired.

His pants and the hem of my skirt are grass stained and filthy. I want him to say, Let's go. Forget the hundred or so pastelitos still left in the basket. Leave it for the hungry, for the men who sleep on the benches when the park's closed.

Watch this, he says. The sun is about to set right behind the globe.

César leaps across the narrow walking path. He leans forward and positions himself so he appears to be carrying the earth on his back. He does this until I laugh.

Then he grabs the basket and calls out, Free pastelitos! Free! He tips his hat, dancing to an invisible merengue beat, giving people—me—a good show. He calls the white women beautiful and the old men boss. And when the basket is finally empty, he tosses it in the air and wears it over his hat. Children nearby clap their hands, along with me.

Stop! I laugh, my cheeks and insides hurting as he plops beside me and drapes his arms over me as limp as a rag doll.

Now we get to play tourist, he says.

Wait, where are we going?

To the Vatican.

He leaves the empty baskets on the ground by the bench and carries me, my arms tight around his neck. Sweat beads by his eyes.

You're going to get a hernia, César! I say, holding my belly, although he makes me feel so light.

We marvel at the humongous dinosaur robot and the Ferris wheel.

Do you think one day we will all be able to fly, I say, and see each other when we make a phone call?

We'll even be able to take a vacation on the moon, Ana Mañana. Imagine us walking on the moon.

Not if we are wearing these clothes, I say.

He finally puts me down when we reach the Vatican's pavilion. The walkway is rolling at two miles an hour. We are on the first row, slowly moving past the large white sculpture of the Virgin Mary carrying Jesus after he was killed. Under the blue lights they look like ghosts. At least we made our money back, says César, and a little more.

I don't think I can even walk to the train, I say.

We're taking a taxi. Call me King Kong!

César lifts me again, like Mary does Jesus—except alive, on top of the world, feeling very much like a part of the future.

PART V

::

I NO LONGER ASK SISTER MARTA LUCÍA WHETHER I CAN use the bathroom. She greets me with her hands hidden inside her black dress, bows her head, and simply smiles as if my pregnancy is a sin. I want to explain that I'm married, but she doesn't allow Spanish. Please, English only.

The class learns to greet each other:

Good morning. How are you?

Fine, thank you. And you?

I also learn: What time is it? and Where can I take the bus?

We learn the numbers and the names of the coins: pennies, nickels, dimes, quarters. We learn directions: right, left, straight ahead, behind you. Up and down, stop and go. And lifesaving words such as dangerous, hazardous, exit, help, emergency.

I'm sorry. I'm okay. It hurts. The body parts: elbow, shoulders, feet, hands. Colors: red, blue, green, yellow. Church, hospital, grocery store, and the names of the vegetables and fruits I don't usually buy or eat—broccoli, brussels sprouts, cauliflower, kiwi. We learn so much each week. The two and a half hours we spend together fly by.

Sister Lucía frequently takes the class outside when the weather's nice. To learn a language is to learn a culture, she says, and learning culture requires interaction.

Ready? She claps her hands for us to follow her to the park on 166th and Edgecombe Avenue, a playground for children, with swings, slides, benches, and lots of bushy trees.

Okay, very well then.

I wait for Sister Lucía's instructions. Who wants to volunteer to try the swings?

I'll do it, I say.

Are you sure? She looks for another volunteer.

But I grab the swing by the chain and settle on the thin wooden board. Only my toes reach the ground. The fact that I'm pregnant doesn't mean I'm an invalid.

Very well then, Sister Lucía says and then to the class: Ana is sitting on the swing. When I push her, you can all say, Ana is swinging.

Ana is sitting on the swing, they say in unison.

Sister Lucía pushes me. Soon, I fly up in the air. I hold tight to the metal chains, worried that I'll pee on myself, laughing uncontrollably. The class laughs with me.

Ana is swinging! they say.

It's good to laugh, Sister Lucía says. Ana is laughing. We're all laughing.

When the laughing settles she tells the class that although they may feel silly playing like children and maybe even embarrassed, the lesson to be learned is that one must try to say things even if one isn't sure. One learns through one's mistakes.

I want to swing and swing, gather leaves, watch the birds, and listen to their names: woodpecker, blue jay, cardinal.

I point to one I recognize from Los Guayacanes and ask Sister Lucía, How do you say?

Hummingbird.

Hum-ming-bird, I repeat it over and over in my head.

Suddenly Sister Lucía claps to signal that our lesson is done for the day. She gives us a sheet with many of the new words we've learned. I follow close behind her, wave good-bye. Is Sister Lucía going off to pray? When people aren't looking, does she take off her habit and smoke cigars? The nuns near Los Guayacanes did. I don't dare tell her when Juan arrives I might not be able to continue taking the classes. The last time I spoke to Juan, he said he would be home in a few weeks. If and when he finds a good flight.

The fighting is almost over, he said.

And ours will resume. The breath will start calling again. I'll learn no more English. I will no longer be able to sell my food to César's friends.

After class is over, I stay behind with a few of the members from the group and give them some pastelitos. Though we only know a few words of English and have little to say to one another, we appreciate each other's company. Someone always brings something. Strange things: spongelike buns with jam inside and flaky desserts made with honey.

On my way home I also offer pastelitos to the elderly who find refuge during the day under the large maple trees, and feed the birds in the square in front of the church. At night, the same square becomes dangerous.

Stay clear of Edgecombe, Amsterdam, and St. Nicholas, I've been warned by Juan, who was mugged once while walking from a parking spot on Edgecombe. Standing at the streetlight on Broadway I imagine a car hitting him at the very moment he crosses Avenida Independencia. Then his plane diving into the sea. Then Juan disappearing in a hot-air balloon into the sky.

WHEN MAMÁ GETS ANGRY THERE'S ALWAYS A TEMPEST.
Everyone thinks it's typical unpredictable Dominican weather, but without fail, every time Mamá realizes she can't cover the sun with one finger she screams so loud in frustration the sky collapses.

Burnt out from all the fighting and sleepless nights, the rebels are now rejoicing. The tempest is a nice break from the war—who can think of war when strong winds are ripping off rooftops? Let the people who have stood by watching teenagers die these past few months fight the impossible war with nature. The flood currents pull everyone from their feet and the palm trees hold on for dear life. The city is a mess.

Those who know about Mamá and her supernatural ability gossip at bars and in beauty salons, asking what in the world pissed her off in such a way to cause all this commotion.

Three days of relentless rain triggered by one uneventful afternoon. After a hardy lunch and leisurely siesta, Yohnny admitted what Mamá had already suspected.

I'm madly in love with Juanita.

What about New York? Mamá thundered. Your dreams of getting out of here?

I'm not going anywhere without her!

First, Teresa falling for a good-for-nothing, and now this?

Rational as she is, Mamá should've known. Juanita and Yohnny started like many cousins who share rooms and beds throughout childhood. Most grow out of the petting and humping. But there isn't much to do or people to see in Los Guayacanes.

So Mamá saw to it that Juanita be placed in a permanent housekeeping position at a house in the far end of the capital. One less mouth to feed. One less girl to fret over. With time, Yohnny will forget and find new tail to chase. She's sure of it. The boy has no car or motorbike, let alone a decent pair of shoes.

But stubborn Yohnny doesn't lose his stride. He quickly begins to do favors for some Yankee army men who patrol the area in their military trucks. With the capital on fire keeping everyone distracted and busy, the so-called peacekeepers look for Communist activity elsewhere. They know that the mosquito buzzing around one's face always has a hidden accomplice that will eventually bite. The bite appears later, when it really itches, when it's too late to swat the bugs dead.

Yohnny calls the Yankees his friends. He hooks them up with weed and mamajuana and local women looking for visas or money. In exchange, the Yankees promise him a visa to New York. There are days Yohnny breaks curfew and returns short of breath and nervous.

Although Mamá is weak-kneed for any man in uniform carrying a gun—except Teresa's El Guardia—she has a bad feeling about this Yohnny-Yankee business. Call it a mother's intuition. These army boys will inevitably be the end of Yohnny. Is he working as a spy? Maybe keeping Yohnny away from Juanita is only deepening his troubles? Maybe, just maybe if she sends him to La Capital on an errand, the Yankees will find another sucker like Yohnny to do their bidding.

Juan has yet to drop off the gifts and letters that I had sent them from New York.

Here you go, Mamá says to Yohnny one morning. Go to the capital.

She tosses him the keys to the motorbike and folds a few pesos into his shirt pocket.

Fetch our things and visit with Juanita if you want.

Really?

The chaos in La Capital has settled. The worst is over.

Yohnny takes Juanita's address and kisses the notepaper.

Yes, of course, Mamá says. Who am I to get in the way of love?

MY BREATH IS FINALLY IN SYNC WITH THE CITY'S. I CAN hear sounds of music. A fire alarm, a police siren, a bus halting at its stop, a garbage truck backing up, and so on. At first they were so loud, almost unbearable, always alarming, but now they sound as pleasant as the radio or the TV or a house full of people. Maybe so many people in New York City live alone because its noises keep them company.

César sleeps through everything. And like all the other Sunday mornings, when he is off work and lazy and fully at my disposal, I wait and wait for him to wake up. Today we're supposed to go to the beach. I resist the impulse to pounce on him like Lenny would do when he wanted my attention. We'd wrestle in the bed and I would trap him, my knees on his arms until he surrendered.

I try not to look at the freckles on César's nose, how they're more pronounced from the sun. I ache whenever he looks at me as if he's willing to do anything I want. Nothing is impossible, he says, even when his eyes are filled with tension. Such an unusual man. How he laughs in the most devilish way when someone trips but is just as quickly moved to tears by a song or kind gesture. I resist being taken by his smell of sweet spices and cigarettes, which slips into everything in the apartment.

When the coffee percolates and the sky turns from aluminum-gray to a warm purple to a bright blue, César jolts up from the sofa and says, What day is it?

Sunday. Remember the beach? I want to go before I get so big someone mistakes me for a whale.

I'm wearing Juan's button-down shirts over one of his T-shirts, which now hugs my belly. My skirt no longer zips up all the way.

César slaps his cheeks to wake himself, rubs the new hair growth on his chin.

I have already packed our beach bag with two bath towels, a small cooler filled with water, some apples and bananas.

Should I also pack some sandwiches?

No, he says, I have a surprise for you.

We take the subway all the way down to Coney Island. The ride to Brooklyn takes over an hour. Fortunately without incident. The news makes it seem as if taking the subway is putting one's life at risk. The villains are often teenagers, same age as me. They're desperate to be heard. The ride's so long, I fall asleep on César's shoulder. Once we exit at the Stillwell station, César carries the mesh beach bag and leads me toward the boardwalk, past the game stands, the jugglers, the clusters of people dressed like peacocks and roosters. Past the ticket booth, the Wonder Wheel and Cyclone.

Wow! I count the rides. Maybe twenty, maybe more.

Close your mouth or you'll eat a fly.

How far is it?

Don't worry.

He pulls me through the crowds. Our sticky arms bump and catch with each other. The boardwalk, thick with people: roller-skating, dancing, kissing. I make out the words on the store signs—Hubba Hubba, Nathan's, Carolina's. The song of the ice-cream truck parked nearby.

Why can't we sit here? Or there? I say, as César takes his time weighing our options along the shore.

You so lazy, he says.

I'm pregnant.

Oh, I thought you ate a watermelon for breakfast.

After our day at the World's Fair, I really can't trust him when he says, It'll only be just a few blocks or right over there. It could mean an hour of walking. The boardwalk has no end, and all the beach looks the same to me. Miles of golden sand, not a palm tree in sight. Bright umbrellas and seagulls dot the shores of Coney Island. Nothing like Los Guayacanes, where dwarfed palms serve as refuge from the sun, and fried fish and sweet potato vendors flirt for business.

Let's find a spot already, I beg César.

César finally takes the nearest steps down to the beach. From the boardwalk it looks packed. But once we get closer to the shore—climb over the sunbathers, the loud hairy men littering the beach with cigarettes, the tilted umbrellas—I see there is plenty of room for us, especially close to the edge of the water. We sit down, butts digging into sand, feet outstretched so when the waves roll in, our toes kiss the water. The breeze combs through my hair. I admire the tight long muscles on César's thighs and giggle over his chicken calves, lighter compared to his face and arms. Our arms touch. I lean in toward him like that day with Gabriel, then move away, tucking my body into a closed fist.

You come here often? I ask.

Who has the time?

The beaches in New York aren't bad, I say. I am still surprised they are even here.

This beach can kiss the ass of our beaches back home.

Well, any port in a storm. It's nice here. Quiet. Dominicans can be so loud. Look at all these people minding their own business, enjoying themselves. Juan only talks about work and making more money. But these people are not doing that. This is the part of New York no one talks about.

So what are you saying, Ana?

That it's nice to see everyone just relax for once. Don't you think?

César ignores me; he's too busy checking out all the women around us. I suddenly feel so overdressed. I lean back. Roll up my shirt to expose my belly. My belly button pokes out. The water ebbs and flows. I dig my feet into the hot sand, and sigh.

The sunsets must be beautiful here.

Too bad we can't wait around for them, says César, sighing too. Once the sun is gone, the guns come out.

It can't be that bad.

Wanna swim?

He's already standing, pulling off his shirt, exposing his broad back and slim waist. The sharp tan lines around his neck and arms.

I don't have a suit, remember?

He doesn't insist like Gabriel had. My breasts are now twice as large. Finally I have something for Gabriel to see.

Watch this! César strips to tight dark shorts and runs into the water, his legs, muscular like a horse's. He dives into a tall wave, disappears, and emerges with long tight curls flapping heavy over his face.

It's freezing! he yells, then runs over to me and shakes his body above me.

Stop it, you wet dog!

Barking hysterically, he digs his hands into the sand to rub my legs and arms with it.

You're impossible!

César stops to take a swig of water from the bag, spreads out his towel, and lies back with his hands behind his neck. His underarm hair is clumped into small bushes. I smell the saltwater on him. I want to lick him.

I spread my own towel beneath me to not get sand in my hair, lay back, close my eyes, dig my feet deeper in the sand, allow my hands to rest at my sides, palms open to the sky. The sun bathes me. Sweat beads trickle on my neck, between my breasts. I listen to the seagulls and waves, the din of the amusement park, the faint screaming of people on rides. I wait for the waves to touch my toes and the breeze to brush my skin, to cool me off, making the heat bearable. My eyes heavier, my arms and legs of lead, my breath steady. I no longer care where I am. I am home, happy.

When I open my eyes an hour later, César is staring at me. His dark curls, shooting in all different directions. His eyes squinting with delight.

Surprise! he says, holding two hot dogs and two Nathan's cups filled with fries, all neatly arranged on a cardboard carrier.

Nathan's, the best Coney Island has to offer.

Every day, I watch the hot-dog man serve a line full of hospital workers. In the winter, clouds escape from his cart and land on my tongue.

The hot dog peeks out from the bread. The taut skin deliciously snaps when I bite into it. The salty juiciness of it, combined with the bread and ketchup. The crispy fries crinkle like an accordion.

It's so good! I say.

His eyes linger on me, happiness on his face. César enjoys my joy. To think that Juan told him to watch over me as if it were a punishment or a chore.

Soon after, seagulls hover near us. A sudden wave soaks our towels. We jump, saving the last of our fries.

Time to go, César says to the seagulls, to me. He wrings out the wet towels and throws them into our bag. We hurry toward the amusement park. The way people scream from the roller coaster makes it seem like it has the capacity to kill and revive a person all at once.

Let's do the Cyclone, I say.

Why not the Wonder Wheel? Safer for the baby.

We can handle it . . . pretty please, César?

He looks concerned, but I make the Lucy face, pouty lips and big eyes.

Okay, okay. Let's do it!

I've survived many a hurricane that tore the rooftops from our kitchen and bedrooms and yanked trees from their roots. Still, I'm terrified of the Cyclone. I don't trust those interlocking pieces of wood. The speed of the carts zipping up and then down makes me lose sense of my legs. My brothers would've been the first in line. How much they may never see; how lucky I am to be in such a place.

César purchases the tickets. I make a note to give him some money later. We punch our tickets and stand on line. We pick a cart. Though I grab the bar, I hold César's hand as the train slowly climbs.

The first dip takes me by surprise. It isn't so bad. The rickety wooden coaster trembles like the wooden floors in our apartment.

The stops and starts, the short drops, the weightlessness of the cart makes the inside between my legs come alive. The wind hits my face. As the cart slowly climbs the last part of the ride, I see the shore, the people like pebbles and among them me and my brothers. We're all together, running after the cane trucks that pass by our house. My brothers squeal and scream. And there's Yohnny running and running, turning back to see how far back we all are. Then the train drops, and César holds on to my shoulders. Our hearts jump in our throats. Together, we scream until the train abruptly stops, pushing brain against scalp. Ana! I hear Yohnny in my ear. Ana! Then a deep silence falls on us. We hold on to each other, hands woven. A smile is plastered on César's face.

You okay? he asks.

My eyes well up.

SOMETHING HAPPENED TO YOHNNY, IS THE FIRST THING
that comes out of Mamá's mouth. He'd gone into the mess of
Santo Domingo.

But what was he doing in La Capital?

I don't know.

Why did you let him go there?

For the first time in a very long time I hear Mamá cry. It unhinges me.

I want to open the door and find myself in Los Guayacanes with
them. They need me.

Hurt. Hurt. Hurt.

I am emptied.

Hours later, husband calls.

I'm sorry, pajarita. I just can't imagine. I have brothers. I fear
for them too. Is César there with you?

He's working, says wife.

I told your mother don't let Yohnny come into the city. But she
insisted. So I said, Tell him to avoid the center at all cost, to come
directly to me because I'm on the periphery of all the mess. If you
only knew the mess, Ana. One day we think it's almost over. And
it starts again. The streets are filled with kids carrying guns. The
power outages go on for days. Everything's being rationed: candles, food, cigarettes. The gasoline! We're blocked. No one's sure
for how long. And who can sleep? I hear the gunfire right outside
my door. I warned her. Tell Yohnny to stay home. But she said
trouble only finds those looking for it. I mean what the hell was
he doing near the Palace? He got caught in a wave of protestors
against the U.S. army and it happened fast. He was just standing

there. They say his arms were up when a Dominican guard shot him right in the back. The bullet went right through his chest.

Wife aches. Sister aches. But husband keeps talking.

Oh pajarita, don't cry. I'm counting the days for this shit to end so I can return home to you.

Husband's voice drops on *you*. It begs for a warm loving response. But wife is empty.

I STEAL A NEWSPAPER FROM THE LOBBY DOWNSTAIRS. I spread the pages on the table and search for any mention of Dominican Republic, of Yohnny. Finally, I see *Dominican* and circle it with a pencil.

> *July 6, 1965*—Porfirio Rubirosa, former Dominican diplomat, international sportsman and playboy, crashed his powerful Ferrari 250 GT into a chestnut tree at 8 a.m. yesterday in Paris. He was alone in the car. The 56-year-old died in an ambulance on the way to the hospital. He was within sight of two of his favorite Paris spots, the race course and the polo club. He was an airplane pilot, a tennis player, a seeker of sunken treasure, and was tagged as the Romeo of the Caribbean, having married, in the span of a decade, five of the wealthiest and most beautiful women in the world.

No mention of Yohnny. No mention of the war. As far as the newspapers are concerned, the war is over, the country secure. For whom? For what? A few months ago when President Johnson announced the American troops landing in Dominican Republic it was big news. But now nobody seems to care. The Americans have left it in the hands of the Trujillistas. Because they're the old puppets? Because they're rich. Because they have a military. And still, people die. Buildings are destroyed. But of course the world only cares about Rubirosa.

When César arrives that night, I'm wearing all black, down to a scarf over my hair. I sit in the dark, without music, without TV, looking out the window, thinking of what I could've done to save

Yohnny. I'd drunk three shots of rum. My head pounds, my eyes glazed. Numb body, heavy feet and arms.

Hermana, no dinner?

He turns on a lamp.

I lay my head on the table. How good the cool wooden table feels against my ear.

What happened? César pulls a chair to sit near me.

They killed Yohnny.

What? Who? He stands up again.

The alcohol swirls inside my head. If I could, I would curl up on César's lap, tuck my feet between his thighs, my head in his neck. Instead, I stand and press my head on his chest and listen to the thump there. My tears soak his shirtsleeve.

Have you eaten anything? he says. Want something to drink? I'll make dinner for us, he says.

He extends my legs on the sofa, placing a pillow under my knees. He turns on the radio. The Beatles will be playing live at Shea Stadium in August.

While he cooks, I take a nap.

César sets the table. He ladles lentil soup into two bowls. Beside them he places slices of avocado and bread.

I'm not hungry, I say.

You have a baby to think of.

He was only sixteen years old. Sixteen!

The lentil soup may need salt.

There really was no one like him.

Stop putting the avocado in the fridge. They turn brown.

And stop acting like bad things don't happen, César!

I throw him the newspaper.

Nobody cares about us, what's happening to our country, about Yohnny. All these words, wasted on stupidities like Rubirosa!

Because this paper is for white people, Ana.

César searches for a piece of blank paper on the shelves and picks up a pen from the table.

Here, write something for Yohnny.

I'm not good at writing.

So use that Rubirosa article as a guide.

I study the blank page on the table. I press the point of the pen on the page and draw a line.

Say it as if Yohnny can hear you. Write it so you hear yourself. Go on.

July 6, 1965.
Santo Domingo: Yohnny Canción died in a cross fire near the Parque de Independencia.

Keep going.

Yohnny, a hardworking young man who helped his family in every way possible.

Be specific, Ana. Tell me how he was helpful.

Yohnny was the first to volunteer in the mornings when his father called on him to work on the farm. He stood up to any man who harassed his sisters. He was resourceful. Even Americans knew him as a man who could get things. He had a soft heart for pretty girls and was tagged as the Romeo of Los Guaya-canes, easy to love. And he could run faster than anyone. He dreamed of coming to America one day to ride the trains, to visit the Empire State Building, to play baseball with Manny Mota and Felipe Alue. Yohnny died immediately without any suffering. Thousands attended his funeral. His cherry-wood casket was buried in the President's burial ground in the capital of Santo Domingo, among other great men who died with honor. His casket is covered in white roses and the guests were all fed passion fruit, his favorite. Just hours before his death, the president

himself was about to grant him a visa and ten thou-
sand dollars to start a new life in the United States.

You're quite the storyteller.

Reality is too depressing. Yohnny never liked school. He
never listened. He always did what he wanted to do. I'm sure he
walked himself right into that bullet, not thinking. He was big-
hearted, though, and so much fun. You would've gotten along
well.

Now write mine.

I don't want to think about you dying. Not now.

Oh, c'mon. Write it as if I'm ninety years old and died and you
found my obit in the paper. What do you see for me, in this very
long life I'll live?

When César's ninety, I'll be eighty-five, and we'll be living in
Los Guayacanes together, spending our mornings drinking hot
chocolate and eating toasted bread, watching the sunrise, rocking back and forth on our chairs and talking about the animals
that misbehave. We will remember all the people we outlived. By
then, Juan will be dead.

I write:

> July 1, 2033. César Ruiz died in his sleep after drink-
> ing a morir soñando. He had been warned the mix
> of orange juice, milk, and sugar was for the youth,
> but he drank it anyway. César was born in the small
> town of Tenares in Dominican Republic and in 1963
> arrived in New York City with three of his broth-
> ers. He went from ordinary factory worker to fash-
> ion designer, inspired by the great Chanel who had
> also launched a career from humble beginnings. He
> traveled the world in his rocket jet and opened the
> first bodega on the moon. In 2013, when he turned
> sixty and was ready to retire, he gave all his wealth to
> the poor children in Los Guayacanes and lived in the

original house of the great Ana Canción, who later
joined him in an effort to start schools and hospitals
for the needy.

César watches me write every word.

You see all that greatness in me?

Why not? Why can't you fly to the moon? Or be a great de-
signer? Why do we have to settle for just this life? I say, surprised
at myself and my own ambition. We have to do it all because
Yohnny can't. We have to make the best of life for him.

And you, what will yours sound like?

Ana will live a long life. Raise a successful daughter. She'll be
happy.

SO I KEEP BUSY. ON TUESDAYS AND THURSDAYS, ENGLISH
classes. Mondays, Wednesdays, and Fridays, I go to the downtown to sell lunch to the men at César's factory. I plan a lunch
menu for each week. On Mondays, pastelitos, thirty with chicken,
thirty with beef. On Wednesdays, pasteles. On Fridays, lunch surprise: sometimes empanadas de yucca, other times quipes.

I prepare and package the foods so the men are able to eat
while standing, like horses, like Americans eat hot dogs or burg-
ers. To inspire customer loyalty, I make food that reminds them
of home.

At night, I marinate the meat and chop most of the vegetables. The following day, I wrap the food into small presents in
Cut-Rite sandwich bags or aluminum foil. I organize them in
my basket, lined with checkered fabric César took from the same
factory where the men work.

I cook as if my cooking will breathe life into Yohnny again. I
cook for him and him only—grating the onions so that he won't
taste them in the filling, pulling out the cloves of garlic so he
won't complain about bad breath. Even César notices how my
food has become more inspired. What's your secret ingredient?
he asks.

Every day, I place my earnings in an envelope in my drawer,
no longer needing to hide my money inside Dominicana. With it,
I still plan to bring my family closer to me, to where they will be
safe and where Lenny can go to school, to where they won't have
to worry about having enough food to eat.

With time, I'll buy a small cart like the hot-dog man's. Eventually a small shop. Then a chain of shops all over the city.

I find César waiting outside the Oven for me, by himself. He's
smoking a cigarette. I'm early. But he's out earlier. Something's

wrong. The men are usually let out at twelve on the dot. I had wrapped slow-roasted chicken thighs—marinated overnight in lemon, garlic, and rosemary—fried arepitas de yucca, spiced with anise, into individual aluminum squares.

I'm taking you home, says César.

He takes away my basket, grabs me by my forearm, and pulls me back to the subway stop.

What are you doing? Where's everyone? I ask.

Immigration shut the factory down. Bastards!

What?

They stormed in but we got out in time. Vicente—you remember Vicente with the bug eyes and butt chin—he jumped out the window and broke a leg, an arm, it was too chaotic for me to know for sure. The cops got him before I could grab him, and I couldn't stick around to look.

But you have papers. They can't do anything to you.

Don't you watch the news? They can do whatever they want.

César pats his chest for another cigarette, curses.

And today's payday too! Those bastards called immigration so they don't have to pay us. It's not the first time.

They can't do that. Can they?

As we walk he pushes against the lunch crowds, swinging about my basket of perfectly wrapped chicken and arepitas.

What am I supposed to do with all this food?

Ana, I lost my fucking job! I was practically managing things. And when the immigration showed, that asshole fed us to them with a spoon.

And just like that my dreams of food carts and a franchise of Dominican food are gone.

César kicks the post office box on the street corner. He punches the air.

Fuck!

Why didn't you call me? I could've saved myself from taking the trip down here.

I lost my job and all you think about is yourself?

But I came all the way downtown.

Please, don't even start with me.

I step back. I've never seen César this angry.

I grab back my basket and walk ahead toward the train station. César grabs my arm and squeezes tight enough to leave a mark.

You're hurting me!

Let me take you home, he says.

I don't need your help, I'll get home fine.

No, Ana, I'll take you home.

He pulls the basket. I pull back. Packages fly across the sidewalk. Heels step into them. I lunge for the basket, stumbling and then falling on my side away from César. A man with a briefcase trips over me and accidentally kicks my leg, and yells, Get the fuck out of the way!

Fuck you! César yells, and punches the man in the jaw.

No! I struggle to get back on my feet.

A police officer appears behind César, grabs him by the shirt collar, twists his arm, and throws him to the ground. I scream as his boot presses on César's neck.

Leave him alone! I want to say. You're hurting him! Why don't you arrest the asshole boss who screwed him?

But Sister Lucía covered none of these words in English class.

Please step aside, the cop calls to the crowd forming around us.

I crouch on the ground nearby, tossing the aluminum packages back into the basket, stretching my hand out to César. I'm looking into the eyes of a captured goat about to be slaughtered.

Run! I say.

I see Yohnny lift out of César's body and run down a road that turns into a stream, with no end in sight. Yohnny runs and stops to lift a middle finger at whoever's chasing him.

Sir, you have the right to remain . . .

The crowd watches him as if César is some criminal.

I yell, I hate you all! You don't know him!

I show my teeth to a crowd that seems pleased by the police-man having caught a black man. An illegal man. A criminal who robbed or killed someone.

I hate you! I continue to scream. You don't know what it's like for us.

How hard it is trying to survive in this big city. How many times César has been screwed, even if he always walks in a straight line.

Ana! César yells. Go home and call Hector.

César's hauled away in a police car. He's holding back tears. He's embarrassed. He's sorry. I'm sorry.

Later that day, Hector calls me to say César got out.

I picked him up from the precinct, so don't worry.

Of course I will.

Thank you, Hector.

Ana, he's my brother.

That night, I wait for César. I rub and rub my belly. The clock ticks, ticks. The store gates all come down. The streetlamps light up. The trash bags are stacked along the edge of the side-walks. The buses gasp. The ambulances wail. Emergency. I rub and rub my belly. Emergency. And me? Where is César? Why does he disappear as if he's without responsibilities? Why can't he call just so I know he's safe? I count the money I didn't make. Count the aluminum packages I saved from being trampled, now stored in the refrigerator. I can't let it all go to waste. All my hard work. All that good food. So I take some of the food and give it to my Jewish neighbor down the hall who has four children, who never even dares to look me in the eye—but a woman with four children will surely be relieved to receive some homemade cooking. Take a package of food to Rose, ac-customed to my surprise visits, who does not shy away from grabbing my arm for help when crossing the street. I drop off food to Mr. O'Brien, to the widowed super, to Bob the porter. The rest of the food I stuff in the fridge. I rub and rub my belly. How long will it keep? I will become so tired of eating chicken and arepitas.

CÉSAR DOESN'T COME HOME FOR A FEW DAYS. WILL HE ever return? When I tell Juan that César was arrested he says, I know. I know. Of course he knows more than I do. But all he says is, now, more than ever, we can't afford to turn away customers.

With Juan being gone, I hadn't seen any suit clients, but when Antonio calls to ask if he can bring some friends over to buy suits, I say yes.

Antonio arrives with three men. For the first time in a long while, the house is full of people. I turn on the radio.

How many months are you? Antonio asks.

Seven I say, happy I'm showing.

His eyes linger on my face. He stretches his arm out to touch my belly. His touch embarrasses me. This is Antonio, who loves his wife. I push him away.

Who wants coffee?

I do, they say in unison.

After they drink their shots of coffee, I ask, How can I be of service?

The younger man chuckles. A dirty mind.

I size him up and say, 46R?

Good guess. Patricio's his name. About César's age. His brother, Jorge Aguire, has a streak of gray hair at his widow's peak. Alejandro, a friend from Juan's work at Yonkers Raceway, is skinnier than the shadow of a wire.

I heard about your brother, Antonio says. I'm sorry.

Word gets around fast even across the sea. Maybe Juan asked Antonio to check up on me?

I haven't opened the suit closet in a while. I pull out suits. The plastic clings to my sweaty skin. When I say it's too hot to try on wool suits, Patricio brushes his hand on my behind. When I look to see if it's a mistake, he winks. I move away and order him to sit on the sofa. Antonio sits on a chair at the table, smiling.

So when will Juan be back? Alejandro asks.

Any minute, I say and hand two suits to each of Antonio's friends.

Go ahead and use the bathroom or bedroom to try them on.

Patricio goes to the bathroom. Alejandro to the bedroom. Antonio and Jorge wait with me in the living room.

You look more beautiful than ever, Antonio says.

He hovers near me, so close I smell his mint breath.

I say nothing, relieved that Alejandro has gone out of the room.

I'll take both of them, he says and doesn't blink twice when I overcharge him by two dollars. Antonio doesn't say anything. The price is still a lot less than they would've paid in any store, even El Basement.

Jorge goes into the bedroom. Soon after, he comes out and asks the price of one suit. And agrees to get it.

Aren't you going to offer to hem them? Antonio asks, surprised.

I'm busy today.

Oh, that would be great, Alejandro says. I want to wear them tomorrow.

You can hem my pants, too, Antonio says, ignoring my glare.

The ones you're wearing?

He stands up to show me. Don't you think they're dragging a bit?

I ran out of thread. And you said your wife doesn't let anyone handle your pants?

Antonio isn't himself today. Though he's supposed to be one of the good ones, he's now acting like a wolf among his pack.

Patricio, you okay in there? Antonio calls for him.

One minute! Patricio yells back.

He's taking too long, I tell Antonio. And I have other people coming.

I turn off the radio. I wrap the suits inside plastic bags. I stand by the front door.

Patricio finally comes out of the bathroom, but when I quote the price, he asks for a discount.

No discounts, Antonio volunteers, and stands between me and the men. He even counts the money and hands it over to me.

Antonio nudges Alejandro to open the door to leave.

Immediately after they leave, the doorbell rings.

It's Antonio again. The men huddle by the elevator waiting.

Did you forget something? I say.

Antonio enters the apartment and closes the door behind him. He stands an arm's length away and looks at me. I stare back, ready to defend myself with the thick plastic clothing hanger in my hand.

He pulls a lollipop from his suit pocket and unwraps it. A bright red globe. He holds it up to my lips.

Try it, he says. I clamp my lips, look right into his eyes, and shake my head no.

I know you enjoy sweet things, try it. He pushes it against my lips. It's sweet, like red soda.

Good, no? he says.

I hear faint laughter coming from the men waiting at the elevator. My heart races, but I plant my feet on the floor, push away the lollipop, and open the door.

Nice to see you again, he says. Send my regards to Juan.

ANIMALS DON'T LEARN IN HINDSIGHT; THEY ONLY LEARN when punished right then. Mamá would've pulled out the meat cleaver and scalped Antonio's shiny hair.

So I count the money and decide to tell Juan that I only sold three suits and not five suits. He won't notice, I'm the one in charge of inventory. And if he does, what can he do? I'm the mother of his child. Even he isn't crazy enough to hurt a pregnant woman. And if Antonio goes into specifics about the sales, I'll go into specifics about lollipops and chocolates.

The phone rings. I leap toward it.

César! Where are you? It's been two days.

I grab the earpiece with both hands as if it'll help me to listen better. His voice has changed.

I found work with this lady in Boston. I'll stay here for a few days.

What job? What lady? What Boston? Why can't you come home? I need you here.

Don't you worry, okay?

He hangs up before I ask more questions.

I turn on all the lamps, the radio, the television. I double-check the doors are locked. On the fire escape, there are still no pigeons. Will they ever return? I leave rice on the plate, just in case. I change the sheets and make the bed for César. I open a can of Chef Boyardee, heat the mushy pasta, eat it with a spoon straight out of the pot. The flavor, so flat and consistent and reliable, is suddenly the only thing I can stomach.

THE CALENDAR: 25 OF JULY. FIVE DAYS, NO CÉSAR. A lifetime.

I prepare another can of mushy pasta and eat it warm, tucking my feet between the sofa pillows. The warm-pudding noodles travel down my throat and to the baby.

A lock turns at the door, then another one—César?

I pull the door open; the chain is still on.

César's hand waves at me through the crack.

Aaaanaaa? he croons.

Open the dooooor.

He's drunk. He'll need a shower. I'll have to feed him and tuck him into bed. Who else would?

Before Juan left, César went from one woman's bed to another. When the women started making demands on him—a little something toward the rent or groceries—he would switch the woman like an old shirt.

Please don't let him come home with the smell of perfume. Please be the same César, my César.

I place the bowl of pasta on the coffee table. Once I unhook the chain, César almost falls on top of me. Yes, drunk. Yes, perfume. Yes, he needs a shower. His eyes red as if he hasn't been sleeping.

César throws himself on the sofa. He looks at me like he's been a bad boy. But he doesn't care. He tells me one of the guys at the factory hooked him up with another job in menswear.

Menswear, huh? I say, happy that he's in my living room again, that everything will go back to our usual routine.

I will make you a tuxedo with lots of room around your fat belly.

He steps back to get a good look at me and says, Damn, you grew in the past few days. Can I listen?

I sit down. He presses his ear against my belly and embraces my hips.

I can't wait to meet you, little shrimp. He lifts my shirt and kisses it. Suddenly he is on his knees, both hands holding my belly.

She's kicking you, I say.

I feel her! he squeals.

I giggle. He continues to rub my belly, his hands firm and soft, skimming the bottom of my breasts. All my little hairs lift. I revel in the way his hands hold me like a gift. The rush of blood, anticipating, anticipating. I want to bite into a peach. Beg his hands, his lips to misstep and fall into my mounting desire.

There you go, he says to the belly. Where the baby pushes, he kisses, his lips lingering longer and longer. My breasts tingle.

I missed you, baby, he says.

The baby kicks, and César rolls onto his back on the floor into a fetal position.

She knocked me out! he says. I throw him a sofa pillow.

Can I fall asleep right here? It's so cool down here.

Soon after, his soft purr turns into a deep snore. I sit and watch him. To dull the ache, I place a pillow between my legs, rock back and forth, until the earthquake between my legs strikes.

Cabronita! I hear my sister snicker.

WITH A GOOD WOMAN, YOU'D BE UNSTOPPABLE, I TELL
César one evening.

He rips the seams off one of my dresses while I stand on the
coffee table. I am his mannequin, wearing half a dress: just a slip
and one of Juan's undershirts.

Don't move, I don't want to hurt you.

César holds a pin with his lips, a tape measure dangling from
his neck, a pencil behind his ear.

I'm serious, you need a good woman to settle down with. Who
will take care of you.

You already take care of me, he says.

If we were birds, César and I could mate, and Juan and I could
mate, and any bird who is capable of not eating my offspring, who
is able to bring me food, to build a nest, who is healthy and has
attractive colors, could be part of my mating community. There
would be no marriage contract, just the game of survival and
pleasure.

But we're not birds. Our days are numbered. Juan has been
gone two full months. He left end of May and it's now almost
August. If he doesn't come back soon, he'll lose his place at Yonkers Raceway. He has to return to pay the rent, of which he only
paid two months up front. He's losing his patience with all the
corruption.

Dominicans are no good, Juan says.

But we're Dominican.

No, really, pajarita, not even family can be trusted. Everyone
sells themselves to the highest bidder. It's hell. Hell. I miss you,
he says. I can't wait to be home.

Every moment with César could be our last minute, our last
day, or week. So I savor it.

César tugs on me, pulls out darts and sews the fabric by hand.

I tell him, I want you to be someone important, César. You deserve that. Any woman would be lucky to have you.

But you're my inspiration. Why do you push me away like that? he says. Raise your arms like Jesus and keep 'em up so you don't bleed to death.

I laugh even more when he sews by hand around my armpit, inadvertently tickling me. He bunches the excess fabric below my breasts, folding it into darts.

I'm sorry, this is the only way, he says. He fusses and tugs around my hips and smooths the fabric on my backside; his hands dip into the small of my back and the rise of my behind, which has grown twice in size since I arrived to the U.S. He pushes the fabric down around my thighs, holds it together, his nose close to my inner thigh, just enough to make me pulse.

Desire. Desire. Desire. I have no other thought.

My arms hurt, I say, to say something.

Well, beauty equals pain. That's what the models say.

So I'd rather stay ugly. Besides, no one sees me. Juan won't even notice.

I see you. You see you.

He offers his hand to help me down from the coffee table so I can look at myself in the mirror. He has taken two of my dresses to make a single one. All this stuff he's learned by working with men's clothing. How to layer the fabric so it gives around the joints. Unlike women, men don't tolerate being uncomfortable.

Look how easily you can move your arms. I gave you just enough space so it doesn't pull around your back. You can also bend down without being afraid to tear open the seams.

Because I'm so fat?

My boss wants to teach me all his tricks. He says he prefers Dominicans because we work harder than anyone else.

Maybe it's because you're special.

Nah, he's giving me an opportunity. Those Jewish guys give us work but keep their secrets to themselves. The Italians, they're more open.

It's amazing how from nothing, you made something.

You do the same with food. Me, I look at all these fabric scraps and think, four scraps make a shirt. Just have to put them together like a puzzle.

I know! When the fridge is almost empty, I invent something. And it comes out good. But I forget how I did it.

Write it down. That's what my bosses do. They're always writing things down. People's names, when they're late. How much they produce. When a fabric does something interesting. That's our problem, we don't write things down.

I do write stuff down.

I go to the shelf to get my notebook and hand it over to César.

My name is Ana, César reads aloud. I like sunsets. I am fifteen years old.

I write every new word or anything I don't understand. Then I look it up. Like what does alligator have to do with later?

César bends over laughing.

Americans and English make no sense, I say.

Juan will be shocked when he finds out how much you know.

He doesn't know about the classes.

Juan's all about school. He's been pushing me to go to school for years.

But Juan gets so mad sometimes. I never know what will make him upset.

César imitates Juan, "If I was your age . . ."

I laugh just a little, struck by the resemblance.

César stands up and expands his chest, purses his lips, and furrows his eyebrows, imitating Juan even more.

Ana, tell me you love me, me, me!

He waits for an answer. Where Juan is hairy, César is smooth. Juan's eyes are round and large and César's almond-shaped. Juan's hair thin and wavy, César's a bush of tight curls. Juan is pale, César is the color of the crunchy skin off of juicy roasted chicken thigh, creamy hot chocolate, buttered toast, dark honey, the broth of slow-cooked sancocho.

Every soul food I crave.

I love you, I say, and mean it. I love César with every one of my bones including the baby's. And if I don't find something to eat soon I am going to bite a piece off of him.

Come here and kiss me, César says, still in character and trying to hold back his laughter.

No, Juan.

Come on, Ana, don't be a banana. César taps his cheek.

I tap-kiss him on the bull's-eye and run off to the kitchen.

That's my girl! César yells from the living room. Now go get an education and become rich so I can stay home with the baby!

I press my back against the kitchen walls, hiding the red in my face from César. In the refrigerator I find half an onion, a tomato, an open can of tomato paste, parsley, some peppers. The soaked beans have to be cooked. Soup, I will make soup. And as César pedals the sewing machine I light the burners, then reduce the flame.

IT'S A RELIEF WHEN CÉSAR SHOWS UP WITH HECTOR IN tow for a meal. It's getting harder to be alone with these almond-shaped eyes and tailor's hands and dancing feet. When the two brothers don't talk about politics they talk about baseball, which I prefer because only bad news comes from Dominican Republic.

I watch the game with Hector and César. They make bets on when Juan Marichal will blow his top and punch catcher John Roseboro, who's really asking for it. But on the baseball field, the nonwhite players have to play nice around whites because the world is watching. Once away from the camera we know that Marichal's fists will come out.

Those blacks wish we'd disappear, Hector says.

The brothers share how they feel the same tension at work. At the bar. On the streets. And even more so after the Americans occupied Dominican Republic and Los Angeles had its riot. Thousands hit the streets. Stores burned down; people broke glass windows and took whatever they wanted.

Those blacks are angry, Hector says.

But we're angry too, César says. We can't rent houses, either. Our schools aren't better. We're paid less. The police harass and shoot us at will. We want to work and be left alone. To be able to live our lives without watching our backs. But the blacks look at as us like, Who invited you to our party?

It's not easy, Hector says, shaking his head in agreement. Getting the side-eye as the new kid at work. And in baseball, we're killing it with plátano power.

They laugh.

So during a game, when Roseboro throws a ball as if he wants to hit Marichal in the face, one time too many, we hold our breath.

Roseboro throws off his helmet. And then Marichal takes his bat and hits Roseboro on the head right in the middle of the field.

We know it will make the front page of all the newspapers to-morrow.

Finally we'll make the news. All the covers.

Is it over for Marichal and his career? the announcer asks TV viewers.

But like the rest of us watching, what satisfaction I feel to see a Dominican stand up for himself.

WHEN I WAKE UP IN THE MIDDLE OF THE NIGHT TO USE the bathroom, César isn't in his bed. It's eleven-thirty. He has to go to work early the next day. After dinner I left him dozing on the sofa. He'd claimed to be tired.

Out the window I see there's still a party going on in the ballroom at the Audubon. The curtains are closed. The display lights of the Buick store light up the corner. I stretch my neck out the window. The night, hotter than ever. Two streetlamps are busted, so it's too dark to see much else. Maybe César is taking a walk? Sometimes he likes to smoke a cigarette on the benches in Pigeon Park.

Bastard. Does he do this all the time, leave without warning?

I go through his stuff for clues, maybe I will find matches from local businesses. I take the shirt he has worn all day and hold it on my lap, stretch my legs on the coffee table. I smell his shirt. César's smell makes me crazy.

Usually, I sleep like a log, but now the baby's kicks keep me awake.

I turn on the television. Nothing on but long loud beeps. Emergency warnings. I get my crochet needle and yarn to relax myself. During all my years in Dominican Republic, Mamá would ask me to crochet doilies to give as gifts, and I hated it. I always lost count and tangled the yarn. But with all the anxiety of Juan returning and the baby coming, and as a way to keep my hands busy and not eat everything in sight, crocheting and counting the lines gives me a sense of control. Besides, the baby will need a blanket come winter, some boots, a hat.

Where are you? I say to the dimly lit void of the room, as if the walls can tell César's secret. I want nothing more than for César to fall in love, make a life for himself. It would simplify everything between us.

I wait for over an hour. How am I to sleep knowing he snuck off at night? We're supposed to be partners in crime. We've seen each other at our worst and best.

Mamá has always said to act the opposite of what people expect, to keep them on their toes. But when I hear the door click I turn off the lamp beside me, turn it back on, then off again.

When he sees me, César screams. I scream.

Are you crazy, woman?

I couldn't sleep.

So you sit in the dark?

I didn't mean, I was trying— Wait, where were you?

I go to him and my belly pushes him back against the wall. I poke my finger against his chest.

I smell a bar.

Ana, it's too hot. I couldn't sleep. I went for a drink.

Why can't you ever take me with you?

You were snoring like a freight train.

I don't snore.

You want nothing to do with that place—there's only people looking for trouble.

Like the Irish who punch you?

The Irish only punch us when they're drunk. And it's two-for-one drinks at happy hour. Don't worry, Ana, if they look at me wrong, I'll go to Mami's. She thinks I'm Cuban and gives me free drinks.

Mami, the bartender at the bar for the blacks who drive Cadillacs. The bar owned by the mother of Sammy Davis Jr., the man who makes music with his feet on TV.

Next time, take me with you, I say.

You're underage. Oh and they changed the Irish bar to Luna Llena. The new sign went up today. Ha, the owner actually said to my face, you spics are better drunks.

Promise me, César!

Okay, okay! I promise to be a better drunk.

THE NEXT EVENING I ASK HIM ABOUT GOING TO THE BAR.
Before Juan gets back I want to see this full-moon bar by the High
Bridge pool.

I'm too tired, César says, not tonight.

I go into my bedroom and turn off the lights to wait until he
sneaks out again. And why shouldn't he? Who wants to hang
out with a fat, married, pregnant woman? In a week Juan will be
back. He already bought his ticket home. César and I are anxious
about it. The last time Juan saw César, he almost punched him in
the face. Because of me. Now the money is right where I found it.
I'm sure once Juan sees it there, he'll forgive César.

Although I have no business going out by myself so late at
night, I wrap my hair high on my head and clip on two fake pearl
earrings. I paint my lips a pale pink. I put on the dress César re-
tailored for me and a short raincoat. It's very hot outside, but I
need armor. I put a few dollars in my bra. A purse, too tempting
to a thief. I hold my keys inside my fist and think of all the times
Teresa snuck out at night.

Usually, riding the elevator doesn't scare me, but when the
copper gates close and the doors rise above my head, every part
of me begs, Go back home. I can't just show up at a strange bar.
César may not even be there. What if he's with a woman? A man
does have his needs. But why can't that woman be me?

I walk on Broadway, on the west side of the street, on the same
path the hospital workers take. I head north, past the parking lot,
the diner, the shoe-repair shop. Without all the incessant noise of
the city, I can hear the suction of bus doors as they open and close.
I watch the lone riders inside on display under the fluorescent bus
lights. Through my shoes I feel the vibrations on the pavement,
of the delivery trucks rumbling past me. I hold my breath as I
pass by hefty garbage piles, soon to be collected by large trucks.
I make note of the emergency room door at the hospital, open

twenty-four hours. Against all the warnings on the news about potential riots, about holdups and drive-by shootings, at this most dangerous hour, I turn east on 170th Street and head all the way to Amsterdam Avenue.

I contemplate whether to walk on the road and risk getting hit by a drunk driver or to stay on the desolate and dark sidewalks, where mice scurry. A chill crosses my nape. Someone has busted the lamps across the street, turning High Bridge Park into a black hole. If I venture into the park I will surely disappear forever.

Finally, signs of life. Men in swanky suits with shiny shoes and slicked hair enter and exit fancy cars. Children and decent women are home, and here I am, pregnant, chasing my womanizing brother-in-law to a bar named after the full moon.

Yes, Ana Ruiz-Canción is officially a lunatic.

I push my belly out to exaggerate its size, as if it could protect me.

The brand-new neon sign of La Luna Llena lights the entrance of the bar. Through the dark windows, red lamps and small tables crowd the room. Behind the bar, a wall lined with colorful bottles. Sitting on barstools are women in skimpy outfits, like dancers in a variety show. The music inside is so loud the windows vibrate, and through them I see César dancing, his arms in the air. Some women laugh, drape themselves on him: loose women, easy women, stupid women. Pink, shiny platform shoes. Long legs exposed. A short plaid skirt so high up my heart sinks. Hector climbs from chair to chair to high-five César. They twirl the women, all laughing, living their lives. They slip in and out of view, as the crowd swarms from one side of the room to another. And then I see my reflection, a stupid fat girl who might as well be herding goats.

Suddenly, all the lights of the bar come on. A waitress carries on her shoulder a big serving dish piled high with spaghetti. César pulls the plates from a shelf as if he's at his second home. The large clock on the wall strikes midnight. César had told me about the free midnight meals served to the drunks before closing. I watch them eat, until someone exits and says, Want to come in?

I clumsily enter and the large fan blows hot air on my face. The bar is crowded, the music so loud I feel the drumming in my chest. Where did César and Hector go? I search for them and finally see César, his back to me.

César? I place my hand on his shoulder. He turns around and I step back and away. It's not César. This stranger holds my arm. A firm grip. My eyes widen.

Hey baby, I don't bite, he says, and with his other hand caresses my cheek.

So I slap him. I feel the sting on the palm of my hand. I look around. No César, no Hector.

You bitch, he says.

Now everyone is staring at me.

I rush out of the bar and hurry back to Broadway like a jealous wife whose brother-in-law she has to get out of her heart, because her husband is due back in a few days.

PUFFER FISH CAN KILL YOU IF YOU EAT THEM, YET SOME people take the risk and die. Keep your eyes open and don't be a pendeja like all the other girls in Los Guayacanes who fall for men with too much sugar in their mouths. Puffer fish inflate into a ball when they feel threatened as a warning to predators. The males work endlessly on designing their territories to attract a mate. Burrowing diligently with their fins, reorganizing shells. They work twenty-four hours and many many days without taking a break. The males have many mates and reign over multiple female territories. Once the female is in his territory and tries to leave he will bite her. The female is only allowed a visitor if the visiting fish mutes its bright blue, yellow, and orange spots so that the king puffer fish doesn't feel threatened.

You get what I'm saying, Ana?

THREE DAYS BEFORE JUAN ARRIVES, CÉSAR TAKES A DRESS from one of the showrooms his friend works at. A sample, he says, made from a new experimental fabric that stretches to the size of the body.

I have to tweak it a little, so it will fit you, he says.

Because I'm not skinny like those models?

No, because you're a real woman.

The scarlet dress has a black band at the waist that lands high on my rib cage. The neckline cuts straight across the shoulder to reveal my neck bones—my best asset, as that treacherous Marisela once told me.

I slip on the dress and appreciate the short length, the way the low neck accentuates my breasts. It hugs all of my body in a way that feels covered but sexy. My hair cascades, thick and full, past my shoulders. I make up my face with fire-engine-red lipstick. I liberally apply eyeliner, mascara, and blush, knowing once Juan arrives I will no longer be able to wear this face.

César waits for me in the living room, holding a rose in his hands. He wears a silky brown shirt under his white suit. This time, he hasn't puffed out his curls, but greased and pushed them away from his face—he is now the man in the Duke pomade ad.

The rose is real. I hold it to my nose.

Olé! César lifts his arm in the air like a flamenco dancer.

What do you think? I twirl awkwardly for César to admire his tailoring work.

It's exactly how I imagined it. Perfect.

You should make clothes for fat pregnant ladies. We always look like whales.

You look more beautiful than a rose. Then he combs his hands through my hair and says, God, I love your hair.

You have too much sugar in your mouth.

Shall we? César presents his arm so I can catch it.

We exit the apartment. My thighs rub together into a sweat. My swollen feet are stuffed into high heels so that my calves tighten and elongate my legs. I want to be at my best for César on our last night even if it hurts. Tonight I am a woman without complaints.

The bouncers at the Audubon, friends of César, let us skip the line. We go up the narrow stairs. César leads me past the offices into the ballroom. I part the long velvet curtains and peek out the large arched windows, surrounding the ballroom, up at my building. How clearly one can look into our apartment at night. I left the kitchen lights on! I see the silhouette of Dominicana at the window where I left her, watching me. All those nights I longed to know what went on behind these same closed curtains inside the Audubon. Now here I am.

The band plays. People dance merengue.

Good music, eh? César pulls out a chair and he sits next to me.

I observe the women with small waists and fresh faces. I don't want to let go of César's hand, can't stop looking at his face: his smile, his happiness, his brilliant eyes.

Want to dance? I ask him.

César extends his arm and we glide toward the crowded dance floor.

My belly is so large that when he turns me, César has to stretch his arms. My back is against his chest. I lean into him and he presses forward, our hips swishing from side to side, our feet digging into the wooden floors, his breath on my neck, his arm over my arms, my hand woven into his. The song starts slow, then fast and then slow and then fast, and the music envelops us. His arms are strong and confident and I trust them when I turn and turn and fall over his shoulder in laughter. Both my arms grab at his neck, my head on his chest. With each turn, my feet lift off the ground. This Ana, so light, so loved, so beautiful. Juan's pending arrival makes the tears come, down my cheeks, gushing onto his suit. César doesn't pull away or ask what's wrong, but holds me tighter, his body pressing onto mine, his hands sliding up and down my back. He pulls out his handkerchief to wipe the mascara from under my eyes. And then he does it. I know it's coming and I should stop him. He kisses me on the mouth, hard and strong, his tongue full in my mouth, my lips locking onto his, my head dizzy, the ache between my legs throbbing in tandem with my heart. My hands catch under his shirt. Desire. Uninhibited, unconstrained, and free.

The band members stop playing. I open my eyes to complete darkness. I hold on tightly to César while we wait for the lights to come back on. Our bodies, one pulse.

What happened? I whisper. Everyone in the crowded room stands eerily still.

Se fue la luz! yells a band member from the stage.

Dominicans are in the house! César yells, and enough people cheer along with him to show that our numbers are growing in this city. Soon there will be more of us in Washington Heights than Puerto Ricans, Italians, Irish, and Jews.

The lights come back on as the triangle strikes and the horns blare, then the piano and drums kick in. César looks at me with love.

I turn myself away so my backside leans against him. His sex, a pistol. I move away. He pulls me closer. I close my eyes. I want to be naked with him, to love him, to feel his hands between my legs, on my breasts. He rubs against me. The crowd thickens with people dancing. The music swallows us in, embraces us. He holds on to me. When we dance, he stays close, closer than ever before. My insides swell and I kiss him. Suck on his tongue, bite his lips, and I am lost to him.

When the song stops, I peel away, my sex burning, my head dizzy.

César, I need to go to the bathroom.

Ana, wait.

In the bathroom, I wash away the makeup on my cheeks, around my eyes. The lipstick is smeared around my mouth.

What am I doing?

Ana! César calls from outside the door.

One minute! I say.

When I walk out, César rushes to me. He pulls me aside to the hallway near the offices, where it's quieter.

Forgive me, Ana, he says.

For what? I'm the one who's going to hell, I say. This is Juan's baby.

But I love you, César says.

And a hundred others.

All I think of is you, he says, putting his hands in his pockets.

Juan will kill you.

César and I are eating the poisonous fish. And to end it right there, I run down the narrow stairs to the exit.

Wait, Ana. Wait.

Outside, the crowd waits to enter the ballroom. A part of me enjoys giving them a show.

Please, César, I say in a telenovela voice, forget about me. I'll ruin your life. Please leave.

César slaps his hand flat across his forehead. By then, we've entered the lobby.

I'm not a dog. You can't just tell me to leave.

He follows me across the street, back to our building. He watches me make a fuss of pressing the elevator button and crossing my arms and tracking the light moving across the numbers.

He opens the door of the elevator before I can.

Please go, I say once we're inside.

César pushes me against the wall. Pins my arms.

Tell me you don't love me.

I love him. I fucking love him. His mischievous eyes, his firm ass, his muscular legs. The way he says my name with bated breath. There's no point in lying. We've been eating puffer fish all along. I look at his lips until the elevator stops on our floor. I take his hand and he follows me into the apartment. The kitchen light is still on. I'm relieved that Dominicana on my window is looking away from me. César and I go into the bedroom. We don't turn on any other lights or say another thing. In the dark with the moon as our witness, I pull off his suit jacket, unbutton his shirt. Touch his clavicle. Undo his belt, his pants, and watch them fall on the floor. I pull down his white underwear, bleached by me. His pistol springs up and points at me and for the first time I don't cringe or look away. I stare at it. Grab it. I want it inside of me. I turn around for him to unzip my dress. To undo my bra. My underwear. All off. All on the floor. When we face each other, naked like newborns, he grabs my belly, round and hard. He traces the dark thin line that runs from my belly button to my nest. His fingers tangle in my pubic hair.

You're so fucking beautiful, he says, and I press his hand and push his fingers inside of me. He gasps into my ear, his curls tickling my face. My nipples harden. He turns me around so that his sex rubs between my legs. He folds me over onto the bed. His chest close to my back. His lips on my neck, on my shoulders. His hands dig into me. I grab him and push him inside me. I don't care if I die right there. I want him to thrust inside of me forever. Let this be our last day. Let us die right here.

WHEN THE SUN COMES UP WE'RE STILL NAKED IN BED. ON Juan's bed. Our bodies are sticky from the heat, from our sweat. From everything. I look at César on his back, his arms above his head, his legs flopped open, his penis small and scrunched like a tamarind. When I stand to put on some clothes, to make coffee, he pulls me in, and in seconds he's hard again. But now it's daytime. Now the light is on us.

Let me make us some coffee, I say. I need to brush my teeth. Wash my face, streaked from the tears and the remaining makeup. Put on some clothes. Recollect myself. My hair from the humidity is shaped like a starfish.

Don't leave me.

I'll be back, I promise.

I cover my body with the sheet and walk out.

While the coffee percolates and the milk warms, my mind races with regret. Juan will be back in two days. Mamá is right. I have been struck by the devil who stole all reason. Love, love, love. What good is it, if it can't put food on the table. Women have to be pragmatic. We had a plan. Cement blocks are already piled high on Papá's property. Teresa may have ruined her life with El Guardia, but I ruined our family's future with my brother-in-law. Why couldn't César have been a stranger, someone I can eventually hide away who won't complicate everything? The coffee comes up. The milk boils over.

Ana! César calls from the bedroom as if he always slept in that room. As if we have always been lovers. And I think about Juan calling, Cari! from Caridad's bed as if it does not belong to her husband. So this is how it happens. This is how.

I carry two cups of café con leche to the room. César, still naked and hard. He's like a teenager after all. His smile from ear to ear. He lights a cigarette and his eyes are full of desire. Not like Gabriel's desire, never acted on. César has a man's desire, the insatiable desire of one who has tasted victory.

I've been thinking, César says, sipping his coffee, smoking. He sits up, props some pillows behind him, extends his legs and crosses them at the ankles. I sit at the opposite corner, on the edge. Drink my coffee nervously, thinking, two days. Two days!

But César doesn't seem to care. As if I'm like any other married woman he's been with.

So I have a friend who moved to Boston.

Again with the Boston. It's always Boston.

She opened her own dry cleaner and she needs a tailor. She asked me if I wanted to move over there. It's only three hours away. She has a house with a yard, like Hector; real nice, white fences, a garage. She told me I can rent the apartment on top of her garage and start working with her. Be like a partner.

So this is his plan, to leave New York for Boston? He talks, but I only hear the police sirens outside the window.

What do you think?

I fight myself not to throw the cup of coffee into his face.

Ana? He waves his hands in front of me.

We should get dressed, I say. There's a lot to do before Juan arrives.

I turn my back away from him.

Don't you want to come with me to Boston? César asks.

He reaches for me, both his hands on my shoulders. In the mirror I see Us. Our hair rebelling, our skin darker from all the hours we've spent sitting in the sun. It's the first time I ever saw us together so bare.

Go with you? The words really land.

Of course, silly.

He climbs around and gets on his knees. His eyes look up at me. His hands fold on my belly.

Let me take care of you and the baby. We can start over in Boston. You can make your food and sell it. I can do tailoring.

Juan will never forgive you. He may even kill you.

I'm willing to take that chance.

And my mother? My father? We can't just leave. They're counting on me.

People do it all the time. They leave for less important reasons than this. I love you, Ana. And you love me. And I don't care if no one in my family ever talks to me again, I want to be with you. We can't go back now and pretend nothing happened. We can't. Please say yes.

I've trained all my life. Pretend, pretend, pretend. Pretend the whippings didn't hurt. Pretend I was listening. Pretend to care about the stories Juan told me and that I loved him. Pretend that I was happy about leaving my house in Los Guayacanes.

To hell with pretending. Yes, I say. Yes.

PART VI

JUAN ARRIVES FROM SANTO DOMINGO. AND WHEN HE AR-
rives to the apartment Juan's already tipsy from the flask Hector
carries in his pocket. They bust into the apartment with Juan's
luggage and bags full of Dominican foods wrapped in gift paper.

Look at you, he says, and slaps my face softly a few times. I
have a surprise for you.

I keep moving about, trying to piece together a meal for three.
What surprise?

Your mother and Lenny will soon have a visa. They may be
able to come even before the baby is born.

What?

Isn't that what you wanted? Juan says.

What I wanted is already happening. César is preparing an
apartment for us. He's stocking up the fridge. He's looking into
playgrounds and daycares. He's looking for a school where I can
study, and a job flexible enough so I can care for the baby. He is
planning to wait two months, until the baby is born. Then we will
run away together.

Where's César? Juan asks, looking around.

Hector explains that César has gone to Boston for a job because that's what the Ruiz brothers do. When there's an opportunity to make money, they chase after it. I close my eyes and appeal
to César for guidance, for protection, for an answer. But rather
than face Juan with me, he went off to Boston, to outer space with
a jet pack.

Doesn't the news about your mother make you happy? Juan's
sausage fingers massage my neck.

Of course. I'm happy. I'm shocked.

The phone rings. I let out a deep breath.

He picks it up and says a few words, quickly hangs up as if he
can't be bothered. His eyes turn back to mine as if he can reach
into my heart.

The brothers take over the house like wild boars. The hard plastic suitcases pop open, are gutted of their contents. Juan pulls out a bottle of rum wrapped in netting.

Barceló Añejo, the good stuff!

I purse my lips and hold back from crying. I should've taken all the money I made and left with César on the bus at Penn Station. The bus would have dropped us off in Boston by a supermarket, where his friend would've picked us up and driven us to the small apartment on top of the garage attached to her house.

Ana, says Juan, get us some glasses.

He pats my behind, pushing me toward the kitchen, his hands looser but less aggressive than I remember them.

I disappear into the kitchen with the rum bottle in hand, in search of calm, in search of order. I open the cabinet doors to find a neat line of glasses, one behind the other, as if on display at a store. I place two stubby glasses on a wooden tray, and another one for myself.

I pour the rum into all three glasses, over ice. I gulp one before I leave the kitchen. Swallow hard. I place the tray on the coffee table, keep my back to them and look out the window to reliable Broadway, to the people on their clocks, coming and going. The same people who stand at the bus stop. The same people who enter and exit the Audubon Ballroom, crossing paths.

Can it be? Mamá and Lenny are coming to New York?

The sharp burn of the rum lingers on my tongue and throat. The warmth of it fills my head.

Ana, sit by me, Juan says, pushing Hector away to the end of the sofa to make space for me. Juan's voice tinged with laughter, so clueless of how I have changed, so clueless of my betrayal. It makes me feel sorry for him.

How was your trip? I ask just to say something.

Smooth. Forgot I was on the plane most of the time.

The last time I flew on a plane I threw up twice, Hector says, because the pilot bounced the plane like a rabbit.

The men laugh as Hector jumps up and down in the living

room. His heavy body shakes the wooden floors and I want Mr. O'Brien to complain with his broomstick.

Juan's hand lands on my lap like a brick.

Let me check on the food, I say, and slip from under him.

What I would give to hear César's voice.

Juan follows me into the kitchen.

Can I help you with anything?

This is a first. Now I have to pretend.

I need the big plate on the top shelf.

He climbs on a stool, gives me the plate. Stands behind me. The narrow kitchen locks us in. My large belly presses against the sink with Juan against me. His hands circle both my breasts.

They're huge.

He squeezes hard. It hurts, but I stand still and say nothing as his hands drop to the globe I carry, hard and full. He nibbles on my neck, catching me by surprise.

I cringe. Maybe it's a mistake to wait until the baby is born to leave.

Juan, this kitchen's too small and hot for three people. Go entertain your brother.

Oh, how I missed you both, pajarita, he says.

I serve the food at the table in the living room and watch them eat from the threshold of the kitchen. Though I'm hungry, I never eat when people are over—only with Marisela, only with César.

The phone rings. I pick up. Silence on the other end.

Caridad? I know it's you, I say, surprised at my own voice.

I hold the earpiece for a long minute, hang up, and lean in toward the living room.

That was for you, Juan.

Juan wipes his mouth for a final time with a napkin and pokes his head into the kitchen while I busy myself clearing dirty pots from the counter.

I have to take care of something. But don't worry, I'll be back later, he says to me, then turns to Hector. Hey, gimme a ride?

Of course.

Hector hovers by the door waiting for Juan, who pulls a small package from the suitcase and tucks it into his jacket pocket.

Did you bring me any letters? I call out to Juan before they leave the apartment.

Look in the suitcase, he says, and as if he'd forgotten something, he turns to me, picks me up, and hugs me.

Stay out of trouble, pajarita. I'll be back before the moon. And remember, you're all that matters.

Then they are gone. And I am able to breathe. I turn off the music. I close all the windows to block out the street noise, yearning for silence.

I scrape the dishes and soak them in soapy water. The phone rings again. I hope for my mother but know it's Caridad.

Aló. I hold the earpiece with my shoulder, continue to wash the dishes, and wait for something, anything.

He left. To see you, I say.

The other end silence, not even a breath.

Say something, you coward! I say and throw a dish on the floor.

I SWEEP THE GLASS, SHOVEL THE BROKEN DISH INTO A dustpan, and toss it in the garbage. Wash the dishes and wipe the stove. Take Juan's clothes and hang them in the closet, place them in the drawer. The dirty ones I stuff in the hamper in the bathroom. I take out the bags of mentas from my mother and the four letters tightly wrapped with twine inside a thin plastic bag. First, I will finish cleaning. Then read. Something about the letters makes me nervous. I pile the packages, favors for Juan's friends with names I've never heard of, on the shelves. When all of Juan's things inside the suitcase find a place, I stare at the two empty suitcases, their open mouths begging me to take them back to Dominican Republic.

Maybe I can leave to Boston before Juan comes back. Send a message to César that I'm on my way so he picks me up at the station. It will take Juan and Caridad three, maybe four hours to make up for lost time. Plus the time of the bus ride to Boston, about four hours. But how do I reach César?

I manically open the drawers and stuff clothing inside of a bag. I can go to one of those places on the pamphlet the doctor had given me, the one with the map that Juan crumpled up and threw away but that I later retrieved from the garbage and hid in a drawer. Red dots signaling safe spaces. But then what?

Because cleaning helps me think, I wring out all of the washed laundry from the bathtub, tie a clothesline from the entrance door hinge to the closet door hinge, across the living room, hang the clothes to dry. I bathe. I shave my legs and armpits. I wash my hair and wrap small sections with rollers. What if I just chop it all off? Then Juan will kill me for sure.

Because I can't leave the apartment with wet hair, I balance the hair dryer on the spine of the sofa and sit under it. It'll take at least forty minutes. Meanwhile, I can make a plan.

I take the letters from my family and hold them on my lap.

One from Yohnny—Yohnny? I drop the letter as if a ghost had written it and place it behind all the others.

I sink deeper into the sofa, maneuvering my head under the hair dryer so the heat doesn't burn my cheeks and the tops of my ears. I open the first letter from my mother. No, How are you? No, How's the baby? It starts with, Now that I've applied for a travel visa you should start looking for a job for me. Lenny will accompany her because he's proven to be incapable of doing anything on his own but read the paper to Papá when he's too tired to read it for himself. And add numbers. She calls him a walking calculator. Just like you. So in exchange for the price of two plane tickets Papá gave Juan another large piece of land.

I put down the letter. My heart aches. What is a man like Papá without land?

Papá's letter is written on a small piece of notebook paper, in pencil. It's the second one I've received from him since my arrival. Like his first letter, he starts with I don't want to bother. I don't like to ask for anything. He then says: You have to take care of your mother now. Take care of Lenny. I handed Lenny a wrench and he nearly cut off a finger.

The letter ends with, Juan is a good man.

He's clearly given up. He too is pretending.

I study Papá's childlike handwriting. He went to school maybe two or three years at most. Yes, Papá, a good man pays the rent, provides for his family, works hard. A good man keeps his word. He cheats on his wife. He almost chokes her to death. He punches, slaps, trips, hurts her. Yes, Papá, Juan is a good man.

How will Mamá and Lenny live with me and César on top of a garage in the one-room apartment in Boston? Mamá will never allow it. Her allegiance is to Juan. Our land's future is tied to Juan. And soon, Papá will have to come to New York because he can't stay there alone. And what about Teresa and poor Juanita and Betty?

I tear open Teresa's letter, looking for answers. No use. She has been caught by the white-shirts who carry the Bible. Just when I thought God had forgotten me, she writes, Miss Ashley

from Texas invited us to eat with her family, to teach us how
they prosper with the Lord by their side. In great and frustrat-
ing detail, Teresa describes the chocolate-chip cookies served for
dessert. And the magical blue boxes of elbows they gave her and
and how by adding hot water to the packet of yellow powder
she can feed herself and El Guardia for a week! How this means
she doesn't have to grate yucca and soak beans anymore, giving
her more time to spread the Lord's name. I have seen those blue
boxes at the supermarket beside the cans of Chef Boyardee. Poor,
poor Teresa, seduced by macaroni and cheese by those Yankees
in short-sleeved white shirts and dark pants who go from house
to house, always in a pack, who hand food to the street children
and lure them into their houses to sit around the living room and
listen to how much God loves them. I have seen the white-shirts
in New York too, by the subway exit. Teresa has always seemed
so strong. It doesn't make sense. As a soon-to-be-mother, even I
know God's happier when his children keep a good distance, and
are not always hanging over him like spoiled children, always
asking him for things.

I hold Yohnny's letter, rub the cream-colored notebook paper
covered in blue ink between my fingertips. The words bleed into
one another.

> My Sister,
>
> How are you? Have you forgotten about all of us
> already? Tomorrow I will deliver these letters to
> Juan, but really the goal is to see Juanita. You're not
> going to believe this but she's pregnant. With my
> baby. I know, I know, a complication. Thank god
> we are second cousins because if not I would've made
> her get rid of it. Is that cruel? But no matter what,
> my plan is to go to New York and take her with
> me. Mamá doesn't know because she's still mad at
> Teresa for sticking her foot in it with El Guardia.
> But what am I supposed to do? I love that woman.
> And did Mamá already tell you about Betty? One

of the American soldiers I've been doing errands for fell in love with her. Our shy, horse-faced Betty. Mamá saw him in uniform, over six feet tall, white like milk, and he looks like he never broke a plate in his life so she acted quickly and sealed that deal. He's taking her to Tennessee. He don't know Mamá put brujeria on him. And you could only imagine Juanita. Jealous like I've never seen her. She wants her baby to be born in America. Like yours. Like Betty's. So that's the plan. Sooner than you know it, I'll be knocking on your door.

Your brother,
Yohnny

I fold the letters, my ears burning under the hair dryer. I touch my hair, still damp. Why hasn't anyone mentioned Juanita and Yohnny's baby? Is it still a secret? And Betty? She's marrying an American soldier and will move to some state in the middle of America. I would've never imagined that possibility. But oh sweet Betty, if she chose him like he chose her, what happiness.

I pull my head out of the dryer.

Once Mamá arrives, she'll take over. I'll no longer have a say about what we eat for dinner or where things should go. From the first day, she'll rearrange everything, I'm sure of it. But what choice do I have?

I hold my belly and speak to it. Soon you'll have a say with my life too.

I undo the rollers in the bathroom and let the rollers and bobby pins pile in the bathroom sink. My ends are still very wet. Coño! Carajo! Long hair is for girls. Soon I'll be a mother. I take the scissors from the medicine cabinet and chop half of the length off. The curls spring up around my face. All the dried highlighted ends from the sun back home are now gone. Suddenly my eyes look bigger. My neck naked. A weight off my head. Let Juan be mad. Let César think I look ugly. It's my hair.

I put Juan's empty suitcases one inside the other and prop

them in the hallway. I need to tell César there will be no more Boston. I prepare a dish of leftovers and sit by the window to eat.

The pigeons are back. A whole new generation. They don't know about the slaughter of Pigeon Betty. I watch the Jewish children stream out of the Audubon, waving their blue and white flags. Why do people have to look so happy?

Soon it will be dark. Soon the store gates will all come down. Soon the crowds will gather for the 7 p.m. movie. Ay, Yohnny, he wrote me a letter. Maybe he's waiting for another opportunity to come back, standing on some line, waiting to leap into a body before a baby is born. Maybe he'll leap inside of me.

I take a breath. At least Mamá can help me with the baby so I can both work and go to school. She will hate my short hair.

AS PROMISED, JUAN ARRIVES HOME BEFORE THE MOON shows itself in the sky. He takes a shower. He eats and then says, I'm tired. Caridad has obviously made up for lost time.

Come to bed with me, he says, and extends his hand. He doesn't even comment on my hair. This irritates me.

Before I can invent an escape he pulls my hand. I have bathed twice. But still César is all over me.

Juan wants to see how much I've grown. He takes off his pants to be more comfortable. He leaves on his socks, his briefs, and his button-down shirt. He has lost weight in Dominican Republic. He looks good and tanned. The moonlight pours into the room, but he turns on the lamp next to his nightstand. There's no place to hide. Juan stretches himself out on the bed. He watches me. I stand there.

That baby looks like it's gonna pop out any minute, he says.

I laugh, not knowing what to do.

Come closer, he says, so I sit next to him. He pulls me toward his chest. My head rises with each breath. Can he tell I'm not the dead fly he left two months ago? Something has changed and my body rages inside, ravenous and hungry. My insides want to push out of my skin, my eyes, my ears, my mouth. Teresa warned me about how one loses control. But César isn't waiting for me in his car in the middle of the night to whisk me away like El Guardia waited for Teresa. César hasn't even called.

Exhausted, Juan falls asleep, and I follow.

A few hours later I wake up and my back is turned away from Juan. He holds me from behind. He surprises me by fingering my hair and kissing my neck tenderly.

I brace myself for a fight.

Now you look like my dark-headed Marilyn Monroe, he whispers.

He unzips the back of my dress, unhooks my bra.

I'm tired, Juan, I say, and scoot away.

I want to look at them, he says, and turns me on my back. Off with my sleeves, down with my dress. My nipples are large and leathery, sensitive to touch. César has sucked on them. Kissed every inch of me, over and over again. Before he left to catch the bus to Boston he said, Don't worry, my sweet thing. Everything'll be okay.

I close my eyes to make Juan disappear. I turn my back to him again. Can't he see I don't want to be touched? Can't he see I'm no longer his?

His sex pokes me from behind. He lifts my skirt. He grabs my hair in his fist as if it's the reins of a horse and jerks my head back so I look at him. I pray to the statue of Jesus sitting on the windowsill, next to the candle of the Virgin Altagracia, and St. Martin. And I imagine myself swelling up into a ball like a pufferfish. Impossible to bite into.

Get out! Get off me! I scream, and kick Juan. I stumble out of the bed. My body trembles.

Juan's sex points to the ceiling. He looks at me befuddled like a stranger. I stand there. Feet planted. I pull the sheet off the bed and over me.

Good to be home, he says sarcastically. He doesn't yell back. He doesn't insist.

JUAN HASN'T BOTHERED TO COME HOME BUT DOES CALL to say he'll be back for lunch. In the past he didn't give explanations. This time he chatters on and on. All kinds of distractions to cover up his night with Caridad.

The sun is hot but the air fresh. ESL class starts in an hour. I place my notebook inside my purse and walk over toward the rectory. There are more police standing around than fire hydrants. The Audubon Ballroom's surrounded by cop cars. Broken glass litters the streets, and business owners board up their storefronts. Children are nowhere to be seen. No stickball. No older couples sitting on lawn chairs on street corners fanning themselves gossiping. I know I should turn back, but I don't want to be alone in the apartment where everything reminds me of César.

At the rectory, a sign reads: Class canceled. I climb the steps toward the church's door. Upon entering, I feel a gust of cool air and a pressure to confess that I'm not sorry for being with César.

In one of the pews Sister Lucía kneels in prayer. I sit next to her. When Sister Lucía finishes praying she holds my hand and frowns. Can she tell I have sinned?

Go home while it's still quiet outside, she says in Spanish. It makes me so happy to hear her speak Spanish.

Wipe that smile off your face. Her voice is urgent, filled with concern.

Last year, the riots happened right outside the church and all over Harlem when an innocent man was shot by the police. So go home, Ana. And lock your door. Sister Lucía waves me away toward the exit.

Outside I examine the grave faces of the older men and women standing guard in front of their buildings. Their anger makes me nervous, but I understand it. To be angry and not have the power to control your life. To not feel safe. To depend on a person who reminds you how they can hurt you, even kill you, at their whim. I understand.

I look out my window for hours, waiting for something to happen. Fires rage on television. Santo Domingo burns too. Out on the streets here, fireworks and gunshots are indistinguishable. Young men are under fire in Vietnam. There's too much fire everywhere, inside of me. Too much.

CÉSAR FINALLY CALLS. I'M SO RELIEVED TO HEAR HIS voice. I'm all waterworks.

Please don't, he says.

I try to imagine where he's standing to make the call. At a phone booth? At his friend's house? Has he shaved? Has he taken a shower? Is the sun shining like it is in New York? Is the air different? What's around him? His shoes, are they scuffed? Who's ironing his shirts?

How are you? he asks when I calm down.

I'm okay. You? I say.

The apartment is a shithole, he says. I found a mouse in the toilet.

We can clean it up, I say, knowing there will be no César and Ana running off to Boston. No Ana making César breakfast before he goes to work every day. No dancing in the living room even when the music is off.

I have to find another place. In a safer area. Closer to the supermarket, so you can walk everywhere, you know. But I need time.

Juan got Mamá a visa. Lenny too.

Don't tell me.

He's booking their trip so they can arrive before the birth. Mamá doesn't know what to do with herself.

And us? What about us?

César?

A click. A pause. Please insert ten cents for another three minutes.

I hang up and wait all day for him to call again, but he doesn't. All day my stomach feels empty. All day I feel a chill in my bones.

THE NEXT DAY, JUAN SHOWS UP WITH A NEW CUSTOMER for the suits—Mauricio—and with him is his wife. I have to unglue my feet from the freshly polished floor at the sight of her.

I hold myself back from scratching out the cat eyes that plead with me to pretend we've never met.

Mauricio is handsome, tall and lean, though he has the face of a sergeant. Marisela meekly follows him, sits close to him at the table that once fed her. They glance around. I offer coffee. They make small talk. Juan plays as if he had never lent Marisela money. Everyone talks to each other, except no one talks to me.

Mauricio looks out the window and says, You can see the whole world from here.

That's why I chose the top floor, Juan says.

You have such a lovely home, Marisela says, ankles crossed under the table.

I excuse myself so I can fetch the coffee.

Do you need any help? she asks me casually, breaking my heart all over again.

No, thank you.

I should yank off her drop earrings, pull on her hair, kick her.

But first, Ana, 40L for Mauricio—that's your size, isn't it? Juan volunteers.

I know how to size a man too, I almost say.

Juan Ruiz, a true pro, says Mauricio.

Relieved to have something to do, I dig into the closet and find a few suits. I hand them over and point to the bathroom so he tries them on. Even when Mauricio has left the room Juan and Marisela continue with the charade.

How many months are you? Marisela asks me.

She's carrying an elephant, Juan responds.

Excuse me, I hear the coffee.

Thank goodness for percolators, for the way they take their time to fill. I serve three espresso cups on a tray and three glasses of ice water, a paper towel wrapped around each glass.

In the living room, Marisela admires her husband.

It looks good, Mauri. You can wear it to my sister's graduation this Sunday.

Don't remind me. Your sister's a piece of work. Been here three months and she already walks with her nose in the air because she's got a typing certificate.

Juan laughs.

School's a good thing. So many more doors will open for her, Juan says.

Why did Marisela even agree to come? Maybe she had no choice. I try to find some semblance of the woman with whom I spent so many afternoons. Marisela doesn't dare look at me. It makes me happy to think she suffers. She makes it seem like she can manage her man, but perhaps we're both fucked.

I heard César found work in Boston—is it true? Mauricio asks Juan, who smiles.

Work? That boy can work anywhere. It's this tipa who has him crazy. She's been trying to get him to move back there with her for over a year.

And before I know it the tray tips over, hot coffee and glasses of ice water right onto Marisela's lap. We all scream. Marisela jumps up to peel away the fabric from her skin, and Juan yanks me away.

What's wrong with you? he says. Get her some towels!

I act immediately.

It's okay. It's nothing. We're on our way home anyway, Marisela says, as nervous as me.

I roughly blot at her shirt with a paper towel.

Are you almost done? Marisela asks her husband.

Mauricio buys two suits but asks to pay for them at the end of the week. I want to warn Juan about how their word is shit, but Juan walks them and the suits to the door. Marisela looks back apologetically at me. I busy myself patting the sofa cushions dry, placing a towel on the floor to catch all the spilled water.

Until soon, Juan says, then slams the door.

I face him and wait.

C'mon, Juan, show me the good man you are. Before his trip he was all sharp lines, clearly defined. Now he's a puzzle, his face and body, shuffled up by witnessing the war. Something has changed him, and like Papá, who never says much, Juan holds back where he is broken. I draw my face closer and stare back at him. He lifts his hand in reflex, stops himself. So I spit into his eyes. *C'mon, Juan, make it easy for me to leave you.* I clench my toes against the soles of my feet to hold my ground. He balls up his fist, bites it, then yells, What's wrong with you?

Go ahead, I say.

Do what you do, Juan. Be like the brute I know you are. Fuck you. Fuck César. Fuck Marisela. Fuck everybody.

He looks wounded by my words. He slumps his shoulders, turns his back on me and sits on the sofa. He turns on the TV. A woman demonstrates a vacuum cleaner to a live audience as if it's the most interesting thing in the world. Fuck her too.

Juan's already gone when I wake up the following morning. He has let me sleep in. This should worry me, but I am tired of being worried. Being so close to my due date, my sleep has become deeper, my dreams bizarre, and often I wake up confused as to where I am.

The most vivid dream is of Yohnny inside our apartment dressed in a karate suit standing in a fighting position. Juan calls for me from the bedroom, drunk and too lazy to chase me. I plead with Yohnny to go home, fearing Juan will kill him. But I'm already dead, Yohnny says. When I extend my arm to touch him I find only air.

Does the dream mean Yohnny is closer to coming back to life or that I'm closer to being dead?

After drinking a café con leche, I narrow my eyes at where the tray spilled yesterday. I dilute Pine-Sol in a small plastic tub of water. I dampen an old towel in the mixture, wring it out, and push it with a broomstick across the floors. The pine scent calms me. When I finish mopping the floors I take another damp towel and dust the furniture. Then I find it, under the doily on the dining table: forty dollars, folded inside a sheet of notebook paper.

Ana,
Please forgive me.
Marisela

THE PAPERWORK HAS COME THROUGH. IN A FEW WEEKS Mamá and Lenny will be eating at our table, sleeping in our beds. If there's one good thing that has come from the war, Juan explains, it's that the embassy sped up the tourist visa applications.

He says Papá will meet El Cojo at the restaurant in the next few days to purchase their airline tickets.

Does this make you happy, Ana?

I hug Juan tight around his neck and he hugs me back.

Hearing an actual date for Mamá's arrival feels certain and real, like a small accomplishment for our family. And I'm eight months pregnant. And Marisela asked for forgiveness. Forget that César may or may not have a girlfriend and that he perhaps pulled a Dominican move, feeding me garbage about looking for a nice place for us and the baby, when in fact he's a coward.

Wow, I have so much to prepare, I say. We'll have a full house, and soon Papá, Teresa, and her son can come. And Juanita? When can they all come?

The super has told Juan the apartment next door will become available within the next year. Once it does, all the family will come.

Mark my words, pajarita, the Dominicans are going to flood New York in a blink of an eye. This neighborhood won't know what hit them.

Thank you, I say, and kiss him in fast short pats all over his face.

It makes me so happy to see you happy, he says, searching for love in my eyes.

Juan is my monster and my angel. In this messed-up world, he tries his best. And I owe it to him to try my best. Maybe with time if César keeps his distance I can make my marriage work. I can ask Mamá to heal me from the poisonous fish. To make me one of her potions to forget César. Maybe then I can even love Juan.

ONCE FALL KICKS IN, THE CITY IS BLANKETED BY A firestorm of leaves. The pigeons are back on the fire escape, pecking at the rice I have left for them. New fashion has skirts cropping up on women's thighs and men opting out of formal suits in favor of black leather jackets and berets.

I count the days on the calendar until their arrival. Juan has already figured out that the school two blocks away will enroll Lenny in first grade. Mamá will work at a lamp factory across the bridge in New Jersey. A van will pick her up and take her there every morning at 7:45 a.m. And when the baby qualifies for daycare, I will join her.

There will be plenty of people to love and to rely on. To make room in the closets for them, Juan sells a bulk of the suits to another vendor. With all of us working outside of the house, no one can take care of the suit business, anyway.

All this waiting—without César, without the suit customers—makes the days unbearably long. Whenever the phone rings, I hope it's César, who will call to say he still loves me, that he misses me, that he's still working hard to figure out a real solution for us. But when the phone rings it's often the breath, even if she knows Juan isn't home, she calls and calls. So I turn up the radio and play songs for her, and she listens before hanging up.

She must be lonely too.

Sister Lucía has gone away to visit her family in Chile. There are no more English classes until next spring. I focus on trying my best not to upset Juan. He's being so generous. There is loneliness during the day but also peace, for once. Going out, even for a walk, is a trial. My bladder is the size of a pea. My feet are always bloated; my soles ache and shoot pain up through my legs and around my hips, especially when I have to climb the stairs. The elevator in our building has a mind of its own and only works when it wants to. If I have groceries, I will wait an hour until the super or the porter volunteers to help me up. How do the neighbor with children and the old lady Rose manage when the elevator is out of order? It's unnatural to live up so high.

To fill my days I write in my small notebook. Writing becomes like talking. I write down my dreams. In them, Juanita sits at my kitchen table, her belly as large as mine. We press our bellies together, becoming a two-headed pregnant beast. It's a comforting dream.

The leaves on the trees outside our window soon become vibrant, bursting with color. For something to be born, Papá always says, something has to die. But pregnant as I am, I can't manage any more loss. How beautiful the leaves look right before their last days. Every year they fall, so the tree trunks rest and the leaves can come back in the spring.

Hold on, I tell myself and rest my bare feet on the floor and imagine them as tree roots.

CÉSAR'S RETURN. THE CONTINUOUS RING OF THE DOOR-
bell blares across the apartment to the kitchen. I run to the door
to look through the peephole. I see no one. The sound of fingers
tapping. César calls my name so softly I barely hear it. When I
open the door, he jumps at me and says, Boo!

What are you doing here?

I pull him in and lock the door, with the chain.

What if Juan was home? I hiss. What if someone sees you?
Why aren't you in Boston?

I came to get you, he says, and we stare at each other. I have to
get on my tiptoes so my face can be closer to his.

I slap him. Now, it comes so easily.

I gasp at what I've done. His look of disbelief and smile of
admiration.

You want to do that again? he asks and takes my hand, holds
it to his face.

He unhinges me. His jeans are frayed, his shirt needs ironing,
his fingernails need a trim. I'm pleased he has all the signs of a
man living without a woman. Men can only perform like men,
Mamá always says, when women are doing everything. We're
invisible little workers so they can puff out their chests.

I walk away from him, frustrated. I want to take off his shirt
and iron it. I have to restrain myself from getting the nail clippers.
Now that Juan is back in New York, everything is changed. The
shell of the pomegranate has been cracked open. There is no way
to make it whole again.

César takes my arm and rolls me into his body. His face is close
to mine. His breath smells of coffee, alcohol, and cigarettes. He
steps back and forward, gently pulling and pushing me. His head
slumps onto my shoulder. His feet are no longer moving, only his
hips. He sings softly into my ear, his weight heavy on me.

Ay, Ana Banana, he says, and sticks his hands under my arms

and tickles me. Tickles me onto the couch until I laugh so hard no sound comes out of my mouth. César tickles and tickles until I pee on myself.

César! I yell, and run to the bathroom. It has only been a small leak, but with the pressure of the baby on my bladder, I need to be more careful—he needs to be more careful.

After, I find him in my room taking out my clothing from my drawers.

Let's go before Juan returns, he says, and pulls out a suitcase from the top shelf in the closet. Unlatches it and it pops open. Inside there is another suitcase and inside that a bag.

Did you find a place for us? I ask.

My friend will be picking us up in less than an hour. We don't have much time, Ana. Where is your paperwork? Once we leave we won't be able to come back here.

My mother arrives in a few weeks with Lenny. I can't just leave.

Believe me, your mother knows how to take care of herself.

He tears open my closet.

I look at the perfectly made bed. The curtains I have ironed. Everything has an order, everything has a place. I have already made room for the baby, for Mamá, for Lenny.

I can't go with you, I say.

But we made a plan, he yells, his voice full of sparks. Fuck!

I protect my face. His arms thrash in the air. His hands pull at his hair. He walks out to the living room and then back into the room. He knows I'm right. If he can barely take care of himself, how can he take care of me? And my family?

What am I supposed to do in Boston by myself?

I don't know, I cry. Come back to New York?

I flee into the kitchen to chop onions, cilantro, and peppers. To mince garlic, to fry a plátano. To do anything to make the ache bearable.

He follows me. I hold on to the onion with one hand. I grip the knife with the other. *Please don't make this harder for me.*

What the fuck are you doing? Put that knife down. We don't have time for this.

I chop, chop, chop the onion into the tiniest pieces.

His hand wraps around my arm so I can let go of the onion, the knife. He leads me to the living room.

Please, he says, his voice softer. Just come with me. Don't you love me?

My feet are rooted. My fists, tight against my sides. My eyes wide open, welling up with tears from the onions, from the fact that we both know I am not going anywhere.

Don't move, okay? He plugs in his record player and looks through his 45s and says, at least dance with me, eh?

I know this song by the Four Tops. Sung by the four black men whose front man looks just like El Guardia. I'd memorized it from start to finish to practice my English pronunciation. It's always on the radio. His body moves as if stepping on the uneven floor of a cloud as he dances alone and sings it aloud. Then he extends his arms toward me and once again I am trapped by his smell, his warmth. We should've run off before Juan's arrival.

I can't help myself

I love you and nobody else

We sway together for a long while. Though upbeat, the song is sad. This is good-bye. I know it by the way our hands weave together and by the way I have to finally let him go. I have chosen my family. There will be no César and Ana forever.

WHEN I TAKE A WALK ON BROADWAY I PRETEND I'M BAL-
ancing a book on my head. I sway my hips, looking into store
windows in search of a fur coat and a string of pearls. Some
sheer stockings and a patent-leather purse. The store windows
are crammed with old furniture in need of repair, piles of bed
covers, sausages dangling bloody red at the meat shop. My reflection stares back at me: hair flat, no poof, no velvety bow barrette
like Miss Kennedy's to hold my hair up. The strumming guitars
and banging of drums loom close by. The crowds swarm around
me, people holding signs, *End War Now.* They shout in unison this
thing and that, pushing me ahead, a riptide under my feet. The
banging of pots. The ominous sound of thunder. I should go home
to avoid trouble, but I throw myself in, allowing the wave to lift
and take me along. Surrendering. *Peace for All.* We march downtown against traffic, filling the streets, halting the delivery trucks,
buses, and cars. Our breaths in sync. The cars honk. The sirens
wail. A helicopter dips low above us. The police hover nearby with
clubs, waiting, waiting. They, like the marchers, multiply quickly.
Lined up, the cops become a blue fence all along the sidewalks
containing us. From my living room window, the protests seem
loud and chaotic, but once inside of it, I feel weightless. A woman
links her arm to mine and I link my arm to a man next to me.
They're much taller than me. We're like a school of fish, not losing
our place, swimming against the current. Alive. I can barely see
anything, the mass of bodies pushing back the traffic, providing a
shore for the march to break into. Turn back! Turn back! Mamá
would say. Don't get involved with business that's not yours. But
our arms looped one into the other, get tighter, stronger. Suddenly,
we're sitting. The traffic jams. There's no turning back. I don't
care that my skirt will be full of street dirt. Chants rip through my
body. *Together we're strong.* So strong. This is why we sit. This is
why we say no. This is why we link arms.

THE DAY MAMÁ AND LENNY ARRIVE I DON'T GO TO THE
airport because there is no room in the car. It's a beautiful fall day
in October, not cold, not too warm. Much better than arriving
in the dead of winter like me. They arrive loaded with luggage
filled with things Juan has planned to sell to a friend, things he
instructed Mamá to tell the customs officer were gifts for friends,
or just their own belongings.

I have left nothing unturned in our small apartment. Everything has been meticulously cleaned, polished, organized. Mamá
will sleep in the foldout bed in the living room and Lenny on the
sofa. At first I suggest to Juan he should sleep in the living room
so when he comes home late he won't wake us up. But it's my
house, he says angrily, a wife should sleep with her husband.

All the smells of home permeate the place. In the oven, bread
pudding bakes. On the stove, a majarete simmers. I stock the
fridge with ingredients Mamá will recognize to ease the transi-
tion. I turn on the radio to the Spanish station. With the money
I have saved, I bought Mamá a nightgown, a pair of slippers, a
dress, some underwear. A net for her hair, bobby pins. For Lenny,
I bought some pants and two shirts. Just enough so they don't suffer embarrassment. Not too much, so Juan won't realize I have
my own money to spend.

I wait for them in the lobby. The elevator is working. Bob
the porter has not arrived yet. I stack the books and papers on
the mantel. I sort the advertising by the mailboxes. I stand by the
door, then sit on the small sofa.

When Juan's car pulls up in front of the building, I run to the
door. My eyes tear up when I see them climb out of the car. Lenny's arms are bare, his pants too short for his legs. Mamá wears a
flimsy dress and a shawl around her neck. I see a few white hairs.
My old lady! Next to Juan, in New York City, they look so small.

Mamá! I call out to them and open the door, waving them into

the building, where it's warmer. She looks at me and through me.
Mamá? I say again and then as if something registers, she waves.
She slaps Lenny on the head and nudges him into the building.

Lenny? I hug him. He's so shy and meek.

What happened to your hair? Mamá says disapprovingly.
Now your face looks fat.

Come, come, I say, and suddenly feel the surrealness of being
with them here in the building, of pressing a button and waiting
for a box to come down.

What about Juan? Mamá asks, turning in circles.

I'm right here, Juan says. He comes up behind us, hauling two
large suitcases with him.

How was your trip? I ask Mamá. To Lenny, Was it fun?

Lenny smiles, looks down at the black and white tiles.

Mamá says, Everything was very nice.

The Mamá in Los Guayacanes is full of words. In New York
City, talking with her is like pulling teeth.

The elevator comes. The gates open. I hold the door for Mamá
and Lenny to enter. Lenny jumps in and the elevator shakes, re-
minding me that it is being held by a few cables. Mamá doesn't
budge, stares but won't enter.

Get in. It's just an elevator, says Juan. I have to go to work.

Juan, I say, not to embarrass Mamá, Why don't you go first,
with those heavy bags. Lenny will keep you company.

Once Juan and Lenny are gone, Mamá seems relieved. Her
fragility makes my heart open to her. Everything I feared about
her as a child, her lioness will, her strict ways are gone. Gone! As
we wait for the elevator to return, I ask about Teresa, and Mamá
rolls her eyes.

Crazy as ever, she says.

And Papá?

He's fine. He sends his regards.

What about Juanita?

You won't recognize her. Fat like you've never seen her.

Isn't she pregnant?

That's what she told some chino she found down the road.

Three times her age, half her size, and he's stupid enough to take her with him to Japan.

Juanita can't take Yohnny's baby to Japan—we'll never see her again!

Mamá shrugs. She looks tired.

You heard about Betty, right? She's gone off with a man who was struck by lightning, pale as milk. We plan and God laughs, Ana.

Would you rather take the stairs? I ask Mamá.

If that's what you want.

She turns and starts up the stairs ahead of me, as if she already lives here. After the first flight, I'm out of breath. The baby's feet press against my lungs. Mamá looks around, making note of the stairs, of the hallways. Complaining about living so high up.

Why didn't Juan get a place on the first floor? Too expensive?

We enter the apartment. Juan has already slapped on some Old Spice and changed his shirt.

What took you so long? he says.

Lenny sits on the far end of the sofa, clearly not wanting to take up too much space.

Will you be home late? I ask Juan.

Mamá sucks her teeth softly, but I hear it.

Explain to them how the water works, he says, and then he leaves me alone with them.

Mamá holds her bag close to her body and looks around to all the corners of the living room, the small television, the radio, at all the mirrors, at the shelves filled with old books and LPs. She walks over to the window overlooking Broadway. I can tell from her face the sight of the bustling street from above makes an impression.

See, Mamá? The higher the floor the better the view. Come, I say, I made you some bread pudding and majarete.

They follow me into the kitchen.

We don't all fit. It's too small, says Mamá. She sticks her finger in the pot and tastes it.

Too sweet, she says.

She puts her bag on a chair. She grabs the broom tucked by the refrigerator and says, What, you don't have time to clean in this city? This floor looks filthy.

And just like that I become a child again, and my impulse is to hide the uncooked rice, the slippers, the hangers, the belts, everything Mamá can find to hurt me. But I can't hide her words; they are worse than a horsewhip.

THERE ARE TWO MAMÁS. THERE'S THE DISSATISFIED ONE,
who makes it clear that I do nothing right and who reminds me
how grateful I should be because she can finally teach me how
to be a good wife, a good mother, how to manage a home, etc.,
etc. And there is La Grande Doña Selena, who has a way with
people like the Ruiz brothers, who suddenly visit every Sunday
because she invites them. Mamá lets anyone who visits us know
what a great man Juan is. And he laps it up, a dog with a full
bowl, starved for attention.

I chop. I pound on the mortar and pestle. I do the grocery
shopping. I mend the socks. I take care of her and Lenny. I am the
one who makes a copy of our electricity bill and Lenny's passport
for him to go to school. With my money, I buy his notebooks and
pencils.

But it's Juan who's the hero. It's Mamá who has her way in
the kitchen. Out on the street she's a mouse, inside the apartment
she's a lion.

To escape her I hide in the bedroom and arrange Juan's ties
and my underwear, by color, by style. Juan's things, she does not
dare touch. They are his wife's territory.

Then I take long baths and let the water move about me,
touching my large belly, all my parts, still remembering the gen-
tle touch of César. Is he still in Boston working with the tailor? I
never asked him where he slept, if he slept alone. Too painful to
even think about it.

I count the days until Mamá will start to work at the factory in
New Jersey so that I can have the apartment to myself again. First
Lenny will start school, all the details arranged by Juan. Then a
man with a van will pick Mamá up on the corner of 165th and
Broadway at 7:45 a.m., Monday to Friday, and drop her off across
the George Washington Bridge to work on miniature lamps.

To bring more light in the world, I joke. You will have to get used to the elevator, Mamá, to know how to get around, even if just around the block.

You talk like I've never been to La Capital, she says.

But she's afraid of the outside. This city's much larger, and at night it wakes her up with sirens and gunshots. In Los Guayacanes, the only sounds at night are of the animals, all beating to a clock she understands. She won't admit that this city is alarming to her. Not to me, not even to herself.

ON LENNY'S FIRST DAY OF SCHOOL I URGE MAMÁ TO COME with us.

It'd be good for you to get some fresh air, I say. You haven't left the apartment in days.

If you were only better at keeping a house I would have the luxury to go outside, she says. Every time I ask her to go anywhere she has something better to do.

Well, have it your way.

I make Lenny put on his coat. Juan is already waiting at the elevator. He'll walk us to P.S. 128 on his way to work. I've walked past the school plenty of times, so there is no way I will get lost, but Juan insists. He and Lenny get on well. Juan wishes for a son.

As we walk on Broadway he takes one of Lenny's hands, I take the other.

When we arrive to the school, a two-story brick building with a play area in front, a crowd of parents with their children is already waiting for the heavy metal school doors to open at 8:25 a.m., not a minute earlier or later.

Don't leave me here, Lenny says. He tries to be brave, fighting back tears. Just weeks before, he was running under the sun, in Los Guayacanes. Everything is happening too fast.

Juan crouches down to look Lenny in the face.

He smiles in a way I have never seen before, and I imagine him with César at Lenny's age, helping him navigate everything. Juan looks around at the crowd; everyone is speaking English. He grabs Lenny's coat collar to pull him close.

You see me? I'm old. All my life I'll have to work like a dog. It's too late for me. But you, you have a chance to get an education. If you study hard, you can become a doctor or lawyer or work on Wall Street like those white people. You hear me, big man?

Lenny nods, fighting tears.

People stare at us, move away from us as if we have a bad odor.

You know what I do when I don't understand what people are saying? Juan says.

Lenny shakes his head.

I nod and smile. For everything I say, Jes ser, jes mam.

Jes se, Lenny says in the softest of voices.

You're young, I add, like a sponge. One day, you're gonna wake up and know three times as much as everyone here.

Lenny hugs him so tight Juan struggles out of his embrace.

It's impossible not to admire Juan at that moment. He knows how to take care of things. He knows how to take care of us.

I remind Lenny that in his backpack there are two sharpened pencils, a notebook, and a sandwich with ham and cheese in a plastic bag. I point to our building so that he sees we are only a few blocks away.

When Juan leaves and the school doors open, I say, I'll be waiting right here when you get out.

Remind me how I say my name again?

Mi neym es Lenny. Okay? Now go. Go.

THE BABY HAS DROPPED. MY BELLY, LOW AND HEAVY, MAKES it difficult for me to stand for more than a few minutes.

You okay? Juan asks.

For once, Juan speaks tentatively, moves about with care, doesn't ask me to get up, as if any movement will make me pop. We both hold our breath waiting for the contractions.

Mamá says, Be strong, your body is made for this. Remember how your sister did it and the next day she went out dancing?

The doctor warns that the pressure between my legs will feel like a bad menstrual cramp, like I need to empty my bowels. She instructs me to stay home until I am three minutes apart. To *just keep moving*. To distract myself with chores. Scrub the floors, wash the dishes, sweep. The doctor says moving is good. Staying still is bad. But Mamá leaves nothing for me to do around the house. I have witnessed many women back home have babies before. I fetched them water, tore the sheets, called for the midwife, fed them ice chips. I have wiped the sweat from their foreheads and upper lips, held their hands. I was there to catch the baby for Teresa. I was there. But now that it's me, I'm scared. And having Mamá and Juan pace back and forth from one room to another asking me over and over again, Is it time, isn't helping.

The phone rings. I hope for César even if it's never going to be him.

Mamá picks it up and yells into it, Alo.

Give it to me, I say. Any distraction from the labor is good. I breathe into the breath. The reliable breath.

Maybe it's Teresa? Mamá says. With a bad connection?

I rock the back of my head against the wall left and right, hold the phone against my chest.

But who is it? she asks again and I smile. To think Mamá is more naïve than me.

It's the woman of Juan, I say, as if throwing a bomb into the living room can stop the pain.

Shush your mouth, Mamá says.

I press my back against the wall and slide into a squatting position. An all-over body ache, a dizziness. The pain blinds me. Juan, I say in the smallest of voices. I'm not sure if the words are coming out of my mouth or floating inside my head. My shirt is drenched in perspiration despite the cooler weather.

When Juan comes home for lunch he finds me stretched on the floor like a foal. Mamá stands over me, yelling at him, Do something. Do something.

Juan rushes me to the hospital, Mamá close behind him with my packed bag.

The doctor says I have dilated, but it will still be a while. Go home, she advises. You'll be more comfortable there.

But I have to go back to work, Juan says.

No you don't. You have to take the rest of the day off, Mamá demands, and grips his arm.

Juan pushes her away. This startles Mamá. She blinks once, looks from Juan to me and back at him.

We go out to the waiting room and sit to figure out what to do next.

I'm okay here, I say to Juan. You should go to work.

Juan hesitates. Mamá is still giving him the evil eye. He fears her a little. Maybe because she's slightly older than him. Maybe because she sees right through him.

Mamá, I say, with the baby coming we can't afford for Juan not to work. Let him go.

She sits with her arms across her chest. The doctors, the nurses, the person at the register all speaking in English make her feel powerless.

I'll rush here after work, Juan says, and kisses me good-bye. Juan takes my packed bag and places it under my feet as a foot-rest.

To get through the pain I focus on Coney Island. How I was

warm and drunk after taking a long nap on the beach. How the waves crashed softly near my feet and the taste of the salty fries lingered on my lips.

For hours, I watch people push open the swing doors of the hospital—a broken leg, a gunshot wound, an asthma attack, sickly children with their parents. I cover my nose and mouth with my scarf. The overhead lights make everyone look jaundiced. Mamá sits beside me without saying a word, watching. But she pats my hands firmly, as if saying, *You can do this.*

I breathe in and out of my nose, fall in and out of sleep. Water touches my toes at the beach; a sharp line divides the water and sky. The waves of pain increase and wash over me from head to toe.

I'm on a boat. A wheelchair. I call, César? I scream, Juan? The waves pound against me. I reach out, my hands open. A nurse catches them. Feet inside of stirrups, temperature taken. One nurse after another spreads open my legs to check if I'm ready. Water. Water. Under water. I push. Push. Push. Emptying my bowels. Emptying my womb.

Altagracia Ruiz-Canción is born 24 October 1965. Named after Juan's mother. Nine pounds, six ounces, all five fingers and five toes; eyes wide open, a head full of newborn curly black hair. What a miracle! So tiny—hands and feet and toenails.

Welcome.

I hold her close to my body, relieved to finally have her in the world. As if recognizing my voice, she cries, exercises her lungs, asks to be fed, to be held—skin against skin, choosing attachment over solitude. She gropes the air, eyes sealed, discovering it's cold and too bright outside of the womb. Her toothless mouth parts, as if smiling. Her fist punches the air with determination. And a wave of love fills every empty corner in my heart. So full, so full. I know now why I survived. For once everything makes sense. Traveling from Los Guayacanes, marrying Juan, without all of it, she would've never been born.

When Juan arrives, Altagracia is swaddled in the nursery. I pretend to sleep. I don't want to see anything that will distract me from her beautiful face. Juan leans over me, kisses my cheeks, forehead, and hands.

You did good, he says. Soon we will try for a boy.

My sweet sweet Caridad,

You warned me about family. That family is chosen, not blood. But all my life, my brothers is all I know. When one is hurt, I hurt. When one is in trouble, I'm in trouble. Ramón has betrayed us all in ways I may never forgive. But he's like a father to me. And César, can you believe it, he won't return my phone calls.

I write to you from this place full of disappointments. I'm living in an alien country without rules. Where will I go if we can't return home? I think often about a walk you and I took by the Hudson River. Remember? When on the grass the shadows of our bodies became one and you said, where you go, I'm with you. Wherever I go, you're with me. Together we will always be home. This is what it really means to be married. We don't need a contract. We don't need a witness. Because we know what we are. I want to believe this with all my heart. I really do. But the reality is that you have a husband who any day now will claim you when he returns from war, and I have Ana and a baby, who need me.

My only refuge is to think about your smell. It's fading from memory, I admit this. The way your eyes light up every time you look at me. You have forgiven me many times but maybe this time you'll understand why I can't, shouldn't see you again. To love you has blinded me from paying attention to my goals. Somehow love has made me soft and stupid. I can't make you happy and make Ana happy. I just can't. You deserve more. So much more. When Ana's brother died I was reminded how we can't live with closed eyes. I love you more than you'll ever know.

Yours,

Juancho

AFTER FORTY-EIGHT HOURS OF REST AT THE HOSPITAL I AM
sent home. I find the apartment full of people waiting to meet the
baby. I count in disbelief: Hector, Yrene, and Antonio. Drinking. Puffing on cigars Juan has brought back from Dominican
Republic. A cloud of smoke hovers over all our heads. I cough. A
shooting pain travels up through my back.

Lenny hides in the bedroom and his head pokes out. Since he
started school he's lost his tongue. Lots of nodding and smiling.
Lots of writing in his notebook. Lots of, My name is Lenny.

Mamá is in the kitchen, banging pots.

You look great! Hector yells from across the living room.

I hold Altagracia, my smile tense, my legs heavy pipes. The
anesthetics wear away. My stitches pinch. I may not have understood the doctor's assessment, but I feel every bit of the damage.
I was ripped open from one side to the other. The doctor called
it a third-degree laceration. I feel feverish and weak, but I smile.
Mamá and Juan want me to be strong.

Juan wraps his arm around my shoulders. We stand side by
side under the arch between the foyer and living room. Smile.
Smile. Smile.

A new beginning for the perfect couple.

Flash. Flash. Flash.

I am with César at the World's Fair. He carries me off in a
taxi to a quiet place with a comfortable bed. He gives me a foot
massage and some of his lentil soup. The baby is our baby.

Smile. Smile. Smile.

Yrene comes toward me and asks if she can hold the baby.
Antonio surprises me with a small pink bag dangling from his
wrist. Chocolates? Of course, chocolates.

This is reason to celebrate, Hector says, raises the volume of
the music, and they all clap.

I should put the baby to bed, I say. Juan pats my back in agreement, pushing me toward the bedroom.

I carefully back myself onto the bed and slide myself into a sitting position, afraid of the shooting pain every time I cough, sit, walk, or stand. The doctors warned me not to squat, not to stretch, not to carry heavy objects. *Take it easy,* they said.

The baby wakes up hungry. I'm hungry too. I unravel her from the blanket, placing her on my breast. I hear Juan laugh over the blaring music in the other room. Take it easy? Here? *A cool glass of water, please. A salt bath to soak in for the pain, please. Some quiet, please.* The baby fusses; her gums tug at my nipple. Lenny shows himself, from under the bed, places his chin on the edge and looks to me.

Does it hurt?

No. It's natural, I say, trying to be strong for him.

He caresses her wrinkly hands and sings, What's going on, Alti, Tati?

I need to relax. I put my nipple toward the roof of her mouth the same way the nurse has shown me. She falls off, her lips rooting, hungry.

Coño, I say.

She cries and her entire body turns a bright pink, stretching all tightly wound limbs, undoing her blanket, her pitch high and incessant. Her cries make my breasts engorge. I start to cry along with her, grateful that the music in the other room is loud enough so no one can hear me—but I forget Lenny is here.

You hold wrong, a voice says from the doorway. I look up quickly and wipe my tears. Yrene walks over and takes two pillows and tells me to lean back. She places another pillow under my arm. She takes my nipple like I used to when milking goats and stuffs it whole into the baby's mouth.

Let weight do work, she says, pointing to the floor. I think I understand.

The baby latches. We both feel an immediate relief, a light-headedness. I could've easily fallen asleep while nursing had everyone not been waiting for me out there. Couldn't they come next week? What were they thinking?

Diablo, Lenny says, staring at me wide-eyed. You're like a cow.

You go, Yrene tells him.

This was much easier at the hospital, I tell Yrene. She was like my little piglet.

Yrene pulls out a tissue from her purse and wipes my nose as she would her own kid. My eyes and cheeks are wet, my nose still full of snot. She hands me another tissue and says, Take time. Not rush baby, okay? She tell you, stop.

Then Yrene stands up, pats Lenny to join her, and leaves me by myself. I think back to our time at Hector's house in Tarrytown, how ragged she'd looked, how short she'd been with me, and now I want to kick myself. There she was, serving us food and drinks, without Mamá to help her keep house. And all I could think about then was Yrene's half-tongue.

I admire Altagracia's beaklike mouth, her tiny hands and fists. I finger her earlobes, still not pierced but ready for her first gold earrings. I catch my pinkie under the thin gold bracelet Juan bought her upon my insistence. The amulet dangles from her wrist: a black coral fist with red trim made for protection.

I won't let anyone hurt you, ever.

After she falls asleep on my breast, I swaddle her and lay her on her belly inside the bassinet. I powder my cheeks and nose, still blotchy from all the crying.

When I reappear in the living room, Juan waves me in and tells me I should eat. I am starving. I shove a piece of bread in my mouth.

Do you need to rest? Antonio asks. I'll come by another day. I only stopped by because I heard Ramón is in town.

No, no, no, says Juan. Ana doesn't mind. My wife's a cannon. Stronger than a bull. We'll have at least five kids, right?

Why not a baseball team? I say, biting my cheek, glancing at Yrene.

That's my girl, Mamá says, carrying in plates filled with root vegetables, rice, and stewed meat.

I fear the stitches will rip open, so I sit down. But as soon as I sit Mamá calls me to the kitchen. Where did you put this pot? Where is the extra bag of coffee? Can you please set the table?

Ana, get Hector some more napkins? Juan calls.

Ana, refill the water pitcher?

Ana. Ana. Ana.

I just had a nine-pound baby, a tenth of my own weight.

Let Hector get his own napkins, I hear Yrene say.

I bend over the sink in pain.

Ana, the baby is crying, says Lenny.

Is the baby crying? says Mamá.

How can I hear her with the music blasting? I yell at her above the noise. I want to sleep. I need to drink water.

The doorbell from the lobby rings. Hector runs to answer the buzzer.

Who is?

No answer.

Who is?

Everyone waits to hear who it is.

It's César. A long sword on his hip, here to claim me in a horse with a carriage where I can curl up to sleep in silence and drink and drink goblets of ice water.

Just let them up, Juan says. We're having a party.

More people? All we need are Marisela and Mauricio. And Gino and Gisele from El Basement.

An empty promise, says Hector when no one else shows up.

Mamá tells everyone to eat already. The food is better warm. And soon everyone is sucking on the bones, eating yucca and plátanos. The men comment on how good the food is, and Mamá laughs it off and says, It's nothing. She's happy to feed them, to be needed, to finally be in control of something after all those hours in the hospital like a fish out of water.

Moments later the phone rings. Hector lowers the music.

Juan picks it up. Since my outburst during labor, every time the phone rings Mamá has been suspicious.

He whispers, This is not a good time. He smiles at us and stretches the cord to the far corner of the room to create distance.

What do you mean you're downstairs? he yells into the phone. Hector raises back the volume on the radio. But we all watch as Juan slams the phone shut and sticks his head out the window. Everyone moves to find windows to look out of. Five stories down a woman at the phone booth looks up and waves for attention.

Minutes later, the phone rings again.

Hector lowers the music and I leap for the phone while the woman's voice screams at Juan from below.

Don't you think I have feelings? I hear her voice in double time. You can't pretend I don't exist. After all these years, do you think I'm going to disappear? I need to talk to you, Juan Ruiz.

Finally hearing her voice releases a tension in my chest.

Caridad, I know who you are, I say into the phone as Juan tries to grab it from me.

Give it to me, Ana, or else . . .

Or else, what . . . Juancho?

He twists my wrists then stops. Everyone's watching.

Ana, give him the phone, Mamá says. Don't be disrespectful. We have visitors.

No. No. No! I yell like American children do in public, and I hold up the phone for Caridad to listen from the other end.

Stop playing games, pajarita, Juan says and laughs to lighten the mood in the room. But even the music sounds hollow.

Tell that to your Cari.

Give me the phone, carajo, Juan says, this time louder.

I wrap the cord around my arm and turn away. The phone is mine. All mine.

In one move Juan snatches the phone from me and with it smacks my top lip so hard I bleed.

Yrene steps forward, but Hector pulls her back and says to Juan, Brother . . .

Goddamnit. Look what she makes me do.

If you'd like to make another call, please hang up . . . And soon the sound of short beeps.

I cover my lip. The blood is bright on the tips of my fingers. I look up at Juan and past him, see Antonio cover his face. I see Lenny by the door. I hear the baby crying.

Mamá pulls me away.

Ana, go to your room and find your head before you embarrass us further.

You always take his side, Mamá. Haven't I done everything you wanted me to do and lived up to my end of the bargain? I say, and glare at him. Go to her, Juan! Go to her and leave me the hell alone, I yell. All of you!

Yrene runs past us to the crying Altagracia in the bedroom.

Juan's cheeks are red, his eyes small. He wants to punch something. He swings his arms and slaps my Dominicana off the windowsill. She flies across the room and shatters all over the floor.

What have you done? I scream.

Juan grabs both my shoulders as if he can calm me, but his fingers dig into me hard.

A sharp burn shoots through me. I feel liquid trail down my leg—the stitches. The stitches.

Stop it, Juan keeps saying. Just stop it.

He shakes me and shakes me.

But it's too late.

Get away from her, Mamá says, and balls the dishtowel she's holding and presses it on me to stop the blood. But it's coming too fast, a fountain.

You monster! she yells at Juan.

Call an ambulance, Antonio says.

No, says Hector, it's faster if I run across the street and get help.

Then he and Antonio run out of the apartment.

Mamá, I cry when I see the blood spread on the floor, the rug, my clothes. My vision blurs. The pain pulls me in and out. I see Yrene bouncing the baby on her shoulder, walking between the bedroom and kitchen. I'm too weak to say, Bring her to me, let me hold her.

Juan paces. Why doesn't she stop crying? he says to Yrene.

You stop your crying, says Mamá.

She goes to yank the sheets off the bed, and then wraps them around me like a diaper. She leans me on her hip to wrap my arm around her neck.

I'll carry her downstairs, Juan says, and tries to move Mamá out of the way.

Don't touch me, she says in a guttural voice. And get away from her.

Mamá bends her knees and lifts me from the floor. They don't know she has lifted animals even heavier than me.

You're being ridiculous. Let me carry her.

Go tend to that crazy downstairs, Juan, before the neighbors start talking. Lenny, open the door.

Can you believe this woman? Juan says to no one out in the hallway as Mamá carries me to the elevator. This is what happens when you get involved with backward people. I told Ramón they would be more trouble than it's worth. But he insisted. And insisted. And I went and married her, trying to make the whole goddamn world happy, but nobody's happy. Nobody.

The elevator arrives. Mamá hesitates but steps in, and leans me against the wall. When Juan tries to enter and help, she says, Don't you dare. He throws up his hands and allows the elevator gates to close.

The small corner mirror distorts our reflection. Mamá looks twice her size.

Down in the lobby, the doors fling open to Hector and Antonio standing beside a hospital medic who carries a cloth cot. They enter the elevator and lay out the cot. One-two-three. They lift me.

I am on a boat crossing a river. Caridad wails from afar like a ship's horn. Juan tries to calm her from up in the clouds. I float downriver, holding Yohnny's hand. Stay with us, Ana, stay with us.

At the hospital Mamá sits close by my bed and watches over me. Wipes the sweat from my brow. Holds my hand. When my eyes finally open, I say, Stay with me. Stay with us.

Of course, I'm your mother.

I need to get to Altagracia.

Get well first.

I feel the same ache of longing for Altagracia I once felt for César when we were apart. When I try to sit up, Mamá presses me back down.

Doctor's orders: rest.

Mamá's hopes have turned. It's now us and only us. And together we brace ourselves, imagining how and when Juan will make us pay for disrespecting him in front of others. Here she is, in a city she doesn't know, thinking the weight of our survival is on her shoulders. She had wanted New York. She had pushed for it.

So this is New York, she says with a weak smile.

Don't worry, Mamá; it's made me strong.

She lays her head on my chest, and she lets me comb through her graying hair. And that's when Mamá's cries come in, a tropical storm without warning, her wail with no top or bottom. Finally she understands everything I have sacrificed, everything I have survived for her and for the family.

LET'S GO FOR A WALK AROUND THE BLOCK, I SAY TO
Mamá. My stitches are finally gone. It's unusually warm for November. The leaves are on fire, the sky blue blue, not a cloud. I am able to move around without feeling any pain. I pack the baby's bag, hook it on the stroller. I make Lenny put on his coat, head toward the door. Mamá surprises me by saying, Fine, fine, I'll go.

We walk to Fort Washington, and I point to the river.

And over to the right, I say, is the George Washington Bridge. And past that, your job.

All of New York makes me think of César. Sometimes he calls to check in and says he'll visit to meet Altagracia, but he never shows up. The Ruiz brothers laugh him off and say he's caught up with some woman in Boston. I ache just thinking about it.

Mamá and Lenny sleep in the bedroom with me. Juan now sleeps on César's sofa. We have no choice. We have to make it work until another apartment opens up, until we make enough money to cover the rent ourselves.

We walk up 164th Street.

Mostly Jewish people live on this block, I say. Cubans and Puerto Ricans too, but soon it will be just us. Soon soon I'm going to go to school and study accounting so I know how to manage all our business. You're going to make your famous dulce de leche and sell them at every bodega. There will be a bodega on every block. And Lenny here, when he's off from school in the summer we'll have him sell frio-frios like we did back home. We'll get the largest block of ice we can find, and everyone will be coming to our cart, from all over, for the best tamarind and lemon flavor shaved ice in the city. We'll make them in every color imaginable. And in the winter, Mamá, in the hours we're not working at the factory and I'm not in school, we can sell your delicious beans: sweet and hot. And pastelitos made with flour, even with yucca. And all these stores on Broadway will be owned by us, catering to us. The bodegas will have piles of plátanos taller than me, and coconut water, and yucca, and bacalao.

Mamá laughs at me or maybe with me. But I don't care. I know one day I will no longer live with Juan. I know that Papá and Teresa and her baby will all be here with us. And we are going to work hard. Especially Altagracia, who will make something special out of herself.

We stop at the bench in front of La Bodeguita owned by Alex, the Puerto Rican. When I'd first arrived, Juan told me never to enter the store without him and I obeyed except for that one time.

You both sit here while I get something inside, I say.

I make Mamá hold on to the stroller.

Once inside, I head straight to the register. The man behind the counter does a double take.

Hey, Dominicanita, I remember you. You're Juan's wife, no? Are you back for some free chocolate?

I purse my lips, hand him my crisp dollar.

Three bars of chocolate, please.

New York looks good on you, he says. You planning to stick around?

I look out to see Mamá and Lenny. They're all bundled up, eagerly waiting for me to return, their eyes wide and fresh.

Yes, I say. Yes, I am.

ACKNOWLEDGMENTS

This novel was inspired by my mother's story as well as all the Dominicanas who took the time to answer my questions about their lives and who opened their photo albums so I could bridge the gaps in all the silences in the telling, often painful. When I told my mother back in 2005 I would write a novel inspired by her, she said, *Who would be interested in a story about a woman like me? It's so typical.* And yet, stories like my mother's, although common, are rarely represented in the mainstream narratives available to us. I am grateful for the opportunity to publish this singular story, knowing very well that so many writers who are women of color do not have this privilege and access.

Thank you to Daniel—you have been so patient with me. I love you so much.

Thank you to the Cruz, Gomez, and Piscitelli families, who generously took on the care of my son, making it possible for me to take time away to write. To Paolo, who fed me art and countless meals. Grazie, Stefania, for providing me una stanza to write. I'm grateful to Texas A&M University and the University of Pittsburgh, who funded numerous research trips in support of this novel. To the fellowships and residencies: Hermitage, Art Omi, Siena Art Institute, and CUNY Dominican Institute. To the following publications for publishing excerpts of this novel: *Gulf Coast, Kweli, Callaloo, Review: Literature and Arts of the Americas,* and *Small Axe.* Thank you, Adriana, for introducing me to my agent, Dara, who reenergized the novel with her brilliant editorial notes. And to my editor, Caroline: wow. Oh wow. Perfect timing. Collaborating with you and the amazing team at Flatiron on this book's journey has been divine.

I am grateful to everyone who read this novel and provided their input and expertise, including the creative and scholarly works that have profoundly impacted the trajectory of this book. So many! But, in particular, for their critical feedback: Irina, for encouraging me to be more explicit, and also for suggesting the title. Jennifer, who breathed fire into the novel with her suggestion to change the POV. Milenna, my tireless, devoted listener. Laylah, for encouraging my rage and for our invaluable creative exchanges.

To my Aster(ix) familia, thank you for the ways you keep challenging me. I am especially grateful to mis hermanas, diosas, and brujas—who, without their many interventions, I certainly wouldn't have completed this book. To Nelly, my astral twin, for being the best line editor ever. To Marta Lucia, my fierce, loving comrade in writing and social action. To Emily, for plotting with me in fiction and in life, and for nudging me to fight for my work. To Andrea, for bringing the light when I am full of despair. And to Dawn, for all the love, beauty, and poetry we've shared; so much of it informed *Dominicana* and its coda:

> Leave wreckage by the roadside.
> Burn all decayed tissue.
> Tightrope from which we emerge.
>
> —DAWN LUNDY MARTIN,
> *GOOD STOCK STRANGE BLOOD*

Yes, yes! Let's emerge!

Note: If you have photographs/videos from the '50s, '60s, '70s, and '80s of Dominicanas in New York City, please submit them to the visual archive on Instagram at @dominicanasnyc.

ABOUT THE AUTHOR

Angie Cruz is the author of the novels *Soledad* and *Let It Rain Coffee*, a finalist in 2007 for the IMPAC Dublin Literary Award. She has published work in *The New York Times, VQR, Gulf Coast,* and other publications, and she has received fellowships from the New York Foundation of the Arts, Yaddo, and the MacDowell Colony. She is founder and editor in chief of *Aster(ix)*, a literary and arts journal, and is an associate professor of English at the University of Pittsburgh. *Dominicana* is inspired by her mother's story.

www.angiecruz.com